PAPER CLIPS WALES

Short stories by writers from Wales

Edited by

SUZI BLAIR

NEW FICTION

First published in 1993 by
NEW FICTION
4 Hythegate, Werrington
Peterborough,
PE4 7ZP

Printed in Great Britain by Forward Press.

Foreword

The advent of New Fiction signifies the expansion of what has traditionally been, a limited platform for writers of short stories. New Fiction aims to promote new short stories to the widest possible audience.

New Fiction collections represent the wealth of new talent in writing, and provide enjoyable, interesting and readable stories appealing to a diversity of tastes.

Intriguing and entertaining; from sharp character sketches to 'slice of life' situations, the stories have been selected because each one is *a good read*.

This collection of short stories is from the pens of the people of Wales. They are new stories, sweeping across the spectrums of style and subject to reflect the richness of character intrinsic to the region, today.

Suzi Blair
Editor.

Contents

Boadicea's Chariot

by

Trevor Morgan

It is a few years now since the Secretary of State decided not to chop Wales up into twenty-three penny packets. We celebrated by making County Hall all hi-tech. In the council chamber is an Electronic Voting Indicator. We call it Boadicea's Chariot. In the old days clerks used to scurry around with voting slips (we didn't trust raised arm voting because there were sometimes more votes than people). Boadicea's Chariot put an end to all that running about.

It was the idea of Howell Dda. Everyone called him Howell Dda because he was father of the council. On each wall of the Council chamber is a huge board, its top space headed

The Motion Is

and immediately below that

The Amendment is.

The lower half of the board shows

Votes For

and Votes Against.

By each councillor's seat are two push buttons, a green *Vote For* button and a red *Vote Against* button. The wordings of motions and amendments appear in lights as they are tapped out on a control panel.

The post of Voting Indicator Superintendent was widely advertised ('canvassing disqualifies'). Howell's neighbour Llewelyn did not canvass but he did pay some social calls. 'Careful of that language fanatic Taliesin,' Howell warned, 'he's crooked. He'll take your money then he won't vote for you.' Llewelyn got the job and Howell Dda got an Arms Park debenture.

One day Howell announced to Llewelyn:

'There'll be some fun next meeting. I've put an item on the agenda asking the council to organise an Eisteddfod of the Marches. Bilingual, of course. We lead and bring in councils on both sides of the border. Straddle Offa's Dyke here in the south.'

'Marvellous,' enthused Llewelyn, 'I'd be thrilled to have an eisteddfod like that.'

Howell Dda outlined his idea persuasively to the council.

'Wouldn't it kill the National?' objected Councillor Rhys-Tomos.

'I don't want to threaten the National, let alone kill it. The Marches Eisteddfod could be held every other year, when the National is up north,' Howell Dda replied. A pause, then he added 'though come to think of it, if the National is that easily killed, it deserves to die.'

At this Councillor Taliesin materialised as if he had come post-haste straight out of Merlin's cave. Even in the air-conditioned, draught-proof, council chamber his locks streamed magnificently behind him as, arm outstretched and long forefinger stabbing accusingly, he prophesied judgment and doom. He suddenly stopped and declared:

'Mr Chairman, I am going to exercise a right that I have never exercised in this council before. I am going to speak in Welsh, even though not all will understand, for the English language does not have enough fire for my thoughts.'

He spoke on in Welsh, with oratory that crackled like lightning and rolled like thunder. Those who did not understand him realised, almost equally with those who did, just why he had won all those bardic chairs filling his home and overspilling into his garage. When he sat down there was the sort of hush that follows a heaven-rending storm. Llewelyn was tapping away silently at his control panel, and before anybody else could speak there appeared on Boadicea's Chariot two sentences, one Welsh, one English. The English read:

'The motion is that on grounds of economy and in the interests of the Royal National Eisteddfod of Wales the Council does not organise an Eisteddfod of the Welsh Marches.'

Howell Dda decided that it would be better to live to fight another day than to risk instant defeat in a vote.

'Obviously,' he said as soon as Taliesin sat down, 'much mature thought must be given to this. I propose an amendment to Councillor Taliesin's motion: that we defer the whole matter for six months.' His amendment was carried.

Afterwards he said to Llewelyn: 'That was clever of you. Directing attention to Boadicea's Chariot immediately Taliesin finished gave me a chance to jump in. He was winning a lot of support and I might have been sunk without trace. Now I've got six months to work in.'

'I'd do anything to get an Eisteddfod of the Marches going,' said Llewelyn, 'Good luck when the council debate it again.'

'I'll need more than luck,' replied Howell Dda, 'Democracy is a plant that's got to be nurtured carefully. I must do some nurturing.'

Both sides nurtured well, Howell Dda's and Taliesin's. One influential waverer found himself in the Birthday Honours List for services to culture and did not have much difficulty in tracing the channels of recommendation back to Howell Dda. Another was gratified to learn that his son was in line for a top job newly created at Howell Dda's insistence. Taliesin was instrumental in having one councillor admitted to the Gorsedd and another promoted up the bardic orders. Howell Dda put around the story that the latter dyed his wellingtons to match the changed colour of his bardic robes.

All in all, there was a great build-up and it was expected that there would be a close vote when the big day came.

Close it was. The motion was simply:

'That this Council organise an Eisteddfod of the Welsh Marches.'

Boadicea's Chariot showed

Votes For 50
Votes Against 49

'Somebody may have inadvertently pressed the wrong button,' pleaded Taliesin despairingly, 'could we vote again?'

The chairman agreed, but Boadicea's Chariot still showed fifty For, forty-nine Against.

Next time Howell Dda met Llewelyn he said: 'You'd better get another job, then resign.'

Aghast, Llewelyn demanded: 'Resign! Why? I believe I'm doing my job well.'

'Too well,' retorted Howell Dda, 'you fixed the Chariot, didn't you? From that control panel. You fixed it so that I'd win.'

'How do you know?'

'Because the vote was the same both times. You're so clever that I had my doubts about you. So on the second vote I pressed my Against button, and Boadicea's Chariot ought to have shown forty-nine for, fifty Against.'

'You took a risk, didn't you? And aren't you glad we won?'

'I'd rather not win like that. That's not a democratic win.'

'That's rich, from you,' scoffed Llewelyn, 'with all your wangling.'

'Ah, that's different. That's nurturing democratic opinion. That's before the vote. But the vote is the expression of democratic opinion. You've interfered with that. Besides you're an official, not a councillor. We can't have too-powerful officials.'

'What are you going to do about it?' said Llewelyn defiantly.

'Nothing. But you're going to find another job, then resign.'

Llewelyn got another job. Boadicea's Chariot turned temperamental at the first meeting after his departure. No matter which buttons were pressed, nor what Llewelyn's successor at the control panel did, the Chariot persisted in proclaiming:

'corrected Eisteddfod of the Welsh Marches
result: Votes For 1
Votes Against 98

We had to fly somebody over from Japan to mend Boadicea's Chariot.

Mother's Hat

by

Gill Bryant

Olwen was fascinated by her mother's hat. Its beauty reflected what she had been and Olwen felt she herself would never be.

Her mother had only worn it once, for her cousin's wedding the day before the accident in which she had died. Since then, it had stayed in her wardrobe, above the suit she had worn with it. Father had allowed all her other things to go, except those. They stayed there, mute reminders that he could not let her go, and that Olwen could never be an adequate substitute.

The hat was covered with feathers; small feathers in a blue shade that was just a bit darker than the suit. Her eyes had been that colour, and the hat had made them as deep as the sea. Olwen's were brown and undemanding.

Father had kept their bed, too, in what had been his solitary room for the last five years. A big double bed, it filled the front bedroom apart from the wardrobe where the hat lay. Since the only other bed in the house was Olwen's single one, this meant that no-one came to stay; none of the aunts or cousins or old school friends.

Not that she heard from any of these now. The aunts had written solicitously after her mother's death, but their interest had gradually waned.

When she had first left school to look after her father, after her mother's death, she had tried to keep up with the girls. But gradually contact had ceased, as it became increasingly difficult to leave him for long, and their interests had diverged.

Olwen had had one friend. She was the minister's daughter, and chapel was one place that Olwen could go to regularly. Her mother had been a chapel goer, and so her father felt it only right that she should go too, even though it did mean that his Sunday dinner was late. Peggy walked home with Olwen, often, and she could make Mr Lewis smile. She had blue, eyes, too, but Olwen didn't think she was as pretty as her mother had been. She went away when she married, and her letters gradually became fewer and fewer.

Now there was a new minister, and Olwen thought that perhaps she might have a new friend, because he had a daughter. She had been in chapel last week; Olwen had shaken her hand as she left, but the other girl hadn't said anything.

She seemed pretty and lively, and Olwen thought that perhaps if she perked herself up a bit she would notice her next time. After all, there weren't many girls her age attending regularly.

So that Sunday, Olwen put on her Sunday best and looked at herself in the mirror. She wasn't happy with what she saw. She had a grey look, with a grey coat tight fitting over a shapeless body, and that old grey felt hat down over her eyes. It made all her lines seem to run downwards too.

No one could want her for a friend.

The long mirror was alongside her mother's wardrobe. She knew what she should do. She slid the door open as quietly as she could, opened the box, and took the hat out. Even now, after so many years, it had a sheen on it.

She put it carefully on her head. She thought that it lifted her up and brightened her face.

She slipped down the stairs and out of the house, calling goodbye to her father so that he shouldn't see her go. She walked with her shoulders back, and found herself humming, 'Onward Christian Soldiers.'

She felt confident enough to walk into the church, instead of going to her usual place at the side. There was a place immediately behind the girl where Olwen could admire her fair hair. She wasn't wearing a hat.

Olwen sang the hymns lustily but couldn't listen to the service. When it had finished the girl went out first with her father. Olwen waited for the shortest time that decency allowed, but by the time that she got to the door the girl had gone and the minister was standing shaking hands on his own.

Disappointed, Olwen wandered down the High Street, pretending to look in the shop windows.

Behind her, came a voice, female, lilting, but sharp.

'Did you see that strange girl? With the funny old fashioned hat with the feathers? It may have been fashionable once, but that must have been a very long time ago!'

Olwen peered round the window. There she was, the girl she had thought might have been a substitute for Peggy, walking along with a young man.

Olwen withdrew into the shop entrance, hoping desperately that they wouldn't see her. She focussed on the window. There was indeed a strange girl standing there. She wore drab but tightly fitting clothes, topped by a ridiculous feathered heat. How had she ever thought that it was smart!

After what seemed like a long time, she looked round to make sure that they had gone, and then pulled the hat off. The girl was right. she had looked a fright, but that hat wasn't the real cause. She had been too busy trying to live up to her mother's memory, when she was a different sort of person. Her hair sprung up where the hat had pressed it down, and she shook it out. She undid the coat buttons, and straightened herself up. That was a bit better, but she really needed quite a different shape, and colour.

She looked at the hat, and on impulse sent it spinning into the brook that ran alongside the street. She watched it, trying to bob along, blue feathers drooping, until it disappeared from view.

Then she turned quite deliberately away from home and in the direction of the clothes shop on the corner. She spent a long time summing up what was on offer, and decided that tomorrow she would have to persuade her father that it was time she had some more suitable clothes.

As she turned away she found to her horror that she was looking again at her mother's hat, bedraggled and dirty, but undoubtedly, that hat. What was more, it was held in the hand of a young man. Not any young man, but the one who had been walking with the minister's daughter. He was smiling, and holding it out to her.

'I'm glad I found you,' he said. 'This was at the edge of the brook. I saw you wearing it in church. Did it blow off?'

Her first impulse was to deny everything. But his smile was kind, and she was through with pretence.

'I threw it away.'

'Whatever for? I noticed it straight away in church, it's such a pretty colour.'

'I looked silly; it was my mother's hat.'

'So you did hear what my sister said.' He looked apologetic. 'It did seem a bit old fashioned, but you wore it so proudly; it was like a flag. You look better without a hat, though. Your hair is so pretty, it shouldn't be hidden.'

So the girl was his sister. As they walked along, she found herself telling him all about the hat, and her mother, and, finally, her father.

'So, what are you going to tell him? Or shall we hide it away?'

She looked at the sodden mess that had been so beautiful.

'There's been enough of hiding,' she said, taking the hat from him. They walked along in companionable silence, until the row of terraced houses where she lived came into view.

Her father was standing at the door as they arrived, looking rather anxious.

'Where have you been?' he said, looking first at her and then at the young man.

'This is the minister's son,' she said. 'My hat blew off and he rescued it.'

Her father looked hard at her.

'I have sometimes thought of suggesting that you should use your mother's hat on Sundays; it seems a waste to leave it sitting there. But you look better without a hat. You have a different style.'

So she had, and he had recognised it before her.

'People don't wear hats to church any more.' she said, and, daring, 'Perhaps it is time for the hat and the suit to go to the charity shop.'

'We don't need them any more to remember your mother by,' her father was agreeing with her. 'Someone will love them.'

'Let me take them,' said the young man. 'My mother will see it goes to a good home, and I can tell you about it next Sunday.'

She went in with them both, smiling, and thinking that she no longer needed to wonder if she could ever be a substitute for her mother. She was Olwen, and she would walk proudly into chapel or anywhere else, with or without a hat.

And the Dove Flew Away

by

Charles Blewett

Then came the day when Owen found his way up through the dark, brown woods to the good place far above the grey town. On the ledge of red rock at the top of the green and pleasant hill dwelt a dove. Owen was not afraid to be where the dove was and so they stayed together - in quietness.

The red rock ledge, for all Owen knew, was an ancient launching pad where many other Owens in their time had found the thrust within to send them soaring to the skies.

There he made a lodge of twigs, of branches and of roots and life was sweet, and life bore fruit. His eyes grew eager, his heart expectant of the wonders that the days ahead could hold. And in his lodge he began to learn - such things as school had never time to give.

Then, at a time when the late light was gold, the white horse came to his lodge and bore him away - away to the misty violet rift in the purple clouds - and through - and beyond... When he returned he had grown.

Always after, when he called, the white horse came.

There grew in him a wonder that others had not found the place and desired it, and he wanted to share and bring Mary there.

When he told her and she saw the strange light in his eyes she was fearful and took his hand and came to see - she had to see! - what pull could draw him from the proper world below and from the magnet that was her.

So he brought her to the red rock ledge, Mary, his love. The dove flew away.

The white horse could not bear them both, for Mary feared strange new ways above all things and the white horse could not bear the burden of her fear. So Owen had to stay, and the white horse went away.

'Come down,' she appealed. 'Come down with me.'

His eyes grew less bright. 'But it's better here,' he protested.

'It troubles me,' she said. 'The quietness troubles me. I'm not used to it.'

'But it's better,' he argued. 'Better than the noise down there.'

'And it's lonely.' She shivered. 'There's nobody else about.'

'I'm here,' he reminded her quietly.

'You know that's not what I mean.' Her mouth inclined to petulance.

'But it's different - it makes you different from all the others.'

'I want to be different,' he said firmly.

She turned her large blue eyes full on to him, amazed. 'Why, then, do you think you're better than all the rest of us?'

'It's not that - but I want to be myself, not just like everybody else.'

'But that's selfish,' she accused. 'What about me? I love you and you said you loved me when you married me and... and...' She started to sob, but only at half-throttle yet.

'I do! I do!' He started towards her. She let him put his arm around her waist.

'But you can't - you know you can't.' She turned the sob control up ever so slightly. 'If you really loved me you'd want me to have my share of the Boxes, and you know you can't get the Boxes without the Tickets, and you can't get the Tickets for the Boxes if you're not in the Race.'

She released two large pearly tears and let them run down her peachy cheeks.

'But I don't want to be in the Race,' he protested. 'I want to live. See how much I would miss.'

'How much you would gain, you mean.' She dried the pearly tears with a pretty handkerchief.

'Oh Owen,' she sighed, 'you're so impractical. Of course I want you to do the things you want to do, but we can't go on without the Boxes. Everyone has them - all my friends. Get them first - the Boxes - then you can please yourself afterwards. People think there's something wrong with you if you haven't got them - the Boxes. They think you're queer.'

'I don't mind that,' he said. 'Besides, I don't think I'd be much good in the race.'

'Oh, you would, Owen, I know you would! she gushed. 'You're so clever, you ought not to waste it on this. You could run as well as all the others. In fact, I'm sure I could help you to run better than most of them. I'd be behind you, darling, and we'd be so happy, and I'd be so proud of you.'

But Owen was not easily to be weaned away from his red rock ledge where the dove dwelt and the white horse came. Only, from then on, he came alone. Yet, afterwards, things were not the same. The dove was disturbed by the seeds of guilt that Mary had sown.

The dove flew away and did not come back. The white horse began to turn grey.

Then Owen talked with a friend, a friend who was in the Race and running well and winning lots of the Tickets which entitled him to a bigger and better selection of the Boxes.

'You're way out,' said the friend. 'You're not with it.'

In the face of this dread accusation Owen's spirit quailed. To the sense of guilt that he was depriving Mary was added the fear that perhaps he was, indeed, queer.

When he told Mary that he was ready to enter the Race she was overjoyed, and immediately employed all her considerable powers to adequately equip him. She clothed him with the regulation dress, and nourished him with the proper nourishment. Niacin and Thiamine and Riboflavin and Nicotinic Acid were not too good for her man, and his shirt was soon several shades whiter.

She provided success drinks for the night and success drinks for the morning. Circles of confidence and cleanliness within as well as without were stored in the bathroom, and they learned to share the deodorant specially made for people like them.

So Owen was entered for the Race and after a period of conditioning thought it wasn't so bad after all, and Mary's rewarding embraces were as good as any of the millions of others gleaned from the glossies.

And the Tickets came their way and increased and soon they moved to a proper Dwelling Box, and as they got more and more of the Tickets they gave them to other people in exchange for Heating Boxes and Freezing Boxes, Music Boxes and Picture Boxes, Riding Boxes and stainless steel Cooking Boxes and many other Boxes too numerous to mention.

Mary grew very happy indeed. After a while, when they had enough of the Tickets, there was a little Owen.

And Owen? In time he grew almost able to forget the red rock ledge. Once he went back, but the dove would not return. His lodge had withered and even before he called he knew the white horse was dead. Owen? Well Owen was... well, he was a success wasn't he?

Then came the day when little Owen found his way up through the dark, brown woods to the good place far above the grey town...

The Intruder

by

Anthony Denton

The chimes of midnight rang languidly in the distance from the old church tower.

On the edge of town a small cottage sat off the main road surrounded by limp, tired looking trees whose copper coloured leaves were beginning to surrender to the first bites of autumnal chill.

A solitary, stooping figure picked its way cautiously through the overgrown grass.

On reaching the window at the side of the cottage he glanced furtively around before prising open the rotting wooden structure. He hoisted himself onto the sill and disappeared inside.

Little light invaded the room. He struck a match and screwed his eyes at his surroundings as the meagre light fought to penetrate the dark recesses. A musty smell pierced his nostrils and the total silence hung like an eerie blanket around him.

He shook his hand fiercely and swore as the dying match scorched his fingers.

As he fumbled for a second match the room was suddenly drenched in light.

The startled youth found himself looking at a wizened old woman. Her witch-like features and lined face contrasted with large, clear, staring eyes. Her bent frame stood motionless in the doorway; her hand rested on the light switch.

She, in turn, gazed at the roughly dressed, unshaven youth before her. Her eyes danced over the array of tattoos adorning his arms and hands. Neither spoke.

Moments of silence elapsed. Each looked at the other assessing how to react.

'Who are you? What do you want?' The old woman spat the questions rapidly in shrill, quavering tones.

The yob, swaying slightly and clearly part inebriated, leered at his adversary. 'Money, Ma, valuables, know what I mean?'

'Get out!' screeched the old woman. 'My husband's here, now get out!'

The yob threw back his head and laughed aloud. Realising that he undoubtedly held the balance of power he proceeded to rummage through drawers and cupboards as the old woman looked on helplessly.

'Come on Ma, save yourself the hassle. Where's the money?' The yob turned and towered threateningly over the old woman. He poked a grubby finger at the tip of her nose. 'I'm losing patience. Where's your loot you old hag?' he sneered. Without answering, she hobbled across the room to an armchair.

Easing herself gently into it, she rested back and stared at the intruder. An impish smile flickered across her thin lips. Her eyes twinkled mischievously. 'I'm not telling you. You'll have to find it.'

The yob found himself taken aback by the old woman's change of mood and by the nature of her challenge.

He pulled out drawer after drawer, strewing the contents over the floor and extracting small articles he deemed to be of any value.

The old woman sat silently in her chair watching his every move.

The yob, clearly angered and frustrated by his lack of success, strode across the room. He knelt before the old woman and slapped a hand across her face.

'Money, old woman. Money!' he growled. His face was contorted with rage.

The old woman gasped at the blow. She cringed in the chair eyeing him fearfully.

'Where is it?' he hissed, holding a tightly clenched fist in front of her face.

'If I tell you, will you leave me alone?' enquired the woman.

'Yeah, yeah but let's have it,' replied the yob. He stood to one side as the old woman rose unsteadily from the chair. She reached the table in the middle of the room. Turning to face him she took a deep breath. Resting one hand on the table, she smacked her lips together several times then uttered, 'I haven't got any.'

The yob lurched towards her. 'Look Ma, stop having me on or I'll give you a bloody good hiding.' The words tumbled from his mouth through clenched teeth. He raised an arm as if to strike her and glowered into her face.

'Don't hit me,' squeaked the old woman. 'I'll find something for you now.'

She threaded her way through the oddments strewn over the floor. The yob watched her disappear into the kitchen. He listened to the rattle of crockery and to drawers opening and closing.

Moments later the old woman reappeared in the kitchen doorway. 'Would you like a cup of tea, young man?' The yob stared at her disbelievingly, momentarily stunned by the irrelevance of her question. Despite the advantage he knew he had in terms of physical power he nevertheless felt a state of confusion creeping over him. He stood motionless trying to fathom out the old woman's mood swings.

'Well, do you want a cup of tea or not?' she repeated.

The yob ignored the question. 'Where's your old man then?' he asked. 'You said your old man was here.'

The old woman looked at him quizzically. 'Did I say that?' She hobbled towards him and held out a battered metal teapot. 'Do you like this teapot? It was a wedding present, you know.' The yob swept out an arm sending the teapot flying to a far corner of the room.

'I don't want any tea,' he screeched. He leant forward and took a handful of the old woman's cardigan in each clenched fist. 'Look, you old hag, I want money or I want to see your old man.' Beads of perspiration were breaking out on his forehead. He gasped the words with breathless frustration. He lifted the old woman off her feet and threw her into the armchair.

His lips contorted into a snarl. His unshaven bristles were embedded in a face that was flushed with anger. The old woman squirmed uncomfortably in the chair as she struggled to recover from the rough handling. Her toothless face with hollowed cheeks pulsated vigourously. 'You've broken my back,' she groaned.

'Ma, if you don't make some sense I'll break your bloody neck!' cried the yob.

The old woman placed a hand on each arm of the chair and, rocking back and forth, eased herself to her feet. She hobbled past the yob and, placing her hands on her hips, stretched her bent frame upright. 'Oh dear,' she said, 'no, I'm alright.'

The yob sat down on a wooden chair. He wiped the perspiration from his face with his hand and drummed his fingers impatiently on the table.

'Where's you husband, Ma!' His voice was flat and emotionless.

'He's in bed, but you musn't disturb him,' replied the old woman. She made her way to the kitchen again. 'I must have a drink of water.'

The yob cast his eyes around the room where they fell on an unlit passage down which he peered. 'You're lying Ma. He would have been in here by now with all this racket. You're on your own, aren't you?'

The yob rose from the chair and crossed the room. He looked at the door at the end of the passage. 'What's in that room, Ma? That's your bedroom, ain't it?'

The old woman's voice rang excitedly from the kitchen. 'You can't go in there!' she screamed. 'My husband's asleep in there.'

'That's where your money is, ain't it, Ma? In the bedroom, of course. That's why you don't want me in there.' The yob strode down the passage. He opened the door and peered into the gloom. 'I'm in here, Ma,' he taunted. His ran his hand along the wall feeling for the light switch. Having found it, he smacked it on with his fist. The single bulb in the centre of the ceiling cast a weak glow throughout the room.

The yob advanced a few paces into the room where his gaze was transfixed by the scene before him.

Lying in the double bed, half covered by a blanket, he made out the figure of an old man. His stony eyes stared at the ceiling, his face twisted in a deathly grimace and a large knife protruded from his heart. The body and bedding were covered in a coat of scarlet liquid.

The yob froze. He felt his flesh creep and his hair stand on end. He stared in disbelief.

Suddenly, from behind him came a piercing, cackling laugh. He spun around with mouth agape.

The old woman lunged towards him. As he took in the devilish, toothless, grin and wild, wide eyes he heard the 'squelch' as the long blade of a kitchen knife was embedded into his chest. He felt a searing pain as the knife was withdrawn. The shock and the impact projected him backwards and he fell to the floor.

He lay there stricken with terror as he watched the old woman advance toward him; her hysterical countenance became etched momentarily into his mind. The blade of the knife reflected a reddish hue in the dim light of the bedroom.

He frantically rose to his knees attempting to crawl from the path the old woman was making in his direction.

As he moved to one side another burst of cackling laughter preceded a second lunge with the knife which was planted with deadly accuracy into the middle of his back.

He let out a last pain-racked scream before collapsing prostrate on the floor.

His limbs jerked fitfully in his death throes as the knife rose and fell repeatedly into his body.

The old woman was, indeed, stark raving mad!

The Object of Charity

by

Douglas Morgan

The well-dressed, middle-aged lady wearing a hat looked out of place in the narrow street with its small terraced houses. She was herself conscious of this and pulled her coat more tightly around her, though the autumn day was mild. She did not greatly enjoy this part of the work, but it had to be done; it was her duty.

She hurried on till she reached no 27. There she tapped briskly, but not heavily, on the brightly shining brass knocker.

A little time passed before the door was opened by a small white-haired woman, evidently well into her eighties, who peered at her visitor. 'Yes?'

The caller smiled. 'Mrs Hemsley? I'm Mrs Pearce. The Vicar suggested that I should call on you.'

'Oh, the Vicar, is it? A nice man. Young, of course.'

'Do you mind if I come in?'

'Not at all, my dear, come along in. Would you like a cup of tea?'

'No, thank you very much. You see, I have a few calls to make, and if I drank tea at every house...'

'As you wish, my dear. Now sit yourself down. That chair's quite comfortable.'

Mrs Pearce seated herself in the well-worn armchair and looked around her. She was surprised by the austerity of the sitting-room. It was spotlessly clean, but the furniture harked back to the utility range available in the early post-war years. There were few decorations apart from two photographs, one of a middle-aged, moustached man and the other showing a youth of about eighteen, probably the old lady's son. In her experience, the homes of most elderly people were these days quite comfortable and even fashion-conscious.

The old lady seated herself on a straight-backed chair at the table. 'The Vicar, you say.'

'Yes, Mr Holland thought it would be a good idea for me to come and see you.'

'I see. Yes, a nice young man. And not so high as the one before him. I didn't care very much for that. Call me Father, he said to me once. I told him that I had two fathers, one on earth and the other in Heaven, and I thought that should be enough for anyone.'

Mrs Pearce suppressed a smile. 'The reason I've come is that I'm the Chair of the Dogsworth Fund which was set up in the last century.'

Mrs Hemsley looked puzzled. 'The chair?'

'Yes, the Chair-person, that is. The fund was set up by Sir Richard Dogsworth over a hundred years ago, and its aim is to help meet the needs of old persons in the parish who are suffering hardship. Of course, it's not a very big fund, as these things go. It comes to not much more than a thousand pounds a year now.'

'Yes, I quite understand, my dear.'

'So, of course, we cannot help many people, and we have to be careful about the people we *do* help. There's rather a lot of red tape, I'm afraid, but I have to make a report to the Trustees, so I need to go around asking a lot of questions.'

Mrs Hemsley frowned sympathetically. 'Yes, it must be very difficult for you. If I can help...'

'Well, tell me now, how are you managing?'

'Me? Oh, I manage very well, thank you. It's a bit painful walking - comes on worse in the damp weather - and my eyes are not very good, but I don't want to complain. I am eighty-six, you know, and in another month I'll be eighty-seven.'

Mrs Pearce smiled her congratulations. 'That's... marvellous. Do you have any family?'

'Well, my husband, he died fifteen years ago. I have one son, Henry, but he's getting on a bit now, of course. That's him in the photograph. Fine young man, he was.'

'What about fin... er... money?'

Mrs Hemsley seemed taken aback.

'I'm sorry,' Mrs Pearce went on quickly, 'I don't want to sound inquisitive, but I have to ask these questions. You have your pension, of course.'

'Well, yes, the old age.'

'Did your husband... I mean, any pension from his work?'

'Oh no, my dear, not in those days. He had some savings, just a little, but they went long ago. Mind you, he was a good man, my Jack, worked hard all his life. I still miss him a lot, I can tell you.'

'I'm sure you do. And your son, does he...?'

'Henry? He's in business, runs a little store down Salisbury way.'

'I expect he helps you.'

'Well, he used to send me a few pounds when his business was doing well, but the way things are now, he's having a struggle to keep going.'

'Does he come to visit you now and then?'

'Not so much, these days. He used to, but with all his worries it's difficult.'

'He's got a family, has he?'

'Just a wife. But she's not much help to him, I'm afraid.'

'When was the last time he came to see you?'

'Oh, I can't remember, my dear. It's quite a while ago now.'

'How about the neighbours?'

'They're very good. Of course, they're out working most of the day, but they do some shopping for me if I need it, when I've been ill, like.' The old lady paused and studied her visitor anxiously for a moment. 'Now, are you sure you won't have that cup of tea? You must be tired, going around like this. I remember when I was collecting for the Red Cross, my poor old feet!'

'I'd sooner not, it you don't mind, Mrs Hemsley. I shan't take up much more of your time. So what it comes to is that you have your pension, and that's really all you have to manage on?'

'Yes, that's about it. But I'm very grateful to have it, of course, and I try to be careful.'

'Well then, thank you, Mrs Hemsley, I think that's all I need for my report. Now I had better be getting on.'

Mrs Pearce half rose from her chair, but the old lady held out a hand. 'Just a minute, my dear, you stay there, I shan't be long. I'm so glad you called.'

Mrs Pearce subsided and watched as Mrs Hemsley shuffled across the room to a dresser. There, she opened a drawer and fumbled around inside it for a while before returning. With one hand, she held on to the table, and with the other she pushed something across towards Mrs Pearce. 'There you are, my dear, for your old people.'

Mrs Pearce looked. It was a pound coin. She could not resist registering a sense of shock.

'I'm sorry,' Mrs Hemsley apologised, 'it's not much, I know, but I'm a bit short this week.'

Mrs Pearce's first impulse was to push the coin back and to explain in blunt terms the precise purpose of her visit, but something held her back. Instead, she murmured weakly, 'Thank you... very generous.' She then allowed herself to be ushered, somewhat dazedly, to the door.

As she stepped into the street, she was already wondering what on earth she was going to say to the Vicar.

The Final Chore

by

Trevor Tidball

Sarah rose from her knees and looked down at the floor tiles. They gleamed brightly after the careful polishing she had given them. She smiled contentedly... she always did when she had finished her chores.

'All nice and clean again. That's what I like to see.' She spoke out loud, although she was alone in the house. This was not unusual. She had been in the habit of talking to herself for quite a number of years.

'Don't be so bloody stupid, woman!' her husband bellowed at her, when he'd first heard her babbling away in the kitchen. 'People will think you're stark raving mad, and I wouldn't blame them one little bit! ... perhaps you are!'

She'd made no reply. She never did when he said things like that to her. In any case, there'd be no point. He of all people wouldn't understand why she did it. He wouldn't realise that she was able to retreat and hide inside her own little world of conversation.

A secret personal world, where words could be made kind and thoughtful, gentle and loving. So unlike the words she was forced to listen to when he spoke. Words that made sharp needles dig painfully into her brain, blotting out all other thoughts and feelings...

'Yes, all nice and clean again,' she repeated.

Sarah was proud of her little home, and enjoyed keeping it spotless. Indeed, she revelled in housework, and it showed. Everything was perfect - in the house, that is but for her, that's where life's pleasures ended.

Right from the start, her marriage had been doomed to fail. Still in her late teens, she had been flattered by the attentions of a man twelve years older than herself. She had imagined a happy contented life together. Sadly, Tom had shown her little or no affection from the outset of their married life. She soon realised that all he wanted was a housekeeper and servant to attend to his needs, not a wife to love and care for. Now, ten long years later, she knew what a terrible mistake she had made.

She had learned to accept and cope with the cold loveless relationship that existed between them. It was the cruelty she couldn't endure. It wasn't physical cruelty - she even felt she could have tolerated some of that. It was the continual taunting, the complaints, the sarcasm and derision to which she was subjected day after day, year after year. It was unceasing. Nothing satisfied. Her ideas were scorned, her cooking ridiculed. Whatever she did or said was wrong. What little confidence she had in the beginning was destroyed. She found herself becoming too frightened to move or speak, for fear of causing some caustic biting reaction...

She was standing at the ironing board when she heard his key in the door. As always, she went to the oven, took out his dinner, and placed it on the table ready for him. As he entered the kitchen the look on his face was enough to tell her that things hadn't gone well for him at work. There was no greeting - there never was. Not a word was said as he sat down to his meal. She watched him while he poked at the food with his fork. Suddenly, without any warning, he pushed the plate sidewards, and sent it crashing to the floor.

'Not fit for pigs, woman!' he shouted. 'It's about time you learned to cook a decent meal. Clean it up and do me something that's worth eating!'

She was already on her hands and knees dealing with the mess before he'd finished yelling at her. Her mind was spinning around crazily. The needles, sharper than ever, began their brain torture once again, and the searing pain in her head was almost unbearable. With trembling fingers, she began to pick up the broken pieces of the plate.

Totally unconcerned, her husband sat at the table with his back to her, engrossed in the evening paper spread out in front of him... and then it happened - a strange but welcome feeling of calmness engulfed her completely. Her body stopped shaking, and the unbearable pain in her head just melted away. She picked up a large jagged piece of the broken plate, and studied it intently, before rising slowly to her feet...

Blood gushed from the wound in her husband's neck as he slumped forward in the chair. His head crashed onto the outspread table. His body twitched twice, and then became still. Very still.

Sarah stood there engrossed, fascinated by the trail of red liquid as it ran slowly to the table's edge and dripped onto the tiled floor. Then she shook her head reprovingly.

'Oh dear! What a terrible mess I've caused,' she said. 'Nevermind, we'll get things ship-shape again won't we? ... Let's get on with it then, shall we? The sooner the better I think, don't you?'

The rhetorical questions ended as she walked calmly towards the kitchen cupboard above the sink. She opened it and took a first-aid box from the shelf. Selecting a wide crepe bandage from within, she placed it on the table alongside the body, Then, unwinding a thick roll of cotton wool, she positioned it firmly over the gaping wound. After binding the bandage tightly around the head, securing the dressing, she stood back and surveyed her handiwork.

All the while she had been doing this, she had been humming a tune. She always did when she was busy.

'There, that's tidied him up nicely... now for the rest of the mess.'

Her voice sounded normal, giving no indication that anything out of the ordinary had taken place. Carefully holding up Tom's bandaged head with one hand, she removed the soiled newspaper, and wiped clean the area underneath before lowering the head back to its former position. Then she turned her attention to the floor.

Once more she knelt and was soon working vigorously, humming and talking as she cleaned.

'The only way to do a floor properly, my girl,' she said 'is down on your hands and knees, isn't it?'

It wasn't long before everything was perfectly clean again. The tiles glistened once more, as they always did after Sarah had finished with them.

'A little more housework than usual today, but well worth the extra effort I think, don't you? And it's only right and proper to have the place spick and span, 'specially when you're expecting visitors.'

She took a last look around checking everything very carefully, before putting all the cleaning materials away. Then she washed her hands, and, after drying them thoroughly made her way to the telephone on the hall table. She looked at it intently for about a minute. A small nerve twitched in her cheek, and her face reflected her indecision.

The telephone was something that Sarah avoided whenever possible. It represented an ominous intrusion, something capable of creating pain and distress. It meant listening to words from someone unseen. A voice that might be as hurtful and wounding as the one she had learned to dread. It was too great a risk to take.

If the phone rang when she was alone in the house, she always left it. She used to sit on the stairs, watching it, willing the caller to go away. The relief she experienced when the ringing finally stopped made the peace that followed even more enjoyable. A peace that helped her to return to her own intimate world of make-believe... but now it was different. There was something to be done and she had to do it.

'Pull yourself together, my girl,' she said sharply, 'it won't take long, so get on with it and don't hang about.' She picked up the receiver, and hesitated for a few seconds before dialling. She took a deep breath and spoke slowly and clearly.

Her call was a brief one. Afterwards, she returned to the kitchen, looked around very carefully once more, and then gave a deep sigh.

The seconds ticked by, and in the distance the wailing of a siren could be heard. 'They won't be long now,' she whispered, 'and we're all nice and clean again.'

She smiled contentedly... but then, she always did when she finished her chores.

Invisible Earnings

by

David J Carrington

'There's a million dollars of Government money in the account, Dave; sorry to dump it on you but I've paid all the bills and you shouldn't get anything major while I'm away.' Gordon Black, the Financial Manager of the Northern Canada Job Creation Scheme, was reluctant to hand over his principal responsibility.

He pushed the ledger across to Dave Worthington. 'Remember, if anything over a couple of hundred comes in, don't pay it; I can't stress this too highly. I'll sort it out when I return.'

Worthington was the Scheme's Resource Manager and the most junior of the four staff at their base in Labrador. He grudgingly signed the certificate accepting the account from his colleague. This was, however, the first leave that Black had taken since Worthington had arrived and so the additional responsibility of minding the books was not a frequent burden.

That evening, Worthington drove Black to catch the Gander flight before returning to the bar of the Labrador Inn. Sipping his drink, he failed to hear the approach of a large man in his late fifties.

'Dave! Just the man.'

'Hi, Joe. Problems?'

'There wouldn't be if you guys settled your account on time.' Joe McShane was the manager of the local Hudson's Bay Trading company with the contract to supply equipment for the Scheme's projects. He was normally jovial but there was no concealing the irritation in his voice.

'A month ago we delivered those snow machines for your winter projects. I gave the bill to Black myself and I've reminded him frequently that we needed payment within seven days. Then this morning, I get the cheque; it's thirty grand short! Now he's gone on leave. I'll have to charge interest, Dave; I've got no choice.'

'That doesn't sound like Gordon; he's usually meticulous with money.'

McShane took an invoice from his pocket and threw it on the bar. Worthington read the scrawled details. 'A hundred and twenty, or is that a hundred and fifty, thousand dollars?' He quickly calculated the total from the entries above. 'It's a hundred and fifty thousand but it's not clear. That's the problem; you should have had it typed.'

McShane shrugged. 'Yeah, well, the clerk was sick... anyway you worked it out in one minute; it took Black a month to get it wrong. No, Dave, I'm charging interest from tomorrow.'

'If I pay you the difference, would you reconsider?'

'Sure, but...'

'I've got the account while Gordon's on leave!' Worthington smiled.

McShane relaxed.

Worthington grabbed the phone on the third ring.

'Hi Dave, Randy Baxter, Royal Bank. McShane's just presented your cheque for thirty thousand; there aren't the funds to cover it?'

Worthington laughed. 'Very funny, Randy...'

'No joke, Dave. The money's not there.'

'I took over the account yesterday. There was a million dollars in it. No one could spend that much in Labrador in one day.'

'There *is* a million dollars altogether, but most of it's on deposit and I need twenty-eight days' notice to transfer it into the current account.'

'But I saw the current account statement. What's the money doing on deposit?'

'Earning nine percent - a rock solid investment...'

'Cut the commercial, Randy. I may not know much about public accounting but I do know it's illegal to speculate with government money by unauthorized investment, however safe. There's something wrong here. What am I going to do?'

'Come and see me and we'll work something out.'

Maurice Laniel, General Manager of the Job Creation Scheme, cupped his hand over the telephone mouthpiece and whispered. 'It's Worthington. He's at the bank. He's found out!'

John Baird, the Operations' Manager, leant forward in alarm, ears straining.

'I'll take it up with Black when he returns,' snapped Laniel into the phone. 'I'll see you in fifteen minutes.' He hung up.

Silence draped the office for a few seconds. 'I knew we were asking for trouble giving him the job,' Baird muttered.

'The stand-in responsibility is in his contract,' snarled Laniel. 'It would have looked suspicious if I'd taken the job myself. Besides, Black assured me he'd briefed Worthington not to pay any bills! Damn!'

There was a tap on the door. 'Come in.' Laniel stared through the window, still concerned about the events of the last two days. Worthington was reluctant to accept the 'new policy from Head Office' explanation that he and Baird had hurriedly contrived.

He sensed a visitor in his office and turned to see a smartly dressed young man who held out his hand. 'George Johnson, Sir. Head Office have sent me to do a surprise check of the public account.'

The words scorched the inside of Laniel's forehead. In a sea of rising panic his mouth gaped stupidly. Johnson continued but only fragments penetrated Laniel's tumbling mind. 'Usual thing... consolidate ledger with bank statement... no irregularities... routine... etcetera.'

'You can't!' spluttered Laniel suddenly. 'Black's not here. You must wait until he returns. I won't let you.'

'I'm here to check your system which shouldn't be dependent on individuals. The employment contract requires the Resource Manager to deputize for the Financial Manager. This is an excellent opportunity to see how a non-specialist copes.'

'But Worthington's a financial disaster. I'm relying on Black to sort the books when he returns. Can't it wait?'

'No. I've a schedule to keep so I'd better make a start. I'll debrief you this afternoon.' Johnson left.

'... and never before have I encountered such a swindle.' Johnson concluded grimly.

Laniel's face was grey. 'Ok. It's like this,' he sighed. 'A couple of years ago, there were only the three of us. We sought ways to improve our lifestyle in this isolated place. Investing the public account in a safe, low interest scheme seemed ideal. Our only problem was to deceive the auditors into believing that the money was always where it should have been - in the current account.'

Johnson listened impassively. 'I will have to report this.'

'How about a quarter share? In four weeks the account will be restored and no one will be any the wiser.'

'You've already tried to sell Worthington a phoney story. Do you think he'll keep his mouth shut? No way! I advise you to put the hundred and fifty thousand dollars worth of interest back into the current account; you've got forty eight hours before I present my report. It will look better if the interest has been returned.

'As a matter of professional interest, how *did* you get the bank statements to show the whole amount apparently still in the current account?'

'Baird was dating one of the bank tellers for a while. She stole some blank statement forms. We just printed our own and put the real ones aside.'

'Give me those blanks; it'll stop you cooking any more books. By the way, Black will not be returning. Goodbye, gentlemen.'

'Hello, Maurice,' said the nonchalant voice on the telephone. 'It's Gordon. I'm back. Can someone pick me up?' This was the third shock to Laniel's system in a week.

Unable to contact Black, he and Baird had made frantic phone calls to their respective banks securing sufficient loans to replace the interest they had creamed from the invested public capital. Johnson had left several days ago but the expected storm had yet to break. A warning bell clanged loudly in Laniel's head.

'Maurice?'

'Oh yes, I'm here. I'll collect you myself. We'll return via the bank.'

Black stormed into Worthington's office. 'Give me the account back, now!'

Worthington smiled wryly and pushed the ledger slowly across the desk. He cleared his throat noisily. 'Ok. You left me with a million. I had one bill to pay of thirty thousand and the balance is in the current account. Here's the latest statement.

Black snatched up the cheque book and flicked through it. 'There are *two* cheques missing!'

'When I ripped out the cheque for thirty thousand, I tore out two by mistake. I couldn't put the unused one back so I destroyed it and marked the stub. That's ok isn't it? I'm not accounts trained you know.' His face reflected the innocence in his voice.

At that point, Laniel burst into the office. Trembling with rage, he waved a piece of paper under Worthington's nose. '*This* is the latest bank statement; yours is a forgery! The cheque that you 'destroyed' was made out to a G Johnson for the amount of the interest that Baird and I repaid. Johnson is your partner in crime. He supplied you with blank statement forms.'

'My statement is as genuine as any of yours,' retorted Worthington.

'I'll get you...'

'You'll do what? Tell Head Office? Sure you will. I've got copies of the real statements too - enough evidence to put you all away. Think about it, Laniel; as far as the rest of the world is concerned, not a cent of public money is missing; the capital in the current account is intact for all to see.'

'You double crossing...'

'Me? No. I'm just an... er... financial disaster trying to boost his standard of living with some, shall we say, invisible earnings?'

The Unionist

by

John Phillips

Pencadoc lies in a valley, happy to be remote, unknown. Everyone who lives in the place knows that it is a village produced by the Industrial Revolution, born to provide coal for the furnaces of the iron works and domestic hearths. It is unpretentious in its style of architecture and its inhabitants are as natural as natural can be.

In the 1880's, a small group of Conservatives gathered together and decided to open a club which they hoped would further their cause. Wanting to avoid open provocation, they decided wisely to call it the Unionist Club. Labour could be Labour and Liberal could be Liberal but in their valley it was better to be prudent.

When the need arose for increased membership, politics were played down and in time the club became as anonymous in its activities and its atmosphere as the other clubs, the main talking points being rugby, soccer, snooker, horse racing and darts. Politics was almost an alien word, one remembered only when some daft ninny brought it up, as happened now and then, such as when four years ago a picture of Margaret Thatcher was hung up in the concert room. Complaints were made to the Committee. 'What's her face doing in a place like this? She's never been a unionist. In fact she's dead against unions.' The Committee understood and deemed it wise not to disillusion good spenders who kept the club solvent. They removed the picture and restored calm.

Occasionally, some bright spark on the Committee feels that it is time that a speaker is invited to give a party address to members. Usually, such rash enthusiasm is dampened and it fizzles out, but two months ago Major John Williams M C the county agent, was invited. A notice was put up on the board announcing that the meeting would open at six pm and that free drinks would be available to those attending. Normally, when free drinks are on offer there is a good turn-out, but few wanted to hear the Major. Eleven turned up, including Jack Thomas who came to find out who this man was who was trying to take over his job. 'I'm the M C in this club and we don't need another one. Who's this Williams, then?'

To be fair, not all the members are as dim as Jack, although Tom Richards has come pretty near to it. Tom is rising eighty-three and joined the club forty years ago solely because it has a snooker table. When he applied for membership and had been 'vetted', he had paid little attention to the questions and barely bothered to read the application form. His membership card shows that he is a member of The Unionist Club in Pencadoc, a card very handy when going for a trip in the summer, but the symbol that indicates affiliation to certain other clubs has no real meaning for him other than it seems to get him entrance.

Tom was walking up Main Street one day when a car stopped beside him. There were four men inside it and one of them asked him, 'can you direct us to the Conservative Club?'

'Conservative Club?' asked Tom. 'Never heard of one around here. You'd better go to the top of this street and turn right into Merthyr Road. There's a Post Office there and maybe somebody in it can help you.'

The car drove off and Tom walked on for another forty yards, came into The Unionist, bought a pint and settled down in his favourite corner. Half an hour later the four men from the car walked in and when they saw him one of them said, 'aren't you the man who said you didn't know where the Conservative Club is?'

'Yes, that's me,' said Tom. 'Did you find it after?' He was given some funny looks which he could not in any way understand. He sipped and cogitated until long after the four strangers had departed. Later on, when Jack Thomas came in, Tom went over the incident with him and summed it up by saying, 'some odd people about, Jack. They wanted a Conservative Club and instead of finding it, they came here. Funny people!' Jack agreed.

Space Invaders

by

Paul Crossley

Extra Vehicular Activity Expert number 1256f/B, Terra authority first class, Coastline specialist graduate and SupaSuit advanced pilot highly commended - or Eva to her friends - strode purposefully through the swirling green fog. The SupaSuit head-dome sensor indicators flickered madly around her peripheral vision. Just below the completely useless visor, a small screen indicated her position, partly with a map projection and blinking red dot marking her position, and partly with a computer enhanced view taken from the suit's 360 degree cameras. She stopped walking, or at least instructed the suit to stop walking for her, and held a begloved hand up to her face. Six inches away it appeared as a dull shadow. Four inches, the outline coalesced into a hand shape. Three inches, yes it was a glove. Three inches of real visibility. How was she expected to work in these conditions?

Eva stared hard at a particular green pulsating *Led*, and then blinked twice. The suit spoke. 'Communication Request accepted. State recipient.'

She spoke slowly, concentrating on every vowel and consonant. The suit audio input system had been playing up lately, resulting in embarrassing wrong numbers. 'Ground to Mothership channel 2, Flight Control Co-ordinator Richardson, Main Ground Surveillance Module 25/14, monitor screen 2. Confirm.'

The suit spoke back. 'Mound to Grotherchip shannel toof ligtco troll...'

Eva snapped out an expletive and instructed the suit to stop the call. Damn cheap rubbish they made these things from. Junk, but junk she relied on all day, every day. 'Just call Mothership central for me, I'll do the rest, okay?'

The suit remained silent.

'Well?'

'Ground Sat Comms inoperative, Ground Tech Support reports Fog vapour ingestion in primary circuits, fix time three hours ten minutes, earliest.'

Another expletive. Eva instructed the suit to adopt a sitting position, and she relaxed down inside the squatting machine, glad to take the weight off her feet. 'Suit,' she slowly enunciated, 'replay my Personal Mission Briefing again would you, and make me a coffee.'

A warm comforting voice filled the head-dome, the voice of dreamy FCC Richardson. 'Eva, your mission today, Neptune Colony year 317, day 12, Terra year 2429, day 302, is to evaluate coastal land erosion progress in sector 127/3, formally known as Wales/Gwynedd/Llandudno.'

Eva sighed. FCC Richardson was so clever, he could say those funny place names just right. She asked the suit for replay and mimicked Richardson's voice saying, 'Wales-stroke-Gwynedd-stroke-Llandudno.' The recording continued.

'Historical records of this area are very confused and many have been lost altogether. It would seem likely that the area was used for recreational activity, though of what kind we are unsure. You main task is to search out a particularly interesting feature, which was briefly visible through the fog earlier this time frame. Previous scans at normal atmosphere density had revealed nothing, however during a particularly violent wind storm we were able to discern an unusual regular shape protruding into the sea. Your drop point will be calculated approximately eight-hundred metres from the object. Advise extreme caution. Today's fog level is particularly high, density expected at 0.95, corrosive element 0.31 and increasing. Good luck, Eva, stay in touch.'

She sighed again. There was a small insistent beeping coming from somewhere in the suit. She scanned the indicators. Nothing was obviously wrong. 'What's that noise?' she asked.

'Coffee's ready. Suck on nipple 2.'

Eva did, but it tasted vile. She ordered the suit to stand up and continue their journey, concentrating again on the display below her nose. Vague shapes drifted slowly by, nothing making any sense. She ordered a gain increase in exterior sound sensor amplification, and stopped to listen. Ah, that was better, her favourite noise, waves washing against the shore, the regular irregularity of it. Wish-poosh. Wish-poosh.

Eva approached the shore end of the mysterious structure. It appeared that a wide concrete path was funnelling down to some sort of narrower walkway. As she started to take her first step onto the changed surface, a loud warning whine off in her left ear and she quickly aborted the forward motion. 'What's that beef, suit?'

'Surface ahead corroded below safety threshold for this model of SupaSuit plus user mass value. Surface ahead consists of fragile wood slats only a few centimetres thick. Structure ahead consists of a supported ramp a few metres above sea surface, and is in distinct danger of collapse. Structure ahead projects out in to sea for many metres, terminating in a larger area, which contains a circular room. Circular room would appear to be...'

Eva waited. 'Well, Suit, spit it out?'

'Circular room would appear to be Fog free.'

'You're kidding, right?'

'Sensors reveal area of pure air, no Fog, no corrosive constituents, normal temperature, Terran breathable, though stale.'

'How are we going for hover fuel?' Eva asked, knowing that to risk the emergency evacuation system on simple exploring was well outside the rules.

'We have three minutes and fourteen seconds available at plus 1.01 G thrust. However this would compromise...'

'Let's go Suit, I won't tell if you won't.'

There was a brief whirring and gurgling sound as the suit started up its small thuster system, then Eva was slowly skimming over the wooden beams, heading out to sea. There appeared to be guard rails along the edge, she speculated that the structure must have had some serious purpose involving the people of its time. The circular building loomed up on her sensor screen. She manoeuvred right up to it, and discovered that part of the exterior wall was made of glass. She pushed the head-dome right up against the grimy surface. 'Exterior lights, Suit, shine straight ahead.'

Sure enough, the beams illuminated not the usual green vapour, but a clear area, a room, a strange room containing many black boxes. 'Suit, probe the floor in there, will it take our weight?'

'Positive. Corrosion heavy on underside, but totally free on top. Estimate safety factor of 25%, acceptable.'

'Right, then how do we get in?'

'One minute twelve seconds of fuel remain. Please wait... Scanning. Threedee projection complete, examining matrix, please wait... Task complete, entry possible, 75% probability of success...'

'For goodness sake hurry up!' Eva barked, 'tell me now.'

'There is a door two point five metres to your left.'

'Well great, get me in there and shut and seal as quickly as possible.'

Fifteen minutes later, Eva was standing naked in the centre of the circular room, slack jawed in wonder. Admittedly the air stank, admittedly even the small ingress of Fog into the room had caused some misting, but to all intents and purposes, Eva was in the original Terran atmosphere, gulping down air unbreathed in centuries. Inside the doorway she had found a pile of pamphlets, each one exhorting the same message. 'Visit the Llandudno Pier End Amusement Arcade, Play Pinball, Pool and Video Games all Day!'

Pinball? Pool? Eva tried to make sense of this, but to no avail. She moved over to one of the strange boxes dotted around the place. 'Suit,' she said, 'come over here a minute.' The discarded silvery pile of material arranged itself into a human shape and tottered over to her. 'What is this thing?'

'Without Ground Sat links to the main Mothership History Banks I am unable to confirm the exact nature and purpose of this machine.'

'Well guess then.'

'I would say, if pressed, that this machine is an entertainment device used frequently in the late twentieth Terran century. It allowed the user a limited expansion of his or her own physical horizons by simulating some unlikely scenario, usually warlike in nature, through which the person could achieve some form of peculiar relaxation. This almost always involved 'killing' pseudo 'things'.'

'It's a game.'

'That's what I said.'

'Can you get it working?'

'It seems to simply require 230/240 volts AC at 50 Hz applied to the power cable at the rear. I can provide this with no difficulty. There would also appear to be copious instructions for the game inscribed around the main display unit. Some form of token is required.'

'Do it, Suit.'

And so it was, as she moved from game to game around the amusement arcade, that Extra Vehicular Activity Expert Eva gained a depth of knowledge and insight into her remote ancestors unsurpassed by decades of more considered study. She learned that Earthmen liked to drive cars and motorbikes very fast, fly planes and helicopters in a furious fashion, stalk dim caverns and fight hobgoblins, wrestle monsters and aliens, race hedgehogs and save lemmings.

After only a few hours the Suit started to chirp its warnings. Energy low, time to return to pick up point short, initial floor corrosion estimate compromised by Eva's jerks and leaps while playing, collapse of structure imminent, and so on and so on.

At the last minute the suit, with Eva on board, soared away from the crumbling building and headed for the store. With the gain turned up full, Eva could hear the terminal cracks and crunches, and eventually the awful groan and huge splash as the Last Amusement Arcade in the Universe slid unceremoniously below the waves.

Simone Says

by

Valley March

Harvey lined up all his shoes: heel to heel, toe to toe. He even included his old tartan carpet slippers.

'Utter rubbish,' Simone said. Harvey had hidden them in the attic, out of sight out of mind.

He had quite a collection of 'utter rubbish'. When she left he fetched the ladder. Proudly he brought down the trophies and set them out about the house. He was positively masterful, now that the mistress had moved out.

Two months now and he sat alone on the throne. Sometimes it hurt like hell, other times he felt honoured. It all depended on how he remembered the farewell scene. Had Simone, propelled by her own ill humour, slammed the door, or was he the instigator? Some days it was clear as the dawn, other times it was murky with the self-doubt that once again she had got the edge on him.

Two months as a male alone. Harvey was heavy with boredom, an existence without excitement. The arguments had definitely been colourful. Now the days were drab with an awful sameness. Harvey would have to admit that they were positively dreary.

But this Saturday was to be different. There was to be an edge of excitement.

He patted his newly-cleaned suit on the shoulder? 'Man, we're going to have fun. And that's no idle parlance. That's a promise.'

He shed his working clothes, as easily and as carelessly as a snake shedding a skin.

'Now you're a slut, Harvey, a real slut.' Simone spoke, but it was only an old record playing.

'Now, Harvey, don't go and wear your red tie. You'll look like a communist. I know one can't make a silk purse out of a sow's ear - but I think you could make the effort.'

He threaded his fingers affectionately through the garlands of ties trailing in his wardrobe. Purposefully he caught the red one, a catch that gave him immense pleasure.

'Oh, Harvey, you're so brash. I like a gentleman.'

He selected his black shoes and took them into the kitchen to give them an added shine.

'Shoes are such a give-away. Scruffy shoes always mean a scruffy character.'

Harvey polished away with such vigour that he could see a mirrored image of himself.

Dressed and ready for the off, Harvey could not resist mounting the stairs again for a final check out.

Opening Simone's wardrobe he stood back smiling at the suited gentleman reflected in the full-length mirror. Cupping the red tie, as if it were a trophy he waved it triumphantly.

'See, Simone, I've put it on 'specially for you. Now, don't I look a winner? And let me tell you, this gentleman's moving into new pastures.'

Outside Maurice made music with a blare from his car horn. Harvey galloped down the stairs, two at a time, in his eagerness to answer the summons.

Sliding into the car, he tapped Maurice on the knee. 'Right, here's Romeo reporting.'

Maurice, dark as a gipsy and as roguish, turned and gave his friend a long and considering look.

'You reckon you're up to it? What if she suddenly came back?'

Harvey gave a wide grin. 'You didn't know I was brilliant, did you? I've actually changed the lock.'

'But what if she came knocking at the door?'

'Oh, I'd cope. If that Simone knocked and knocked and knocked at the door, I just wouldn't answer.'

'Phew, very masterful,' approved his friend. 'You're really starting to come alive again. Who knows, you may even strike it rich right away. This computer date could turn out to be another Marilyn Monroe.

Harvey gave a small shrug of his shoulders. 'Sorry mate, but curvaceous blondes don't usually come my way.'

'Hey, careful. You're going soft again. Remember, there's always a first time.'

'And I'll end up marrying a Monroe?'

'Now watch it, Harv. Who's talking about a prison sentence? Haven't you had more than enough with Simone?'

'But, honest, she could be a delight.'

'She could also be a right little devil. Look, let's not sit here strumming guitars. When there's that Marilyn waiting out there for you.'

It had been Maurice's idea to fill in a questionnaire for a computer date. Maurice was always so full of ideas. Roving around the countryside as a salesman, he was forever changing his dames and his digs.

They sped out into the darkness of the country.

Harvey kept shifting about in his seat and tugging at his tie.

'It seems a long, long drive. Have we taken a wrong road?'

'Oh, for goodness sake relax, Harvey. Told you it would be fifty miles - so fifty miles it's going to be. Don't you forget it, I'm not piloting Concorde. For goodness sake, don't get jittery like a dame. Just try and relax. Marilyn Monroe is going to love you.'

'I gave my shoes an extra polish.'

Maurice gave a loud guffaw.

'Shoes - who's to care about your shoes? It's your baby blue eyes that she'll be looking at. In baiting a bird, then bricks and mortar are a real come on, so mind you mention you own your own house.'

'Look, do you like my red tie?' Harvey was tugging at it again. He had put it on in an act of bravado, now he was not sure that it suited.

'Hey, I'm not a cat, seeing in the dark. Anyway it's not for me to fancy you. I've told you already, you're a gentleman. I've set you up and now it's over to you to make all the right moves.'

'The Chequers' was in the main highway. Maurice cruised by it, urging Harvey to take notice.

'Pull yourself together, Harv. Now, you said you'd meet her in the Lounge Bar. Can you see the entrance?'

'Yes, yes, but it doesn't look as if we can park there. There's too much traffic.'

'True, but it's not me who has the date. You've two legs. You've only to push down the door handle and you can be out and on your way to Marilyn. No.' He put out a restraining hand. 'Don't try a suicidal leap now. I'll slow down. Now, up and at her.'

Marilyn was like little Jack Horner, in the corner. She sat with her back towards the entrance, which gave Harvey some heart. So she wanted him to take the initiative and make the approach. It would be a change having the lead role in a relationship. Would he be able to handle it?

I'm a gentleman and a householder, he told himself.

'Next year, Harvey, you must paint the house Old Gold.' Simone could always trespass on his thoughts.

'I'll paint the house next summer. Perhaps a crimson?' It was another bravado. He hoped it would stimulate his approach to the blonde.

Perhaps the blonde was not his date after all? But he was only teasing himself. She was after all wearing the colours he had been told to expect: emerald green costume with green shoes and handbag - and that lovely long blonde drape of hair wriggling down her back.

Again he straightened his tie, after all he must look his best. First impressions and all that ... now he was ready to make the introductions and see that her eyes were the promised blue. Then, again, quite unexpectedly, he was thinking that he would like to marry again.

'Who would ever want to marry you, Harvey - only a lunatic?' Simone had a very direct approach.

He had taken the necessary steps and now gently touched the blonde on the shoulder.

'Excuse me, but I believe you must be Angela?'

She acknowledged the name with a soft 'Yes, I'm Angela.'

Then turning round her blue eyes widened in surprise. But then, swiftly, the wonder was replaced by a glare.

'Harvey...'

Her anger was contagious.

'Right, I'm not the John you expected to meet, but neither are you Angela.'

'Oh, Harvey, what a dirty, dirty trick you've played on me.'

'Surely, no dirtier than yours?'

'And you're wearing that ghastly red tie.'

'And you've got your blonde wig on.'

Then, Harvey, leant over and with great satisfaction, he swiftly scalped her.

Treasures of the Gods

by

Liz Muir

A strike in the dark. A twist of blade and lips. The evil deed was done. No disturbance, no breath of air, just a glint of a cold red and green jewel in the blanket of night. The orb shimmered, the attacker turned and was gone.

Sif stretched, revelling in the softness of her velvet dream. She lay between her subconscious and the surreal, cushioned by the satin cocoon. Something was wrong, she felt light-headed.

She stumbled out of bed and across the floor. Catching her image in the mirror, she stared in horror and screamed! The reflection blurred as she sank to the ground, her face a sparkling mass of tears. Who could have done this? She grimaced in pain. She knew!

Thor was pleased: pleased with the deal, pleased with his minions, but most of all pleased with his new wife. She was beautiful. He had seen the metamorphosis from the subtle beauty of spring's be-dewed, chrysalic figure to the stunning radiance of her summer's voluptuous form. She was his imago of femininity. A contrast between the slight and leonine magnificence of her hair. Just as the lion wears his regal crown, so too did she. A tumbling mass, her golden crowning glory, truly made her the perfect beauty.

Thor returned to his marital hall. There was no sign of his wife. Concerned, he climbed the great spiralling staircase. He heard a noise. A soft murmuring whimper. He doubled his pace, prepared to beat back any intruder. He opened the bedroom door and shock and anger drove the colour from his face.

There, lying lifeless, separated from the rest of her body, was his wife's beautiful hair; Sif's beautiful hair! He felt sick, it had like a dying creature lost its golden lustre.

Sif faced him. She was still beautiful, but her radiance lay in a heap by his feet. Her gentle weeping tore the very essence of his being. Moving forward to embrace her, he too knew the identity of the evil perpetrator.

'I am an insensitive worm,' squeaked Loki.

'Again!' Thor gave him another violent shake.

'I am an insensitive worm.'

'Again!'

Loki could hardly force the words out. He couldn't squeeze enough air through his strangled trachea. The agony of another of Thor's jerks gave him the incentive.

'I...am...an...in--sens--i-tive...w..worm,' he wheezed. He could feel the gradual detaching sensation of his consciousness beginning. He was scared. 'What are you going to do about it?' roared in his ears. He couldn't think, couldn't answer. He saw before his eyes a swirling mass of hallucinative colour spiralling in a frenzy to an infinite point of darkness beyond his focus. He slumped into it.

Before him rose a mountainous landscape in a haze. He was cold and soaked to the skin. His vision cleared a little and he saw ominous structures in the landscape. A high prominent peak with three dark wells positioned around it. Another bucket of water landed on him and he recognised Thor's face inches from his own.

'You didn't kill me?' he asked amazed.

'No, but I will,' came the menacing reply, 'if you don't appease my wife.'

He understood. His voice was hoarse, his body weak, his throat blue and swollen, but he raised himself to his feet and crossed Bifrost Bridge on his way to seek for the dark hell elves.

Asgard lay leagues above him, as the smothering, volcanic heat left his bruised throat parched. But on he struggled through the cavernous maze passed cauldron-lakes, lying deceptively calm.

On the uppermost level of Hel's empire of night, he paused. A flash! A searching beacon of red and green light and Loki found his path. He crossed the darkness and entered the Ivaldi brothers' home.

Swearing to return great favours and friendship to the dwarves, Loki marvelled at their accurate premonition of his need. To aid their ally, the brothers spun gold into silken strands, sculpting a flowing sea of hair that rode the breath of air as one, but broke waves upon Loki's arms.

Finishing their wondrous gift, the brothers quietly explained the true magical delight of the gold head of hair.

'This is not just a pretty piece of woven precious metal, this is a living, breathing, work of art where we have shown our mettle. For entwined in the gold strands are spells of such invention, that grow like nature's own, it will and on her fair head it will be still, When Ragnorok is done.'

Loki gathered the wonderful wig into his arms, thanked the brothers for their mighty work and departed pleased that his task was completed. But as he left the Ivaldi domain Hel's evil influence captured him again.

He pondered the problem of what to do. He was assured of the incredible attributes of the gold hair and wondered if he might wager them with Hel's darker minions for greater reward. He turned aside from his chosen path and allowed his sense of smell to lead him down to terror. The darkest depths enveloped him and sulphurous mists caressed his skin, but on he ventured in solitude. He steered away from sulphuric lakes guided by the twinkling reflection of ruby red and emerald green.

Eventually he saw a flaming glow and he came across the den of Hel's dark elves. The creatures, hunched dwarves, appeared. A moving mass of deadly sin, they approached him and covetously pawed the gold hair. Loki stood and enjoyed their envious inspection.

'It is a piece of stunning beauty,' Loki cunningly said, 'the most wondrous work the worlds have seen, wouldn't you agree?'

This angered Brokk and Eitri, the brothers who heard his words. Full of pride they both replied, 'In our gluttonish hoard we have procured more gold than your imagination full can see. With skills and spells and sorcerer's knells we gather it here to be our company.'

'This is but a pretty trifle,' said Eitri.

'A nothing. A mere tit-bit of skill,' added Brokk. 'Our own work is far superior to this.'

'Surely not,' the schemer smiled. 'The world would have to see such work to believe your boast.'

'What of that?' the slothful pair replied, 'we do not need to be believed. We desire gold not acclamation.'

And so, Loki was forced by avarice's hand to offer a wager for their handicraft. 'I propose you make a piece more valuable than the hair and we set the great beings, Odin and Thor, to be the judges of our competition. As winner I would take your piece, as loser I would give you this,' and before the brothers' eyes he waved the wondrous wig.

The temptation of the offer was great, but the brothers made a lustful alteration: 'We propose a different scam that everything be as you said, but if you lose, we win your head!'

Loki, although not pleased by this demand, was confident in the great skill of the Ivaldi brothers and hence agreed.

The evil pair decided to compete on a more military level. They saw the perfection in the gold hair and wished to strive for art in a different direction. Satisfaction stoked their burning hearts. Of course, two warring beings would fully appreciate the sanctity of iron. Saving themselves a wealth of gold, the brothers began the creation of a great weapon.

Sensing his impending predicament, Loki transformed himself, by a series of verbal incantations, into a fly. His bulbous, jewel-like eyes enabled him to target Brokk. Viciously he attacked the evil elf and stung his eyelids. Dark rivers of blood burst forth, gushing down the channels in his face. Blinded by the gory flood, he strove to save the weapon.

The heat seared his hand, but still Eitri grasped the glowing metal and withdrew the magnificent hammer. Stemming the flow of blood with his hands, Brokk peered through narrow slits to view their work.

'Too short in the handle I fear,' said Brokk.

'But in time of war I would want it near,' replied Eitri, 'it is a glorious weapon, brother. Let us name it Mjollnir, our symbol of destruction.'

The brothers agreed and, taking the hammer to Loki, decided that Brokk, for he had suffered most, should accompany Mjollnir up to Asgard.

Quickly Odin followed Thor, since the deal had made him second in command, Thor had proved himself a mighty power and his father wished to keep him in his new seat. So, to mollify his son's erupting rage, Odin obligingly questioned nothing, but hurried to Asgard's Hall.

Sif was seated, still weeping, next to her husband's throne. Thor himself stood by Odin, while Loki and Brokk explained the wager. Thor was only too pleased to judge the future of Loki's head, and so the presentation of the gifts began.

Handing Sif the wondrous wig, Loki told of the magical power it had. Once placed on Sif's head it became like an all-encompassing ray of sunlight, making her truly as radiant as before.

Appeased to some extent, Thor listened to the dwarf, 'This hammer, lords, has hidden power. No one can break it, or lose it, no creature can stand against it. Its only fault is lack of length, which does not effect its use of strength.'

Instantly the warring lords decided, despite the glowing beauty of Sif's gold hair, that Mjollnir's strength was beyond belief.

Stepping forward, armed with blade, Brokk recited 'If you lose, we win your head. I pronounce my claim!'

Swiftly the cunning Loki replied, 'It was my head I wagered and not my neck. Discard your blade.'

Furiously the dark elf acknowledged his mistake, by tossing the blade out of Asgard, but still he advanced. Aided by Thor, who saw the plan and pinned Loki to the ground, the evil dwarf grasped his awl and, violently swinging Mjollnir, dashed it through Loki's lips.

The fiery pain was worse than Thor's great grip about his neck had been and the humiliation, when the dwarf threaded leather thongs through his lips to keep his cheating tongue still, was almost unbearable.

At last he escaped into the black wings of night. He tore the irritation from his lips, gasping in renewed pain. He paused, then his lips twisted and his eyes glinted emerald and ruby fire, as he began to imagine his revenge.

Dysgu Cymraeg

by

Jean Parry

If you decided to move to France, Germany or Spain - on a permanent basis - would you try to learn the language? Of course you would. Well, I didn't move to France, Germany *or* Spain. I moved to North Wales - on a permanent basis - and I did learn the language - after a fashion!

I moved to Gwynedd where English is definitely a second language. It's a language to fall back on when the visitors pour in, as they do in great numbers in the summer. When autumn arrives, Welsh takes precedence again and Wales is very anxious that their language remains predominant. To that end, there is a great variety of methods offered to 'incomers', old and young. No excuse then not to have a go.

The method I chose was to follow an Wlpan course. This aims to have you speaking some Welsh from the start so I joined a hopeful band of willing victims in the classroom. Three retired teachers, three ladies with Welsh husbands, a bank clerk newly transferred, an elderly American couple and a social worker from South Wales. With the exception of the social worker, we were quite unprepared for the task ahead.

The first hurdle was the alphabet. Forget your K, X and Z but add a 'Ch' and the 'LL'. Now remember that U, W and Y are all pronounced quite differently from the English. Are you getting the picture? Wait until you tackle the mutations! These are the little monsters that change the beginning of a word when it follows certain other words.

'Why?' you ask, in your innocence. Just be satisfied with this answer please...

'Because it sounds better that way.' Oh, for a Celtic soul that demands music in its speech.

I'm not teaching you the language. Find your own class and stick with it. You will discover more than just a new language. You'll bask in the approval of your Welsh friends and neighbours; you'll confound your English friends by smugly correcting their pronunciation of Welsh place-names. You'll read signs, understand notices, translate advertisements that will gain you entry into your village life - for if you think that there is no social life in a village, you are much mistaken. One more thing, and it's the unexpected bonus, you will make some real friends in class through your mutual struggles.

We laboured with the changes in the sight and sound (oh, those sounds) of the new alphabet and before the first session was over we could introduce ourselves *in Welsh.*

Marion, Phyllis, Linda, Martina, Flora, Bob, Joel, Edwina and Catrin - and Jean, that's me.

During the next few sessions, I learned that Joel and Edwina were here researching Joel's family tree. Bob, the bank clerk, was engaged to a local girl and anxious to ingratiate himself with her family, as well as improve his job prospects. Marion and Phyllis shared with me a background of marriage, children, grandchildren and teaching before retirement. Linda is pregnant, Martina wants to start a bed and breakfast business and Flora runs a dance class. Catrin has a little Welsh already, which sufficed in the South but is inadequate for this area where people in trouble prefer to use their mother tongue.

We meet three times a week and, although conversation is very limited in class as yet, the coffee break releases us to English and helps us to know each other quickly, finding some common ground beyond the difficulty of learning as adults. It may seem unlikely in such a disparate group, but find that ground we did.

At the end of our first year, we had come to the realisation that this particular language was like no other. Familiarity with second languages, learned in school, were no help at all. Nevertheless we had acquired enough to converse in stilted, pre-prepared sentences. If we went into a shop, rehearsing our requirements first of all, we were able to ask for a white loaf, twenty fags or a pound of apples. We all agreed that Welsh people were lovely - so sympathetic with, and appreciative of our attempts - *but* the torrent of words in which they replied left us gasping at our inadequacy and the rest of the transaction was conducted, sadly, in English.

'It will come,' we were assured.

The second year is the Pellach, or further, course. We have lost some of our group now. The Americans went home, satisfied that they had traced their link with this strange and beautiful land. Catrin went back home with promotion, having at least learned enough North Welsh to appreciate the differences, and there are many, between that and South Welsh. Two countries in one, really, Wales - the 'Gogs' up here and 'Hwntw' down there. Flora and Martina have discovered other interests as young women do! Linda has her baby now, a little girl called Haf meaning summer. She joins us in class with little Welsh gurgles. Bob is with us, bearing loving Welsh shackles now.

This is the year of examination - the Lefel O (for adult learners). It is an optional test, of course, but we're game for anything. This is a goal to keep us up to scratch and maintain a competitive spirit among us when we really feel like giving up. This is the year of reading novels and newspapers, of holding quite complicated conversations about past, present and future events. This is the year of living with a dictionary, of writing essays and being interviewed, of intensive residential short courses. This is the year for homework and more homework. This is the year when *us* against *them* gradually turns to *us* becoming *them.*

We all passed, much to our mutual satisfaction and perhaps a little amazement on the tutors' part. You may think this is *The Happy Ending?* Wrong! it is only *The Happy Beginning* for it is only now that we feel confident in doing more than comment briefly on the weather or ask, incorrectly, for forty instead of four pounds of carrots. We can even handle the replies instead of slinking away, defeated.

Indeed, we are into our third year - Uwch, the higher course. What more can we learn? Are you ready for this? We are unlearning. In fact, now that we know how it *should* be said, we are finding out how it *is* said. We are learning idiom, the abbreviated forms of everyday speech in this particular area. Like England, each area has its own distinctive way of 'mangling' the language. Can you blame us for not catching what people said to us before this?

For this year we are joined by two more students who have reached our level by another route - intensive ten-week residential courses at the University. They are intimidated at first by our 'pieces of paper' until they find we are speechless in the face of their fluency.

Linda is expecting again and so is Bob, with three honorary Nains to cluck about it - in Welsh, of course. The newcomers are quickly absorbed into the extended family. Bob is pleased that he is no longer the sole male, our new classmates being John, a doctor, and Mark the vet. So it's onwards and upwards, our meetings an established part of our lives, a social club really.

Remember the hidden bonus - the language cementing the friendships? Already we are looking towards our fourth year - the Meistroli, the master class. Will we ever be that good? Well, someone has to carry on the good work. I hope I've done that in a small way by writing down our experiences. Come and join us, The Learners, and help to preserve a language which supports a culture as old as the land itself. A culture which can only really be appreciated in its own tongue.

A Game of Deception

by

Karen Brown

She studied him. The last move was unexpected - a bluff, a trap or a mistake?

Nothing. A blank response, an impenetrable wall of silence. This was unnerving her and she knew it. She thought quickly and smiled. It was her move, that much she did know, but what did he expect?

This game was keeping her awake at night, toying with different strategies. She decided to sacrifice a pawn in the hope of revealing his intentions.

He laughed. It was a clumsy move and they both knew it, but he was tempted to give her a clue for the sheer audacity she had shown. No, he realised that she would not appreciate that - she would want to win against the odds and who was he to deprive her of the chance?

However, he had no intention of losing, because he enjoyed the power that he could command over his opponent too much.

He was stalling.

Faced with black on white, it should have been clear to him - obvious, but strategies seldom are and the stakes in this game were high. Forgetting the game momentarily, he paused to study her. She was frowning with a perplexed intensity, considering her next manoeuvre. It pleased him to see his opponent so involved in this test of wits. They were well matched, for although he had considerably more experience, she had a youthful enthusiasm and impetuosity that he found a refreshing challenge.

He could sense her growing restless and felt obliged to make a move without thinking through the full consequences of such an action. Almost the moment he'd done it he realised his mistake - and so did she. She grinned at him. He had left himself wide open to attack, for he stood to lose almost everything if she decided to introduce a little used rule. He didn't think she would, because in the long run they'd both be losers. However, until she committed herself to one course of action, he was unable to move constructively for the fear of playing straight into her hands.

She perceived his dilemma and slowly contemplated the options available to her. She could eradicate every principal piece in his side, but there was no real satisfaction in that. She didn't really want to beat him out-right. Her intention was to manipulate the game so that he'd have no alternative but to concede to her superior gamesmanship. The only doubt in her mind was that he might not give in graciously. That being the case, she would not only be wasting her time, but there was also the possibility that she could come out of this confrontation damaged in some way.

True to form, she decided that the power that success would undoubtedly bring was worth the risk.

Within three moves he guessed her ploy. He realised that his only hope now was to counter-attack. He had to obtain some sort of a hold over her to limit the options available, so he would have some idea of her intentions.

He was unwilling to sacrifice his Queen at this stage, in case he had misjudged her. Conversely, she could not risk trying to get at him, to break down his other defences with her to protect him. The question facing both players was how important was his Queen to him. Now was the time for decisions. If he wanted to continue the game he would have to sacrifice this piece, as it was the only constructive move left open to him.

She watched him intently during this period of indecision. Would he do it? Was he actually prepared to risk everything in this game? Drawing a deep breath, he stared into her eyes, shook his head and slowly moved his Queen into a vulnerable position.

Squinting her eyes slightly, she nodded slowly as a sign of understanding, and her face broke into a smile. Now it was her turn to decide. The game was coming to a climax and she was the master of her own destiny.

She knew that now she could have him, if she so desired, but did she want him? She was intensely flattered by his attentions and attracted by his flirtatious nature, but what would he expect? Yes, she wanted the excitement of a torrid and illicit physical relationship with a married man. The stolen kisses behind half closed doors and secret meanings to every look, smile or phrase, but this would be a new game with new rules and higher stakes. Not just the humiliation of rejection, as before, but the fear of being discovered with him and discredited. She was in an emotional turmoil, caught between the desire to play a more exciting, complex game and the need to maintain a wholesome, professional image.

The game was currently in a stale-mate situation and only she could determine how it would end. He looked at her with questioning eyes. She could concede the game even now, it wasn't too late. She looked from her King to him and back again. All she had to do was lay the King down and the game would be over. Alternatively, she could obliterate him completely, and be the out-right winner, but she had grown to respect, admire and even love her opponent, as he had grown to love her, during the course of their toying with emotional pawns. He touched her hand, no one could win this game without being a loser as well.

She studied the board and then made her move. With one movement her Queen replaced his and the two players met in a passionate embrace, and so the next game began.

Gracie's Afternoon

by

Lesley Morrison

The rain formed liquid crystals on the small, square window panes. With a slight nodding of the head she awoke, reality emblazoning itself in the coals of the fire. There was little warmth in the glowing embers and even less in the December sunlight reluctantly penetrating through the ancient wooden frames of the living-room window. A street-light shone, but not for her... for some last minute shopper on Christmas Eve, laden down with bags, boots marching quickly in order to escape the pursuing rain. The quiet voice of an unfamiliar News-reader captured her attention for a second. What was he saying? Too quiet, too distant ... the picture on the television showed the remains of a battlefield, while the only clearly audible sound was that of gunfire. The television was as alien to her as the rain on this depressing Christmas Eve.

On the table was a half-eaten box of chocolates. Very nice, a tasty gift from the Salvation Army, very nice... but very difficult to accept. The chicken and mince pies were safely put away in the pantry... perhaps she would eat them tomorrow ... perhaps. She rearranged the shawl around her knees to reveal the fluffy blue slippers on her feet. A Christmas gift from her sister, the one in Ireland. They had arrived by parcel post two days ago, a welcome reprieve from the monotony of boredom.

She wanted to hear the television, but it was pointless turning the sound up anymore. If she did the neighbours always came around, standing on her doorstep and shouting at her. Often the woman from next door ignored her altogether when they passed on the street. She didn't really mind, except for the days when it would have been nice to have someone to talk to. Even the permed, bingo-mad head of the neighbour would have provided a pleasant interlude.

It was almost four o'clock, nearly time for tea. She decided not to wait. Why should she wait, there was no-one to please but herself since her Alb died.

She placed the shawl neatly on the arm of the chair. Mistily she stood and looked at the chair. She had sat on the arm many times, dangling her legs over the side while sitting on Alb's knee; they had cuddled in that arm-chair, kissing sloppy kisses and laughing as they made their way up the stairs to make love. The sounds of their loving re-echoed in her head. The rafters remembered the joy of their lust in the small terraced house.

The house had rung with her laughter once upon a time, but once upon a time like all good fairy tales had ended long ago.

She walked the few steps to the kitchen, her legs ached and the pain shot through the base of her spine.

'That damned factory,' she spoke aloud and supported her back with her free hand, holding the kettle with the other.

The factory had been hard work, but there was a war on and the women had to work - besides that she felt that she was doing her bit for Alb. Alb fought in Europe, he was there when the British troops liberated Bergen, Belsen. He had fought his way through France and Germany and when he came back he was different. She had made, she thought, enough bullets and bombs to fight four world wars and her legs and back suffered premature arthritis through her zealous efforts.

Without realising what she was doing she wiped her eyes. There was a handkerchief in her apron pocket. She always carried a hankie.

'Never get caught without a hankie' Alb had said. That was the day he proposed to her - before the War. He put the ring on her finger. She stopped crying and smiled at him. They were outside the Cinema, her eyes and teeth gleamed at her marvellous fortune. She looked down at the stone glinting on her hand.

The light caught the rain on the window pane, the distraction of the kettle boiling dulled the memory.

'This back of mine' she uttered. She liked to hear her own voice. There were days when it was the only voice she heard. Bingo at 'the Pensioners' hadn't quite appealed to her, it reminded her too much of the woman next door whose quality of life depended on whether or not she'd had a 'win', her moods revolved around her good or bad fortune.

She poured the boiling water into the tea-pot. Her hand shook, but she knew she would not spill the scalding water. The strains of child-like voices fought through the cerebral padding of her mind.

'My imagination' she said, but the sounds continued. She left the tea to stand and hobbled back to the window in the living-room. The tuneful voices ceased when she pulled back the curtain, just an inch or so, just enough to see out. In horror she dropped the curtain as she saw the young Carol singers.

'Hmmph' she snorted, 'where are their parents letting them out on a night like this.' She hurried back to the teapot, but her face betrayed the emotions within. They could still cause her to panic, after all these years she was still affected by children. There was still that ache inside her barren womb that threatened to reach out and suck her into its depths. A dismembered hand that touched the futility of her reproductive organs and mocked their very existence.

It had just never happened for her and Alb. Making love with Albie had always been good, but a baby had just never happened. Besides, after the war he'd lost all interest in having a child. In their latter years she found the courage to ask him why he hadn't cared about their sterility.

'I've seen Belsen,' was all he would say. Then he'd go into his quiet moods and sometimes he'd drink until he fell asleep in an alcoholic stupor. She would put a blanket over him and he'd sleep off his drunkenness in that oh so distant chair, while she went alone to the redundant bed.

'Now that was loneliness,' she said aloud. She poured the tea and took it into the living-room. The fire threatened to go out... it didn't matter. She would go to bed early.

Her grey hair wisping onto her face she brushed it away, the sight of that old hand displeased her. She would not look into the mirror if she could help it, there were far too many wrinkles there. She'd had friends who'd had children of course. They were always complaining about sons-in-law or their son's new girlfriend. Ah, for the chance to complain about someone besides the bingo-mad neighbour. She told them she sympathised and how glad she was that she had remained childless. They were never convinced, neither was she. A sound from the TV set caught her attention. The manic laughter of a game-show audience stirred her reflections. She couldn't see what was so funny.

She replaced the shawl over her knees... what would it matter if the fire went out... she had her shawl and a cup of tea... and sleep was never too far away...

'A few more steps... nearly there,' said a disembodied voice.

She was walking and the steps were easy.

She could hear her own laughter and it was a young woman's laughter.

Through the mists of the dream Albie's face appeared, it was young and untroubled... as it was in the beginning.

'Alb!' she shrieked.

He was laughing, the dimple appearing with his smile. In her dream they fell together, arms locked in embrace. He felt so good. The tears were wet on her face as she kissed him.

'Don't say anything' she said 'don't spoil it... I don't want to wake up yet, I don't want it to end.'

'Oh Gracie' he spoke, 'it won't this time my love, not this time.'

The Parting Gift

by

Linda Bitvus

'You expect too much from people Sabrina,' her mother chided her. 'Men won't tolerate being 'just good friends' once a relationship has ended.'

'That's where you're wrong, Mum,' Sabrina remembered her passionate indignation. 'Mike doesn't mind that I've chosen Peter instead of him. We are still very good friends. He bears me no malice.'

'I'm sorry, Sabrina, but I just don't believe it. There isn't one man on this earth who will submit passively to being discarded by the woman he loves for another man. Look how shabbily you treated Mike! How did he react when he first realised you'd been two-timing him for Peter?'

'Okay,' agreed Sabrina,' he didn't like it, but Mike has borne me no grudges since. He knows that Peter and I are right for one another. He's pleased about our engagement. He indicated as much to me over the telephone.'

'He still rings you up then does he?' Sabrina recalled her mother's resounding disapproval.

'Yes, and I ring him up too,' Sabrina spoke cagily. 'I rang him up to see if he would fix my nose in time for the wedding. He was only too happy to oblige. He said it would be his parting gift to me.'

'Mmmmmmm, he always was soft where you were concerned!' It seemed there was nothing Sabrina could say to alter her mother's views on the subject.

Sabrina was lying in the darkness of the hospital recovery room. Her face was bandaged and she felt as if she'd been punched in the face. This was Mike's parting gift to her, some six months prior to her wedding day.

Mike was a plastic surgeon and a very skilled one. Sabrina had known him from the time when she had worked as a nurse in the same hospital. Their initial working relationship had quickly blossomed into romance but it was always more intense on Mike's side than on Sabrina's. He had proposed to her within three months of courting her, but she turned him down flat. The trouble was, he wouldn't take 'no' for an answer.

He became fiercely and tiresomely possessive of her, a thing Sabrina hated. It was partly because of this and partly because of the fact that she had met Peter, that she split with Mike.

It was true to say that Mike had been devastated by her rejection, but despite her mother's thoughts, Sabrina prided herself on the fact that she had remained on friendly terms with him, even when she had openly declared her love for Peter.

Mike's first explosive reaction to the fact that he had been cunningly two-timed for a month had subsequently simmered. Not that he had any real choice in the matter, since Sabrina had chosen Peter and not Mike. And now they were to be married.

'How does it feel, love?' Sabrina's mother was at her bedside, her manner, cherishingly concerned as she bent over her only daughter's bandaged face.

'It's sore Mum. The bandages come off tomorrow and then the cast over my nose the following week. The bruising will take three weeks to disappear. After that, I'll be as right as rain...'

'And as beautiful as ever, Sabrina,' her mother stroked her forehead gently. 'You'd better rest now. I'll come tomorrow when they take the bandages off.'

'You won't be able to see the transformation until the cast comes off at the end of the week,' Sabrina informed her.

'Transformation?' her mother sounded dubious. 'There was nothing wrong with the nose you had before, Sabrina. All our family have that characteristic little bump running across the bridges of their noses.'

'All but one,' Sabrina reminded her triumphantly. 'Mike showed me the shape of my new nose on the computer monitor. It's going to be perfect! Smaller, aquiline and without the bump!' Sabrina was insistent.

She knew Mike's skill as a plastic surgeon was widely recognised. His parting gift to her was bound to be a first-class example of rhinoplasty. She might even be featured in cosmetic surgery leaflets and brochures.

'If you say so, Sabrina,' her mother abstractedly fingered the bump running across the bridge of her own nose.' Has all this been done for Peter's sake or for the sake of your own vanity?'

'Both,' Sabrina admitted honestly. 'I don't want to look ugly on my wedding day.'

'Oh, that's wicked Sabrina!' Her mother sounded quite shocked. 'You have never been an ugly girl.'

'Maybe not in your eyes,' Sabrina paused. 'But now I shall be happy with the way I look and not afraid to have side-profile photographs taken on my wedding day.'

'Tut, tut!' Sabrina knew her mother's patience was wearing thin.

'I can't wait for the cast to be taken off, Mum!'

'Well, you will just have to be patient. Time will be the greatest healer.'

The two days in hospital passed quickly for Sabrina. Just before she was due to leave, Mike came to see her on his morning rounds.

'I won't be there when they take the cast off, Sabrina,' he told her quietly.

'Oh?' she queried his statement.

'No, I've decided to take a job in the new Burns Unit opening in Wiltshire.'

'You're moving away from the area Mike?' Sabrina's surprise was reflected in the light of her green eyes.

'Yes,' his expression was dull. 'Well, now I can't have you, there's nothing to keep me here anymore.'

'Oh, shame!' Sabrina pouted her lips coquettishly at him.

'You've got such pretty lips, Sabrina,' Mike looked at them in a moment of painful reminiscence. Then his voice hardened.

'Just make sure Peter is there when they take off the cast,' his eyes gave her a searing look. 'I'm sure he'll appreciate every last detail of my handiwork. Every careful stitch marks one degree of the pain you caused me.'

'Stitch?' Sabrina looked alarmed. 'I thought the stitches were internal and wouldn't be seen.'

'I'm speaking metaphorically,' he laughed. There was nothing natural about his laughter. It was a cackling, cruel tortured laugh. 'Remember, Sabrina, your new nose is my parting gift to you. It's my way of expressing everything I feel about you. I just came round to say goodbye.'

'We can still be friends, though, Mike, can't we?'

For once Sabrina sensed his bitterness.

'Friends? Oh we can still be that.' He smiled as he left the room but there was a sourness in his words that lingered and Sabrina had the deep feeling that perhaps her mother was right. She had wounded him by not marrying him and he had never really forgiven her for spurning him in favour of Peter.

She ran to the door and called down the corridor after him. 'You won't ever forget me, will you?'

'No, nor you me,' he waved and was gone.

The great day arrived. Sabrina returned to the hospital as an out-patient. Her mother was there and Peter held her hand as the cast was slowly removed from her nose.

Sabrina's eyes were tightly shut as Mike's handiwork was unveiled.

'Oh my God! Sabrina!' her mother gave a piercing shriek. 'What has he done to you?'

'It's his parting gift to me,' Sabrina spoke confidently as she reached out a hand for the mirror. Peter's iron hand gripped her wrist.

'No!' he was emphatic. 'Don't look!'

'Wh...What? What are you talking about?'

Sabrina grasped the mirror out of Peter's hand and held it up to her face as her mother began to sob convulsively.

Her hand shook as she gazed disbelievingly at her reflection. Her new nose was gross, bulbous, deliberately scarred and savaged by the surgeon's knife. The parting gift of a man spurned beyond his reason and endurance!

Dinner is Served

by

Jill Bristow

'This dinner table looks very posh,' said Graham as he passed through the dining room into the kitchen, 'it's only your sister Dianne who's coming to dinner you know, not Princess Diana!' Julia felt her husband's arms tighten around her waist, she stopped cutting the meat and swivelled to face him.

'I know that, but Dianne seems really serious about this new boyfriend of hers, so I want to make a good impression,' she said.

Graham laughed, 'with the meal you've cooked tonight, the Queen herself would be impressed!'

Julia was feeling quite nervous about meeting her younger sister's new boyfriend. Dianne was twenty five years old, and it was the first man she had ever appeared serious about.

The doorbell rang dead on eight o'clock, 'Oh my God, they're on time! Quick, Graham go and answer the door!' Julia waited anxiously for them to come in.

Dianne walked in full of smiles, wearing a little black dress pulled over her dainty figure like a glove. Following behind her was a very well dressed man with blonde wavy hair and the clearest complexion Julia had ever seen. The pride shone from Dianne's face as she introduced her new boyfriend to Graham and Julia.

'This is Nigel.' Dianne beamed from ear to ear. Nigel shook Graham's hand with a polite greeting. Julia held out her hand, but instead Nigel put both his hands on her shoulders and kissed her heavily on the cheek. Julia blushed with embarrassment and rushed off to the kitchen to see to the meal.

During the main course Julia could not relax, she did not like the way Nigel looked at her. Nigel was a good looking man, but there was no doubt that the only person he was in love with was himself.

'So, you're a solicitor are you Nigel?' Julia tried to hide her uneasiness by making polite conversation.

'Yes I am,' smiled Nigel, his well spoken accent was harsh and exaggerated, 'I live and work in Gatacre.'

Nigel told Julia and Graham all about his four bedroom house with large gardens, and the fact that he would not live in any other part of Liverpool amongst the 'riff raff' as he called it.

Dianne cut in, 'Nigel's house is gorgeous, he's got a pond in the back garden which looks like a lake, and the bathroom's got a jacuzzi. Oh and you want to see the...'

She was cut off in mid-sentence by an impolite glare from Nigel, 'that's enough babe, I'm capable of telling your sister and her husband my own life story!'

At this, Dianne's eyes glistened with tears and she dropped her head, 'Yes Nigel.'

Julia could not believe the obedience of her own sister, this was not like Dianne at all, she was truly under his spell. Julia's liking for this man was rapidly deteriorating, she could not understand how Dianne seemed so blind to his 'smarmy' personality. What did she see in him?

During desert, Nigel and Dianne were hugging and kissing each other rather a lot. It was amazing how quickly Dianne had bucked up when Nigel had 'buttered her up', calling her things like 'babe' and 'sweetness', this sort of talk made Julia's stomach turn over.

As Julia picked up her last piece of black forest gateaux, something touched her ankle, this made the piece of gateaux on the spoon jump off and land on her taffeta dress.

She looked discreetly around the table, her eyes fell upon Nigel, and he was smiling at her. She felt her face burn with anger. How dare he make a pass at her while he is courting her own sister! She stood up quickly.

'Julia, are you alright?' said Graham noticing the flushed look on her face. She turned and walked towards the kitchen, her voice shaking, 'Yes, I'll just get the coffee.'

In the privacy of her kitchen, she put her hands on the sides of the sink and took deep breaths to try and stop herself from shaking. She then proceeded to make some percolated coffee.

As she put the filter into the percolator, she was aware of somebody standing behind her. She turned to see Nigel grinning in the doorway of the kitchen like a Cheshire cat, he was carrying a handful of plates.

'Hi Julia,' he said in his annoying hoarsy voice, Julia said nothing and turned back towards the coffee percolator.

'I thought I'd give you a hand with the dishes,' he said walking over to the sink and placing the dishes into the bowl.

Julia spoke without turning around, 'there's no need, me and Graham will do them later.'

Nigel walked over to her and stood by her side, whispering in her ear, 'Did you know you're sexy when you're angry?'

Julia could not believe her ears, she felt herself beginning to shake again.

'What!'

'Oh come on,' whispered Nigel, 'I know you like me, I could see the way you were looking at me across the table.' He was smiling, feeling very pleased with himself, Julia felt sick. Trust Dianne to pick a snake like this!

Julia turned to face him, her eyes fiery with rage, 'you really think a lot of yourself don't you?' She lowered her voice, 'I want you out of my house.' To her amazement, Nigel smiled throughout her speech. She froze in horror as his hand made contact with her arm, he rubbed his hand along it and up to her shoulder.

Julia's voice took on an almost inhuman tone, 'take your hands off me!' Nigel took his hand off her arm, but he was totally unaffected by her reaction. His sickly smile returned once more.

'I know you want me, but you are holding back because your husband is around.' He turned and walked towards the kitchen door, looking back when he reached it, 'There will be other times.' He raised his eyebrows and left the kitchen.

In disbelief, Julia stared at the space where Nigel had just stood. How could she tell her sister that the love of her life was nothing but a dirty parasite? Well surely he would leave now, after her telling him to get out. She went on making the coffee as if nothing had happened.

Graham came into the kitchen to find out what was taking her so long, Julia did not mention Nigel's behaviour because she knew Graham would not be very pleased at all, and might make a scene. Graham helped to make the coffee.

Julia did not expect to see Nigel as she entered the dining room. But to her shock, there he was sitting as large as life caressing Dianne, kissing and whispering in her ear.

Dianne was giggling, she turned and smiled ecstatically as Julia and Graham entered the room. Julia made an effort to smile back, she handed out the coffee's and sat down.

Dianne, who was still beaming, stood up and pulled Nigel to his feet, 'Go on then Nigel,' said Dianne, urging him to speak. Oh good, thought Julia, he is going to make an apology... but she could not have been more wrong.

'I'd just like to say,' said Nigel with his Cheshire cat grin, 'I have asked Dianne to become my wife, and she has accepted willingly.'

Graham stood up to shake hands across the table with Nigel, 'Congratulations mate.'

Julia was frozen to her seat, her mouth agape. Was this all a dream? Surely this poor excuse for a man could not be so two faced! That was it then, her sister was marrying the original Don Juan!

'Well?' smiled Dianne happily, waiting for a reaction from Julia. She rose feeling very unsteady, and turned her mouth up as best she could to make it look like a smile.

'Aren't you happy for me?' said Dianne excitedly. Julia saw the euphoric expression on her face, she could not ruin this moment for her.

'Of course I'm happy for you,' said Julia, moving towards her and giving her a peck on the cheek.

Dianne and Nigel left soon after that. Julia knew she would have to tell her sister, but she could not spoil it for her tonight.

As Julia and Graham saw them both to the door, Nigel smiled at Julia as if he had won some sort of battle over her. Julia gave the same smile back. You've won the battle, she thought, but you haven't won the war!

Margaret

by

Aphra Jones

Margaret walked uncomfortably along the High Street carrying her morning shopping in a large plastic bag in one hand and balancing a bright red brolly and her handbag in the other. It wasn't raining more than a light mist but she wanted to keep her newly-set hair unruffled for the party tonight. Well, it was Robert's party really, one of his business dinners for his younger executives and at the age of fifty-five last June 20th - she was beginning to feel so much older than those bright, clever young wives with their confident partners. They pleased Robert with their youthful enthusiasm and deferential good manners and they spoke kindly to Margaret assuming of course, that she did not understand their business talk but as their boss's wife she must claim their brief attention. She 'was a darling' they said to one another, 'a motherly sort' who enquired after their families, the children's recent illnesses and their holiday plans. Life was so difficult these days for working mothers and fathers, so many domestic problems interrupting their careers. The days were simply not long enough they said, with no time to eat together except possibly on Sundays when the grandparents could help. There was the shopping, cleaning and laundry besides all those swimming, riding and tennis lessons which had to be squeezed in somewhere. And of course, they needed their golf to help them 'wind down'.

Margaret leaned her heavy shopping on the sill of a large plate-glass window... strange how she had never noticed this shop before she mused, as she stared absently through the window.

'Why was the car park always so far away?' she asked herself irritably, and suddenly conscious of her own reflection in the glass she studied the middle-aged image before her. Her dark hair framed a serenely rounded face with slight shades of grey showing at the temples, her loose coat hid a gentle plumpness. 'Not bad ankles' she thought, looking down into the bottom of the window where she saw reflected a slim pair of legs and comfortable town shoes. Robert liked her 'that way' he said, aware that she did not challenge his own professional image. She glimpsed the slight wrinkling of the skin over her bare hands as she stooped to pick up the bag of shopping from its precarious resting place. Robert rarely kissed her these days she thought, and no wonder with so many signs of her own departing youth. He had an irritating habit of saying 'cooking lasts, kissin' don't!' which made her feel more like a wife whose sell-by date had nearly arrived.

He responded lightly and with brilliant flashes of self-assured wit to the conversation of colleagues wives whilst admiring the cut of expensive clothes over their trim young figures. They flattered him with their attentive good manners which concealed their opinions and ambitions from both him and their immediate contemporaries. Margaret in her quiet corner of the social scene had seen it all before and marvelled at her husband's innocence in the face of such youthful skills.

Margaret was about to turn away from the window when she saw inside an evening skirt draped elegantly over a small golden chair, isolated in its corner display. It had a deep blue shimmering elegance as the pleats flowed over the seat to the floor where a casual string of peals lay amongst the petals of a small bunch of white flowers. It glimmered when she moved to one side and allowed the pale winter sun to shine through the window, almost instinctively she folded her umbrella and entered the shop where she asked to see it. She didn't really need any evening clothes, she told herself Robert always liked her in black it 'became her position' he said. The girl took the skirt out of the window and spread it across her arm displaying its unique elegance which captivated Margaret. When she tried it on in the tiny fitting room it curved smoothly over her plump hips making her look slim and youthful and curled over her hand as she looked at the material giving a transparent glow to her skin. Of course she would like to buy it she said to the young assistant who shook her head saying, 'we only hire, madam and this skirt for one evening only.' Margaret hesitated, she had not hired anything for years, only in those early hard-up times when image and ambition ruled their lives and Robert wouldn't like the idea. Well, he needn't know! she thought, as she paid her deposit feeling a new sense of adventure as she watched the girl pick up a dark blue cardboard box from under the counter and saw the skirt slide into the soft tissue paper like a green-blue snake of paradise. It nestled and glowed through the creamy folds of paper, disappearing from view as the girl closed the lid and tied a silver ribbon securely around the box. Clutching her parcel, her handbag, her shopping and her umbrella Margaret stepped lightly out of the shop and in no time at all it seemed she had found her way to the car park.

Once home, she unpacked the skirt and laid it across her bed carefully matching it to a black chiffon blouse - her favourite. It was perfect she thought, feeling like a girl again as she found a dark blue belt and scattered the string of pearls which Robert had given her for their tenth wedding anniversary against the neck of the blouse.

Those were the days, she thought, when he would put his arms around her, holding her close and declaring his love for her. She used to feel beautiful as he kissed her fair skin and stroked the dark cascade of her long brown hair. Today, he will pat her affectionately on the arm saying, 'are you ready, old thing?... time to go!' Ever courteous he will open the car door for her and drive to the Club and there he will be lost amongst the throng of glittering executives saying, 'just a word dear, with James, or Tess, or that pretty new wife of Tom's,' and she will not see him again until it is time to go home People will speak to her briefly, politely passing on to another colleague with scarcely concealed ambition guiding their footsteps, and after dinner Robert will speak wittily as he introduces his guest-of-honour.

She couldn't remember who it was going to be tonight so often they were boring, so self assured and told such dreadful jokes. Everyone will laugh of course, and Robert will call on a chosen colleague to congratulate the speaker with his own brand of good humour and bonhomie. She will talk a little more about nothing in particular, flatter the speaker and let him drift onwards to the person he has been watching over her shoulder whilst she was speaking with him. After a while Robert will take her arm and flushed with success and secure in this business world he will shake hands with their guests, kiss the pretty wives goodbye, congratulate the staff on their good work and leave for home.

Home where she had waited for the children who had left long ago, for friends to call and remind her of her charity obligations, to answer the 'phone diplomatically when Robert was home but did not want to reply... this comfortable home where she felt... well, so redundant.

That evening as she and Robert changed for dinner, Margaret looked in the long mirror watching herself brush her hair, heard the soft hiss as she sprayed the waves carefully into place and skillfully applied a touch of lipstick to her slightly wrinkling lips. More eyeshadow?... perhaps not, Robert did not like her to wear too much.

Picking up the blouse she dropped it swiftly over her head adjusting the gentle ruffles around her neck, she slipped the evening skirt over her petticoat and fastened it comfortably around her waist. Now the belt, her matching pearls and earrings and finally she put on her favourite evening shoes which flattered her slender ankles.

Robert paused as he came into the bedroom suddenly caught by the glowing image of his wife as she stood before the mirror. She looked strangely different more like a young girl, the slightly bored air was no longer there. she looked stunning, he told himself and looked past her at his own reflection. Clearly and with dismay he saw for the first time the tired lines under his eyes, the middle-aged corpulence beneath his well-cut suit, his thinning hair skillfully cut to hide its fading line. Margaret looked back at him in the mirror with an amused expression as if she were hiding a little secret. It was a long time since he had noticed the brilliance of her eyes and... what was it about her dress?

Spontaneously, he put an arm around her shoulders disturbing the faintest drift of perfume and as she turned towards him he felt the soft swirl of her skirt around his feet. Margaret responded to the loving touch, she glowed with a lively vivaciousness when they arrived at the party and seemed to float through the crowds offering a gentle charm to all around her. The young wives were daunted by the change in her, their conversation sounded suddenly brittle and trivial to Robert. He felt older, impatient and surprisingly bored by the occasion. After the dinner was over he took Margaret's arm saying, 'I've left Charles to do the honours... no need for us to stay to the end, let's leave it to the youngsters!'

It was a long time since Margaret had felt so relaxed and happy but she was also a little tired and glad that they did not have to stay till the end of the evening. She had left the speaker to be entertained by Robert's pretty secretary and making their apologies they had escaped homewards. Robert talked to her companionably with no trace of his usual monosyllabic pre-occupied manner, it was more like a sharing of a long friendship which had seemed so nearly forgotten in recent years. Once home they had a warming cup of coffee by the fire with Margaret wearing a long apron to save the skirt from any accidental stain, laughingly she showed Robert that wherever she walked it seemed to peep around the corner of the striped cotton. He smiled at her childish imagination, amused by such nonsense.

Finally, when she undressed that night she placed the skirt on her bedroom chair near the cardboard box on the floor. When she returned from the bathroom she noticed that it had fallen in soft coils amongst the tissue paper, silently like a vanishing spirit. In the dim light of the bedside lamp it seemed to lose a certain shimmering quality as if it were resting and as she walked past the box, her dressing gown caught the slanting lid so that it toppled on to the base hiding the creamy paper. The silver ribbons lay in a half-knot across the deep blue top which melted into the darkness of the night. Tomorrow I must take it back, thought Margaret contentedly drifting into a companionable sleep beside the already slumbering form of Robert... what a strange and happy day it has been, not like any other she had ever known.

Romancing the Past

by

Lewis Terrie

Robert looked down from the black precipice. He searched the broken bodies for signs of life. He wanted to shriek in anger and despair.

Instead he tore his eyes away and slowly, so painfully slowly groped his way blindly down the treacherous rock face.

An ever tightening band round his heart told him there was little chance of survival. It was that small seed of hope that prevented him from letting the wind take him to join her.

He pushed the vivid memories to the back of his mind. She was still fighting for her life.

Sitting by her bed he leaned towards her. His eyes roved over her face. 'I love you Pennie,' he whispered. 'I know now I've always loved you. From the first day I saw you.'

But it was too late.

How well he knew these situations. How often had he given advice. How different it all was on the other side of the coin.

He tried to speak but his mouth was dry with a taste of antiseptic. He reached for a glass of water and drank thirstily without taking his eyes off the prostrate figure.

'Pennie,' he croaked. He cleared his throat and tried again. 'Pennie. Do you remember the first time we met? It must have been twenty... no... thirty years ago... Where has the time gone? ... That was the day you moved into the house next to ours. Mother asked you all over for a cold drink. You didn't say much then did you?'

Robert was surprised how vividly the past came crowding back...

Pennie was standing at the gate waiting for Robert. 'Can I walk to school with you?' she asked shyly.

'Yes. Ok. Sure you can. Your first day isn't it? Are you nervous?'

'No. I'm looking forward to it. Besides I have you to protect me.'

'Yeah. Of course you have. Just let me know if anyone bothers you. I'll sort them out,' he said breaking into a comic boxing match with his shadow. Pennie smiled shyly...

Robert shifted in his chair. He scanned the instruments and rubbed his eyes, eyes that reflected the pain he felt in his heart.

'The following years slipped by,' he whispered. 'We spent so little time together. My rugby and your netball kept us apart. It was your fifteenth birthday when I first became aware of the feelings you aroused in me.'

'You asked me to your party as always Pennie. Only this time things turned out differently. I walked in. The lights were low, music playing. Everyone was dancing. You wore a blue skirt and white blouse. Funny I should remember that after all this time...'

As soon as she saw Robert, Pennie's eyes lit up and she hurried towards him.

'Sorry I'm late.'

'Did you win?'

'Of course,' he replied with a grin. 'Here. Happy birthday.' Self consciously he pushed a small packet into her hand.

'Oh Robert. Thank you.' Her eyes were deep mysterious pools, her perfume just strong enough to reach his nostrils. She opened the little box. Inside was a small pendant on a silver chain.

'It's beautiful. Put it on for me... please.'

Her excited voice sent shivers down his spine. His fingers turned to thumbs at the touch of her alabaster skin as he struggled to secure the clasp.

'That's got it,' he mumbled at last.

Pennie turned and standing on tiptoe kissed him full on the lips, her arms snaking round his neck.

Robert pushed himself away and held her at arms length. They had never kissed like that before. He was confused by the strange sensations which had sizzled through his body. He felt overwhelmingly happy and at the same time weak at the knees.

A knock on the door broke 'l'esprit de l'escalier.'

'C... come in.'

A nurse entered. 'I have to see to Mrs Edgerton. Why not take the opportunity to have a coffee Mr Stelling. You look as if you could do with a break. I'll stay until you return.'

Robert stood up and stretched his aching limbs. 'Thank you nurse. I think I may do that.' He walked out of the room.

'Hello Bob. You look tired. Why don't you take a rest. You've been with her all day.'

'Oh. Hello Dr Andrews. Yes. I am taking a break. For coffee.'

'I'm going that way. She'll be all right. Just a matter of time.'

'I keep telling myself that. It doesn't help you know. Ah. The refactory. Will you join me?'

'Sorry Bob. Wanted in Casualty. Don't worry. She'll make it.' Dr Andrews gave him a friendly pat on the shoulder and hurried away.

Robert watched the retreating figure before pushing open the door.

In the recovery room the nurse finished her checks and made her patient comfortable before settling on the chair beside the bed. Every now and then she glanced at the array of equipment.

Robert hurried along the corridor and entered the room flushed and hot. He stood holding the door handle as if for support. 'I have not kept you too long I hope nurse,' he said. 'Any change?'

'No. No change I'm afraid.' The nurse walked to the open door. 'If you need anything just press the buzzer.'

Robert waved his hand. 'Thank you.'

Left on his own Robert prowled round the room looking closely at each piece of equipment. He felt restless. He knew talking to her might strike the vital chord which would bring her out of the mysterious dark never-never land into which she had sunk.

He slumped into the chair.

'Pennie. It's me. Robert. I'm back.'

His eyes searched for the slightest flicker of response.

Nothing.

'Where did we get to Pennie? Ah, yes. Just before I left to attend College...'

'I wish it could be like this for always,' said Pennie with a sigh as she nestled in his arms. 'It's so peaceful.'

Robert ran his fingers through her soft brown hair. 'I love having you to myself. When I have finished College we will do this again.'

Pennie half turned towards him. 'Promise me Robert. Promise it will be like this again.'

'I promise,' he replied softly, kissing her lightly on the nose. 'And to show you I mean it I want you to have this. My pledge to you.' He handed her a small box.

Pennie's eyes misted over when she saw the pin crowned with two inter-connected golden hearts. 'It's lovely,' she cried. 'I'll keep it always.' She flung her arms round his neck and kissed him.

'Whooee. That was some kiss. Any more in there like that?' Robert gasped.

'Oh, yes. I don't know whether I should give them to you though. They make me feel all funny inside. No, no, no,' she said as Robert made a grab for her. 'I have something for you too.'

Robert found himself holding a gold tie-clip surmounted by a cluster of oak leaves.

Pennie choked back a tear. 'I thought it would remind you of your roots.'

'I shall cherish it always,' he told her as he held her close...

He had been staring into space. He shook his head and looked round guiltily. She suddenly reminded him of Sleeping Beauty and without thinking he kissed her.

'No miracle this time Pennie,' he said with a thin laugh. 'If this had been a film you would have opened your eyes then.'

'Why did it have to be her,' he felt like screaming, 'Oh God. Why did it have to be her?' Robert stretched to relieve the aches in his shoulders and back. He glanced at the monitors for perhaps the hundreth time.

There was no change.

He leaned closer to the still form. 'I had to operate Pennie. I couldn't face losing you again.'

He stopped, hardly daring to breathe.

Had an eye twitched?

He felt pressure on his hand as her fingers slowly curled round his.

An eye half opened, followed by the other until they were both staring up into his.

She slowly smiled. 'Hello Robert,' she croaked.

'Pennie my love. Will you marry me,' he blurted out.

Her hand squeezed his. 'Yes. Oh yes,' she whispered.

Birthday Greetings

by

Don Jarvis

Being married to a country vet can be a very traumatic experience, especially for a twenty two year old girl who has lived for most of her life in a town. But this morning Susan was on top of the world: it was her birthday, the postman had brought her three birthday cards and a parcel, and Andrew was taking her out for a meal that evening.

They couldn't really afford to go gallivanting out on the town, for they'd only had the practice for two years, and as Andrew said, a lot of their clients were even worse off than they were - in fact many of the small-holders often paid their bills in kind - which was how Susan had acquired ten hens, three ducks, a goat, a very spirited young collie bitch, and of course the kittens - all three of them.

She opened the parcel, and then smiled for nestling in the tissue paper was a hat. It was from Aunt Dora of course - it had to be, for Aunt Dora was the only person nowadays who would send a hat for a birthday present, especially a hat like this, wrapped in tissue paper and packed in an enormous box.

Standing in front of the mirror in the hall Susan tried the hat on: turned it this way, and then that - tilted it and tweaked it - and it still looked ridiculous.

Andrew came bustling in. 'Going up to Bensons to look at their pony,' he said, 'then to Charlie Wrights: his heifer's due to calf sometime today.' Suddenly he stopped and stared at Susan, and the hat.

'Oh my God, what's that?' he asked.

'Aunt Dora's birthday present,' Susan said, and she couldn't help giggling, 'it came by post, wrapped in tissue paper and packed in a box.'

'Well don't let the chickens see you in it - it'll put em off lay for weeks,' Andrew said, and he went out roaring with laughter.

Susan put the hat back into the box, making a firm resolve not to laugh, or even smile when she thanked Aunt Dora for it. The old dear was so touchy.

The phone rang; it always seemed to ring just after Andrew had gone out, but it was only Sergeant Jones the local bobby. 'Sorry to bother you Mrs Thomas,' the policeman said, 'but Mrs Blanchard has reported her cat missing; it's female, a tabby, and I wondered if anyone had bought a stray in to you.' The sergeant cleared his throat with a little suggestive 'humph,' before he went on. 'She's a very dominant female - Mrs Blanchard that is, not the cat - in fact the cat seemed just like any other tabby to me, far as I can remember, but the good lady's playing hell up, like.'

Susan stifled a smile, and murmured something about the RSPCA. The sergeant heaved a sigh, 'I've already tried them,' he said, 'let me know if anything turns up - please.'

Susan went into the kitchen to make herself a cup of coffee, before starting on the bookkeeping - then dashed into the garden - the goat was in the flower beds again, and Penny the collie bitch was rounding the chickens up in their run for the tenth time that morning - she couldn't help it - it was born in her.

By half past four she felt pleased with herself: having finished the books, but soon she became apprehensive, for they'd got a Surgery at five, and there was no sign of Andrew.

At twenty to five the door bell rang: the house door at the front, not the side-door to the Surgery, and Susan had a strange ominous feeling as she opened it. Two children stood on the step; a girl of about twelve, and a boy a year or two younger. The girl was pretty, with wide appealing eyes, the boy had a school cap askew on his head with tufts of tow-coloured hair sticking out from under it - he looked just like the character from the pages of 'Just William'.

'Our cats bin run over,' he said, and he sniffed.

'And it's bleeding,' the girl added sadly, 'it's head and it's foot - and it can't walk.'

'Can you bring it to the Surgery,' Susan replied, 'Mister Thomas will be back in a few minutes.'

'Ooh I can't pick it up - I can't,' the girl wailed.

'It's only just here,' the boy said, pointing to the lane that ran at the side of the garden.

Susan sighed: it wasn't the first time that she'd had to cope with an emergency. 'Wait here,' she said, and dashed through to get the First Aid Box - it was an old black Gladstone bag really - but it had plenty of bandages and dressings, and antiseptic in it, which was all Susan needed.

The cat was lying under the hedge on the grass verge. It was a very ordinary tabby, well cared for and very fat, but as the girl said, one of its ears was torn and bleeding and one front paw had most of the fur missing. Susan stroked it gently, just a little wary because some cats have a habit of lashing out with sharp claws at strangers, particularly when in pain.

Suddenly the cat gave a little hoarse 'miaow', and Susan stopped very still with her fingers resting on its tummy. 'Oh dear,' she said, looking at the girl, 'I think you're going to have a lot of little cats soon.'

'Told yer she was in the family way, didn't I,' the boy sniggered.

'Shut up - you're horrid,' the girl replied.

'Now stop bickering, the pair of you,' Susan said, 'look, she's trembling - we need something to put her in.' She turned to the boy and said 'there's a box on the table in the hall, go and get it, quickly.'

Just-William ran like a hare: so quickly that Susan hardly had time to call after him, 'take the hat out of it...'

It was after five o'clock now - there was still no sign of Andrew - and there were two people in the waiting room.

One was an elderly gentleman with an equally elderly collie bitch - 'worms,' he said - and Susan heaved a sigh of relief - the other person had a budgie in a very large cardboard box - budgies claws - Susan positively smiled as she got out the clippers and the left hand of what had once been a pair of very nice black suede gloves... she put fifty pence in the tin box, and then wasted ten precious minutes getting rid of the budgies garrulous owner - wonder if the budgie can talk like that she mused - suddenly Andrew was there.

'Much happening?' he said blithely.

'Where've you been,' Susan wailed; then she lifted her head defiantly. 'Collie bitch with worms, and budgies claws - all done.'

'Wonderful,' Andrew said, he bent down, gave her a peck on the cheek and walked over to the two children hunched over the box by the stove.

'And what have we got here... apart from Aunt Dora's hat,' he chuckled.

'Oh my God,' Susan wailed.

'Stupid,' the girl screamed at Just-William, 'the lady doctor told yer to take the hat out - and take yours off in the house,' and she snatched the cap from his head, screwed it up and flung it onto the floor.

'All right,' Andrew said, 'quieten down.' He peered into the box. 'This cat's got a collar on - how long have you had it?'

'Three days,' the girl replied, 'but I've looked after it and fed it.'

'I have, you mean,' Just-William shouted, 'I'm the one that got the tanning off Mom for pinching the milk.'

'But I pinched the tuna,' the girl pouted.

'Yeah - but you didn't get found out.'

Suddenly the door opened and Aunt Dora's face appeared. 'Hello dears,' she said, 'we were just passing, thought we'd drop in and say Happy Birthday; we've been helping our friend Amy look for her pussy; you know, Mrs Blanchard, she's so upset - the poor things been missing for three days.'

Uncle Albert raised his eyes to Heaven in a gesture of despair - Susan looked helplessly at Andrew - and the children huddled together and tried to appear invisible.

But suddenly Aunt Dora saw the box. She glanced inside it, and then to Susan's surprise clapped her hands together in delight.

'Oh you clever dears,' she gushed, 'you've found Amy's pussy.'

All eyes turned on the nondescript tabby lying snugly in its nest of tissue paper amid the ruins of a purple velvet hat in the box.

'Er, yes, well,' Andrew stammered, 'it was an emergency you see - but I think Susan, er, coped very well.'

'Oh, but it was the children who found it, and looked after it,' Susan said, 'I think they deserve a reward.'

'So do I dear,' Aunt Dora replied, 'and I'm sure Amy won't want all these kittens - the children should have one.'

'Each...' Just-William said firmly.

'Shame about the hat,' Andrew said, grinning all over his face.

Aunt Dora glared at him. 'Who cares about a hat when a life is in danger,' she said, and then added, 'Amy can take us to town as a reward - and Susan can pick a new hat.'

Susan twitched her nose at Andrew in a private gesture that mean, 'see... smarty pants.'

The cat purred and nuzzled its young; the children hovered over it like doting parents.

'The white one's mine,' the girl whispered.

'Mine's the ginger tom,' Just-William said proudly.

Duel of the Dual-Carriageway

by

Alan John Copner

It was another Friday afternoon, the end of another hard week's work, that I wearily made my way home from Cheltenham to Abergavenny.

At last I've reached the Raglan roundabout and I'm only ten minutes from home. The dual-carriageway is clear and I start to drive the last ten miles of my long journey. I suddenly become aware of a car in the distance, as I close I can see that it is in the middle of the road, straddling both carriageways.

I indicate to overtake, and manoeuvre my car into the outside lane, the car in front makes no effort to pull into the inside lane. I quickly motor up behind, and being relaxed and in no hurry, I refrain from using my horn, deciding to wait for the driver to pull over. A short time elapses, and the dozing driver in front becomes aware of my presence behind, and sharply pulls into the inside lane.

I gently start to overtake this vehicle, and I notice that the driver is irate and shaking his fist, obviously not too pleased being woken up. What the heck it's a Friday afternoon, the sun is shining, I'll ignore him.

On finishing my overtaking manoeuvre, I return to the inside lane, and I am aware of the driver behind flashing his lights and still shaking his fists. Almost as pure reaction, I make a silly gesture to the driver, which boiled down to meaning, 'stop being a prat.'

The driver behind, quickly overtakes me, and I was soon to determine that I was not dealing with a normal rational person.

He pulls in front of me, slows down, and adjusts his rear view mirror. I can see from his frame that he's a stockily built chap, probably a weight lifter. I soon become aware of piercing eyes, looking at me from his rear view mirror.

He points at his rear view mirror, motioning that he means me, then holding up his left hand, forcibly hits it with the clenched fist of his right. By now the adrenalin is starting to take effect, I can feel my heart pounding, and the perspiration on the palms of my hands. The dual-carriageway is unusually quiet, and I get this feeling of being alone and vulnerable. My mind races to find a solution out of this serious situation, is there any escape.

Think, think, what can I do, my train of thought is interrupted by the brake lights of the car in front. We are both approaching a lay-by and he indicates for me to pull over. He obviously wants to give me a good thumping, and I had forgotten to pack my baseball bat.

He pulls into the lay-by and I drive straight on, pressing my foot hard on the accelerator, the chase begins.

My speed increases, sixty, seventy, eighty miles per hour and he's still catching me. The whole situation is becoming unreal.

Finally with me travelling in excess of ninety miles per hour, he overtakes and resumes his position in front of me.

The threatening motions of punching his left hand, continue for the remaining three miles of the dual-carriageway. Thinking hard I cannot come up with any escape plan, there are no exits, I cannot stop, I have no option but to continue following behind.

In what seems like an eternity, we are coming to the end of the dual-carriageway, and I can see the Abergavenny roundabout in the distance. Oh no, what's this, he's slowing down, and stopping. We are both still on the dual-carriageway, and I bring my car to a halt. As I wait, the following thoughts are going through my mind, why isn't there anybody else on this road, and why is there never a Police patrol car when you need one.

I watch from my car as he opens his door and starts to get out, is this show-down time?... I'm not waiting to find out. As soon as his right foot makes contact with the tarmac, I quickly select first gear and with harsh use of the accelerator and clutch, I wheel-spin from rest and overtake him.

I decide not to continue into Abergavenny, as I could lead him to my home, so I joined onto the Heads of the Valley road to Ebbw Vale. With the aggressive driver now back in front, we approach the Llanfoist turn off, and I have an idea on how to lose him.

I start to slow down and indicate to turn left, giving the intention to leave the Heads of the Valley road at the Llanfoist turn off. The driver in front sees this and indicates to turn off also, good, I wonder if he is fool enough to fall for this old trick.

He enters the turn feeder lane, and I follow still pretending to turn, I check my mirror, nothing behind me.

I continue following, and wait until I verify that he has committed himself to the turn. Yes... got you! I quickly check my mirror, pull out of the feeder lane back onto the Heads of the Valley road, and drive straight on. I've outwitted him, a sense of relief comes over me, phew! That was a lucky escape.

I look at the deranged driver as I pass, he looks at me, and a big fat smile develops on my face. Before he disappears from view, I can see him fiercely thumping his steering wheel. This driver certainly has a serious attitude problem.

I continued home unscathed, but with a important lesson learned... I always keep a low profile now, and ignore drivers who become irate and start making gestures. Indeed

I think this approach tends to have the effect of making them embarrassed of their actions, and the incident quickly diffuses.

The Butterfly

by

Francis P Xavier

The old village church was situated at the end of a long winding lane, and was often difficult to find. The little graveyard, that was tucked away behind the stone building, was even harder to locate, much to the consternation of visitors. Quite often, a funeral service could be interrupted many times, as mourners who had not been able to find the entrance or the cemetery arrived late. This unfortunate occurrence often caused raised eyebrows as friends or relatives furtively slipped in through the rusty hinged gate, murmuring some apology or reason for their tardiness. But today that had not happened and the service was proceeding quietly and according to everyone's anticipations.

The still afternoon air seemed to accentuate the quietness of the little graveyard. The only sound was the measured tones of the preacher, the Reverend Alister Smythe, as he intoned the time worn phrases expected by the gathering. The words he directed at the casket by the graveside were outmoded, irrelevant, and as lifeless as the body that occupied the wooden box.

'Ashes to ashes, dust to dust.' Monotonously, he droned on, seemingly oblivious to all else except his role in the final chapter of this one man's life.

George glanced sideways at his redheaded sister, Muriel. He could almost read her thoughts as she looked broodingly at the casket containing the body of their Uncle Bert. She and Uncle Bert had similar natures, both blunt and outspoken, both impatient and quick to take offence, and as he looked at her bowed head, he could imagine what she was thinking.

'Get on with it,' Uncle Bert would have muttered. 'We haven't got all day to stand around here, listening to this drivel.'

Muriel had complained to him again, that very morning, about the necessity of holding a funeral service.

'Why can't we just lay him to rest with a simple prayer?'

George had gently remonstrated with her, explaining although they both knew Uncle Bert's views about funerals, the rest of the family had to be considered.

Finally, she had accepted this argument, but evidently her feelings remained the same. His more placid nature riled her at times and, unable to understand his enjoyment of the simple things, she denounced his passive lifestyle as uninteresting and unrewarding.

His attention was diverted by a sudden breeze sweeping across the graveyard. It rustled through the grass, scattering the loose leaves, stirring the flowers on the wreaths, and bringing with it, a butterfly on wing. It was just an ordinary butterfly, the common garden variety which no one bothers to identify. But beautiful, nonetheless. It settled on one of the wreaths, closed and opened its wings a few times, then remained motionless.

How strange, he thought, that a newly born creature would alight here at the scene of death. Yet, life and death seems inextricably intwined, as if each depends on the other, and maybe that is how the balance is maintained. The slanting rays of the afternoon sun highlighted the vivid colours of its wings, reminding him of another time, and another butterfly. It too, had been associated with death.

His mind slipped back to the time he had been on a camping holiday with the local youth group. On the last day they had been asked to prepare a small talk about the highlights of the camp, and what they had gained from the experience.

George had sought a secluded area down by the river, away from the noise of camp and the other children. He wandered along the river-bank, his father's binoculars slung around his neck, till he found a quiet area and, sitting down on the pine needles, leant back against the broad trunk of a tree. His intrusion was soon accepted by the forest creatures, and before long the birds were hopping around almost at his feet.

A flash of colour on the shimmering surface of the river caught his eye, and he turned to see a brightly hued kingfisher swoop across the water to land on a fallen tree trunk. Beneath its perch, the river had formed a small backwater where the flow was momentarily slowed, to form a swirling eddy of twigs and fallen leaves. Some of the debris was caught on the rocky outcrops, as the water noisily spilled over the edge to join the mainstream again.

A faint breeze rustled the leaves for a moment, but it moved on leaving everything quiet again. George could never remember feeling so at one with nature, and he choked down a lump in his throat as he wiped his misty eyes.

Across the river, a clump of willow trees clothed the bark in silvery green foliage, its long trailing branches almost reaching the water's edge. George trained the binoculars on a blackbird as it landed on one of the branches, and he caught sight of a cocoon fastened to the bole of the tree. He gave it a cursory glance, then followed the flight of the bird as it flew away. As the blackbird disappeared into the forest, he felt his eyes drawn back to the grey sac on the side of the tree. At first, he thought it was an optical illusion, or maybe that he had imagined the cocoon had moved slightly, but then he was sure.

He had seen some movement. Fascinated, he adjusted the lens to zoom, and focused his attention on the cocoon. The text book description of metamorphosis paled into insignificance as he watched this miracle of rebirth unfolding.

Slowly, and with great care, the butterfly extracted itself from the ugly grey sac, and clung to the rough surface of its former home. George could see the wet film covering its body, and as he watched, almost breathlessly, the butterfly began to stretch its wings. At first, the movements were painfully slow, as if the creature was struggling to unfold itself. Then suddenly, the wings were fully opened. The brilliant colours vividly portrayed the creature against the dull grey of the tree trunk, and George felt a sigh of relief escape from his lips. He gazed with wonder and admiration as the butterfly extended its wings fully, allowing the sun to dry the last remaining moisture on them. Then, the tiny creature flexed them once or twice, strengthening them for flight, and poised to fly away. It lifted off the tree trunk and hovered nearby for a few seconds, before settling on a branch a few metres above the water.

George was totally unprepared for what happened next, and almost rubbed his eyes in disbelief as the butterfly disappeared. Within the first brief moments of its life, the creature had fallen prey to a passing bird. With barely a perceptible pause in flight, a kingfisher had swooped in and plucked the butterfly off the tree.

Totally immersed in reliving the event, George saw the bird fly off with the tiny creature in its beak, and clapped his hands over his mouth in horror.

'Oh, my God,' he gasped.

His exclamation brought him back to the present, and he looked up to see everyone staring at him. Everyone, except the preacher. Still oblivious to everything but his own importance, and his role in the proceedings, he droned on,

'The Lord giveth, and the Lord taketh away.'

Red Flannel

by

Elizabeth M Humphreys

I was given the name of Moonflower, I am the last of my totem - The Moon. Our ancestors have lived in this land since time began. Our mother The Earth has provided for us, and our father The Great Spirit has protected us. We have fished the bountiful rivers and hunted in the teeming woods, taking only that which was needed.

Then the white men came, we laughed at them when they traded goods in return for land, for the land belongs to all and what man can sell his mother?

We took their red flannel and made tunics and long skirts for our women and fine shirts for our warriors, all members of the tribe had a garment made from it, for it was warm and rich with colour.

Then the sickness began, we shivered and sweated and the red spots covered our bodies, and the people of the tribe began to die.

Our Shaman drove out the evil spirits and purified the sick, and our Medicine Woman used all her skills, but in every tepee there was sickness and death. Our Shaman journeyed to the world of spirit and brought back some of our brothers and sisters, but some of those who returned could not hear the call of the owl or the song of the bluebird, and others could no longer see the beauty of the dark green pine woods and the wide blue lakes. Still the white man moves nearer, he has cut down the trees where we hunted, and wounded the breast of The Mother with his plough. My heart is desolate as I look at my village and my land.

Tonight, when my sister the moon rises, we will burn our tepees, the trade goods and the red flannel that brought the gift of death, and leave for the mountains. There, in the pure air, under the protection of the Great Spirit we will grow strong again.

This is our story and it has to be told.

Elin

by

Perry Siddall

Elin hobbled down the stairs, travelling as fast as she dared in her overworked moccasins. She landed flat-footed on her right foot and barely touched the tread with her left. Her bunions were playing her up as usual, so it wouldn't have taken a genius to know who was coming down.

'Is that you Mam, how's Da tonight?' James stuck his head around the kitchen door and continued to munch on the chicken leg he'd obviously taken from the fridge.

'Your dad's all right, now that the fog has lifted he's breathing a bit easier. Why don't you pop up and see him yourself?'

Elin waited expectantly for the usual excuse.

'Can't now Mam, I'm in a rush, the lads are waiting for me at the corner. We're playing a match at eight, so I'm just grabbing a quick bite, then I'll be off. I hope you weren't keeping the chicken for anything? Anyway, there's a wing left. Lucky that dad hates chicken. Have you washed my kit?'

Elin said nothing, James was all right, just a bit thoughtless. I suppose it was her own fault, but he was the youngest and the only one left at home, now that the others were married. Soon, he'd be off too, if that 'flighty bit' he was going with at the moment had anything to do with it. This time Elin knew her 'pride and joy' wouldn't escape. Well, Cassie would put up with nothing, if Elin read the signs right, so James was in for a rude awakening. It would probably do him good too. The front door slammed and James was gone.

Elin paused for a minute at the bottom of the stairs, her head slightly tilted. She could still hear the stentorian breathing of her husband. Shuffling into the kitchen she surveyed the mess. James had certainly been in a hurry - there were plates piled on the draining-board, the kitchen carcass was plonked in the middle of the table and the breadboard with its half-eaten piece of bread, had been dumped unceremoniously on the work top. Gritting her teeth, Elin squeezed a dollop of washing-up liquid into the basin and ran the hot water, while at the same time she began to gather up the dirty dishes. Just as she put her red, roughened hands into the water, she heard herself being called.

'Elin? Elin!' came from upstairs. Quickly wiping her hands on the back of her skirt, Elin started up the stairs again for about the umpteenth time.

'What is it, Gareth, what can I get you?'

Elin's Gareth lay propped up on four pillows on their double bed. He looked emaciated under his shock of grey hair. Although only fifty-five, he had the aged appearance of a man of at least seventy plus. His bedside table was covered under a layer of pill-bottles and sundry inhalers. Beside his bed also, stood an oxygen cylinder with its little, plastic, perspex face-mask draped over the headboard.

'I need some oxygen, Elin,' he panted, 'help me with the mask.'

Elin passed him the headpiece and helped him to adjust the elastic strip around his ears. She then regulated the air flow and watched silently as he gasped it in. She moved to the door but just as she reached it, Gareth called her again. He'd removed the mask.

'I'll just have a couple of pulls now, will you pass me the fags and lighter, please?'

Rushing to turn off the oxygen supply, Elin protested. 'Please, Gareth, don't! What about blowing up the house with your smoking while the oxygen is running, think of what the doctor said. Please!'

'To hell with what that bloody doctor said,' Gareth gasped as he swore, 'I may as well be dead if I can't smoke. I'll smoke if I like - they've done all the damage they're going to do, so I'm going to enjoy the simple pleasures I have left.'

Elin grabbed for the cigarette as his outburst brought on a paroxysm of coughing and left him hooting for air. Silently she stubbed it out in the nearby ashtray and reached for the oxygen mask yet again. This time he kept it on for some time and sucked in the air gratefully. Elin limped downstairs and put the kettle on. Within ten minutes she had climbed the stairs again with a cup of sweet, milky tea and a slice of cherry cake.

'I had cherry cake this morning,' Gareth grunted peevishly, 'I'd prefer some of the apple-pie.'

Elin removed the plate and went down to fetch the pie. She glanced at the clock on the mantelpiece and saw that it was almost 'News Time'. In another hour it would be time for Gareth's night drink and his sleeping pill. She'd just have a quick glance at the News to see what was happening in the world outside. As soon as it had finished, she started to put the milk on to heat for the Ovaltine. This routine was unchanging. Gareth had to be tempted to eat, so the doctor said, but at least while he was having his regular milky nightcap, he wasn't losing any strength. Elin filled the half-pint glass with the hot milk and added two teaspoons of Ovaltine powder and two spoons of sugar. Stirring it well, Gareth hated lumps, she placed the glass on a saucer and trudged upstairs.

'You took your time!' Gareth griped, as she placed the glass within his reach.

Elin said nothing as he unscrewed the vial which held his sleeping pills. Taking out one Mogadon, she handed it to him. Gareth clutched it in his bony hand and then placed it in his mouth. She helped him hold the Ovaltine as he sipped it to swallow the pill.

'Don't forget to clean my teeth, they're in the glass ready.'

'I won't, Gareth.'

Sitting quietly beside the bed, Elin waited for the pill to take effect. Within twenty minutes he had visibly relaxed, his eyes were closed but his breathing was as loud and tortured as ever. Still, that's how it is with Emphysema, there wasn't a cure - just drugs to make it a bit easier. The doctor had explained to her how the end would be - like drowning in your own saliva, he said. Sounded very unpleasant indeed. Sighing deeply, Elin reached across Gareth and took up her own pillow. Holding it with both hands she placed it across Gareth's face and pressed. He started to twitch but she increased the pressure. She waited for a good ten minutes after the twitching had stopped and his chest no longer moved. Then she took the pillow away. It was amazing how quiet it was when he was no longer breathing. He ought to be happy now, wherever he was. Elin looked at her watch, almost ten o'clock, just time to catch the late News.

The Italian

by

Sammy Coombs

I don't know what caused me to wake that night. I tossed and turned in my bunk before deciding to take a walk on deck. The wind was beginning to pick up and I gave an involuntary shiver as I walked over to the handrail and looked out to sea. A fog was starting to creep along the surface, threatening to engulf us into its midst.

I hadn't noticed the man as I had come up on deck but he was staring out to sea, just as I had been a moment before. A man of average height, his greased black hair combed closed to his head, around thirty I guessed and from where I stood, his clothes looked old-fashioned.

He walked over to join me, 'Couldn't sleep?'

I shook my head 'I suppose it's the lazy days of the cruise.'

He looked back out to sea, leaning heavily on the rail and we fell silent.

Feeling uncomfortable in the stillness I asked 'Is that a French accent I detect?'

'No, my friend, Italian. I am Gino Minetti from a town in Northern Italy named Bardi. You heard of it?'

I admitted I had not and he continued, 'Today is an anniversary for me, but there, you don't want to hear stories from an old man.'

I laughed at that remark and urged him to tell his tale. His accent was pleasant and his voice soothing. I listened intently as his story unfolded.

'The tale begins many years ago' he stared as if seeing the past in the darkness beyond, 'when I was a boy. We heard stories, in Bardi, from the valleys in Wales, of how the miners who dug for coal used our trees for their pit props to strengthen the walls and ceilings of the shafts. There was talk of how men from other villages were travelling over to find work.

I was young, adventurous and faced a future of farming. That night as I helped Mama to prepare the supper, I told her of my plan to leave Italy and find work in Wales. She called me her bambino and I remember shouting at her, 'I show you all, prove to you I am a man. I'm going to .Wales, make fine ice-cream and cool lemonade to ease the miners throats that are filled with the black dust. You will be proud of Gino, Mama, proud do you hear?' I grasped my mama around her not too slender waist and waltzed around her kitchen, my anger quickly turning to gaiety. She thought it just a dream, in my head, and she looked so pretty as we danced around, laughing and singing, I didn't have the heart to say goodbye... I never saw mama again.'

My companion stopped for a while and I shivered a little as the fog rose higher. Cold as I was I couldn't leave, I was eager to hear this gentle man's tale.

'I took enough food from the larder to last a couple of days and one weeks wages. I left a short note to say not to worry. I was off to seek my fortune, and I was gone before first light - to find work and more than that - adventure! Sounds stupid - no? At sixteen it sounded magnificent! ' He paused a moment before continuing. 'I made enough money doing odd jobs to make my way further North to the coast. When I reached the dockside they were taking on ships crew, so I signed on working in the galley. The final trip sailed into the port of Cardiff, a busy and thriving place. So, here I was at last. The Capital of Wales and I could see before me truck upon truck of gleaming black coal. I asked where the coal came from and as you can imagine, got all sorts of answers until someone told me a name. It sounded so strange to me, this foreign tongue, this peculiar accent. I made for the highways and walked towards the Rhymney Valleys. It took me several nights of sleeping under hedgerows and several days of foot blistering hills before I reached the mining village of Trefeddyn, where I was to settle.

At first I could only stand and despair its blackness. The houses came down in rows like giant pathways cut through the slag, their roof tops indistinguishable from their background. One house joined another, each one a replica of the one before, all along a row until its end, and then they would start again until they came to rest on the main street which led to the blackest thing of all - the mine. 'I would bring relief to this dark and miserable place, I thought'

The man laughed allowed as he remembered the arrogant and vain ideals of a younger self. 'I thought to bring so much to this desolate place, but I was to learn that this valley town had a colourful and cheery nature that no black coal dust could ever dampen or eradicate.

I was given lodgings by a widow with just one daughter who was then in service. 'You can have her room willingly,' she said to me, her accent thick and her English stilted from so many years of speaking only Welsh.

The widow wasn't one to shut her eyes to an opportunity to add to her meagre income. 'I've got a parlour you can use' she volunteered when I told her of my business intention, 'for a couple of extra shillings I could let you rent it, to sell your ice-cream and all.'

'On the very next morning, the widow woke me at half past four, I leapt from my bed, thinking there was a fire, flood or worse but she laughed and explained, 'There'll be men coming up from that hell hole, you might serve up some tea save them waking their own house, like. I'm not saying it'll work, but there if you don't try you'll never know will you?'

'From that day my business venture took off. I worked from dawn to dusk serving each shift and in between the retired or injured men, even men on their day off would gather to drink my mother's recipe of fine lemonade and talk and discuss with one another. My room became a temperance bar and I made many friends among the local customers.

I soon needed larger premises and found a shack-like building nearer the mine.

I decided to go to the manager's office and ask to rent the near dilapidated shack; Mr Jones' reaction was anticipated - he laughed and laughed, 'no boyo, you can't rent that bloody old shack, I can do you better than that. The shop on the corner of your street is for rent. You and your wife can move into the house behind and *we* can have a good a shop as your 'cousins' in the next village.'

Everyone seemed to think that all Italians were related!

I looked up open mouthed and managed to say, 'but I don't have a wife.'

'I don't think a little thing like that will stop you, Minetti. There's plenty of girls here, come back when you find one. I'll leave it for one month.'

'I was dismissed. I thought that a problem had been overcome. Now I was presented with the biggest problem of my life, I told my landlady later. She went very quiet, then pulling herself up to her full five foot announced she had the solution. I was no longer to worry, it would be resolved within seven days.'

The man's grin widened as he relived this part of his life. His eyes took on a gentleness and a wonderment as he thought of the 'solution'.

'The very next morning I awoke to find an empty house. No fire lit, no breakfast cooking, no note of explanation. I had to wait two more days for her return - accompanied by her daughter Megan. The old lady looked like the cat who'd eaten the cream, the daughter a little sheepish and I thought there were signs of crying. I shrugged this off as being 'their business'. Until the widow spoke, 'Here's your solution then, boyo,' she said 'don't look at me stupid now, you need a wife to get your shop. You can tell old Bill Manager, it's all fixed.'

'We had three weeks of getting to know each other before our wedding and most of that time was spent in renovating and reorganising the shop, but we had a wonderful marriage and three beautiful children - it would have blossomed into a long and happy life - but the war came.'

The man fell silent and I felt a foreboding in the approaching fog. This was a sad man, his pleasant memories distant, the painful ones crowding in. I gave an involuntary shiver, he went on.

'I heard stories. They had taken some Italians, Germans too who had lived, worked in the community, married within their villages. I did not want to believe that my turn would come.

When the local policeman called to the cafe, naively I turned to my urn to make his tea, but his hand was on my shoulder. Do you know there were tears in his eyes as he told me I had to leave everything that was dear to me, everything I had worked to achieve.

I was taken with other Italians and some Germans to a ship bound for Canada. We were to be held there until hostilities ended. Maybe I could see my beloved Megan soon, hold my babies to my breast.

It was here, in the middle of the ocean that we were torpedoed, didn't stand a chance, really. Ironic that a German U boat would knock a ship out of the water carrying their own sons, but that is exactly what they did. Not one man survived in this foggy, freezing sea.'

The fog had engulfed us in its damp and eerie midst and I glanced to my left. My story teller had disappeared into the fog, swirled up into its cold and clammy clouds.

I wept, for spirit eternally lost and I prayed he would find his Megan one day and she him, so that he may truly rest in peace.

Hand Picked

by

Stephen Mouncher

Ashley Trope stared at the lift doors and blinked nervously. The corridor was desolate, the dim, after hours light forming shadows within shadows. He couldn't do this. Earlier he had been strong and defiant, ready to brave anything. New Years' Resolution; start taking the elevator. Right now he was what he had always been. Scared of lifts. Not a claustrophobe. Just stupidly scared. Of lifts.

He gave up and barged through the exit doors, feeling instantly buoyant and relaxed. As he trotted down to the sixteenth floor he slowed a little and noticed the lights, three floors below, flicker into darkness. It was then that he heard the footsteps.

Ashley stopped and stood quite still. He peered over the edge, sixteen flights spiralling away below, and rolling up the cold, concrete steps came the regular clacking of someone's shoes, shoes coming up the stairs that were always empty around this time of night. Coming up. Towards him.

Ashley blinked and swallowed down a stone dry throat. It was the cleaner, he thought. It had to be the cleaner.

'Hello?' Ashley called.

As he spoke the steps paused in their ascent and a bulb, just two floors below, whispered into dark silence. The footsteps began again. Only this time faster and somehow..eager.

Ashley stepped back from the edge. His hands were trembling slightly. He didn't like this. It was damn unusual for someone to be coming up these stairs at this time of night. He glanced around and noticed the lift was sitting on this floor. He hesitantly approached the doors and glanced nervously at the glowing light on the wall. He couldn't do it. He just couldn't step in there. He glanced back to the stairs. One floor below the lights failed and the footsteps didn't slow for a second. Ashley slammed his palm against the call button. The elevator doors rattled open like the yawning jaws of an underfed beast.

He peered into the well lit interior and, with the footsteps behind him nearing the top, stepped in, spun on the spot and stabbed his finger at the button marked 'G'.

As the doors shuttled together Ashley could just make out a shadowy figure standing at the top of the stairs, no longer walking, just standing. And staring at him. Then the elevator doors were shut tight and with a distinct vibration the lift descended.

The smell hit Ashley almost without warning and there was no mistaking the stench. Urine. And by its violent pungency he also knew that it was fresh.

As the lift fell Ashley steadied himself against the hand rail and began to count to one hundred. It was an old, childish trick, but it seemed to work and after a few seconds he was grinning at himself.

He was okay now. He had been a little rattled by some stupid cleaner but he was fine and in control again.

The lift screeched around him, metal gouging into metal, and vibrated to a sickening halt.

Ashleys breathing began to speed up harshly. The lights above him flickered once, twice.

'Oh no..' Ashley murmured, his eyes fixed inexorably on the fluorescent above.

With a final stammer the light squeezed itself into blackness. Ashley stood alone in the dark.

The lifts' walls seemed to crush in on him. He felt the air being squashed from his lungs and the all pervading reek of urine rammed itself up his nose and down his throat.

He started to gag on the vile taste. He began to breathe in short, sharp gasps, the hyperventilating making his head rush and swell.

He shuddered as he screwed his eyes shut and wished he hadn't given up smoking three months ago. What he wouldn't give for a few drags, just to take the horrendous taste out of his mouth.

The emergency button.

He could reach across and press the emergency button.

The thought popped into his mind, startling in its level-headed simplicity. Mike the night-watchman was still on duty. He would get things rolling again and Ashley would be out of there in no time.

He gripped his hands together to stop them shaking. When he pulled them apart they did seem to be a little steadier. He reached out for the button and felt someone breathe against his cheek.

Ashley screamed.

The sound flailed impotently around the metal shell and echoed along the lonely lift shaft. Ashley flattened himself against the wall, his legs shuddering beneath him, his eyes wide and goggling, trying to catch even the slightest of movements in the near absolute darkness.

He had no idea what was happening to him.

'Is..is someone..there?' he whispered.

There was no answer . The only sounds Ashley could hear were his own ragged gasps. Of course no one was there! he scolded himself. When he had stepped in, the lights had been on, and Ashley had been quite alone. He was just panicking at being stuck in this bloody lift! He was making an absolute arse of himself and if anyone could see him now they would be wetting themselves with laughter.

He chuckled shakily at himself then bit on his lower lip. He reached out to the panel.

Its black surface felt cold under his sweaty palm and he traced his thin fingers over the raised ridges of the buttons. He felt for the largest circle, and after a half dozen strained seconds, he secured the knob and pressed hard against it.

A red light flickered above the button and for a brief heartbeat the panel was illuminated. Then the light went out and Ashley could only hope the message had been received. He took his finger off the button and let his hand fall to his side.

Someone took hold of his fingers and squeezed.

Ashley's throat constricted, strangling his scream in its foetal stage. His eyes bulged in his head and his temples pulsed with the increased pressure.

Someone was holding his hand.

'This... this is not happening. This can't be happening,' Ashley whimpered out loud, his voice cracking.

The darkness spat back no reply.

But the hand, that wasn't there, clutched his sweat encrusted palm more painfully. A whole minute later Ashley started to cry with the terrified passion of a scared four year old.

As the tears split the blemish free skin of his cheeks in pitiful twin rivulets, the lift lurched around him, and, with a keening squeal, shifted downwards.

Suddenly, the grip released itself and Ashley snapped his eyes open. The lift was moving! He was going to be free! Even as the box lurched for the second time, the doors crashed open and he staggered out into the sanitised light of the lobby.

He spun on his heels and whipped his eyes around the lift's interior.

No one there.

No one at all.

He slowly turned away as the first nervous chuckle rippled through his chest. By the time he was halfway across the lobby he was shaking with uncontrollable laughter.

'Everything alright, sir?'

Ashley jerked his head up and peered at the night watchman.

'No it's not alright! I've been stuck in that bloody lift for what felt like ages! Where the hell were you?' Ashley did nothing to restrain his spiteful anger. The old man studied the younger with a droll and arid patience.

'Sorry. Moved as quick as I could,' he muttered.

Ashley stared at the night watchman with barely concealed disdain. Then, forcing a civil grin, he held his hand out. The stupid old fool had got the lift working in the end, after all. And whatever those crazy hallucinations had been up there... well... they were over with now.

'Sorry Mike. Got a bit rattled. No hard feelings?' Ashley said, lying effectively.

'Ah, that's okay, sir.'

He moved to take Ashley's hand but stopped in mid-movement, wrinkling his brow.

'What...?' Ashley began.

'Your hand. You've done something... to your hand.'

Ashley looked down and he could see a thick droplet forming on the tip of his elegant finger, a single bubble of dark liquid, swelling even as he stared at it.

Ashley slowly turned his hand palm upward and he felt the room slip away under his feet.

Blood.

His hand was full of blood.

And no matter how hard he looked, no matter how furiously he dug around in the sticky, warm fluid with his left finger, he couldn't find any cut or break in his own skin.

His perfect hand was full of blood.

And none of it was his own.

Last Train to Brighton

by

B Gerad O'Brien

Richard Mann braced himself against the cold wet night and dashed across the road to the little red letterbox buried in an old brick wall. The trees rocked wildly and the rain blew in darts across the solitary street light as he checked the letters one last time. Identical envelopes, identical handwriting, but two different addresses, and two very different notes inside. He sighed deeply and dropped them quickly through the slot.

It had to be done. Sooner or later it had to be sorted out and it might as well be now. Back in the car he wiped the wet from his face and brushed back his hair, his mind going over and over the words in the letters that were timed to arrived by first post on Friday.

The first was to Helen, his wife of twenty years, flame haired and slate grey eyes that he thought were the most beautiful in the world. But somewhere along the way the light went out and now they looked through him with total indifference. And tonight would be the same as every other night. When he got home she would have already eaten, and she would ask politely how his day went as she put his meal on the table. But then she would turn away and carry on doing something else as his answer drifted past her. He'd have a shower and read the paper and she would watch TV late into the night. Maybe if the children were still at home, maybe if... well, it was too late now. One way or another it was coming to a head, and Richard Mann had already rolled the dice.

The note simply said; 'you know in your heart this had to come, and I only hope we can part with dignity. By the time you get this I'll be far away, starting a new life. You won't ever hear from me again. Richard.'

The second letter was to Rebecca, a special person who was filling his life. They had worked together for years, but it was only when they both ended up in the same department that they spoke more than two words. Then when a major crisis hit the company they were thrown together under enormous pressure, and through it all they could find time to laugh, her hair as black as coal bouncing with the fun of it all and her eyes wide and full of understanding.

But after the crisis was over they found they couldn't let go. What had been snatched tea breaks now became lunches, then stolen moments on their way somewhere else, until it eventually became lies and late nights at the office. Courses that they 'had' to go on suddenly appeared until in the end it was consuming them both.

They talked a million times about making a break. A friend even offered to rent them a couple of rooms. But for Rebecca it would be a terrible sacrifice. Her husband Tom was a giant of a man, kind and loving, and she swore he already knew something was going on, but when he put out feelers she couldn't face him with the truth and would deny that her feelings had changed towards him. He worshipped her, so she had no way of knowing how he would react. One thing for sure, he would be violently hurt, and he would never let her take the children. It would be a hard choice for her to make.

Friday was her day off, so she would be home when her letter arrived. It, too, was brief.

'Babe, I know this will be a great shock to you, but I'll be taking the 6.15 to Brighton this evening (Friday). I've got a new job with a lot more money, and a company flat. I'm sorry I kept it secret all along but I couldn't tell you before because I know after all that's been said and done it won't be an easy decision for you to make. In fact I've told no one where I'm going, especially at work, that way no one will ever find us. So if you want to make a new start, begin a completely new life, then meet me at the station. Love, Richard.'

So on Friday he took a taxi to the station as early as he could leave work, but still they hit the rush hour, and when he ran into the platform the noise from the train was drowning out the muffled announcement from the Tannoy. Doors were already being slammed as he pushed through the milling throng of commuters, straining to catch any sign of her. He scanned the windows of the train, then across to the waiting room. She wasn't in the cafe either and a dread filled his heart. There was no time left. If she wasn't here now, then the answer was clear.

He looked back to the train, and froze when something sharp pressed into his back.

'Richard...'

He turned sharply.

'Tom?'

'Steady. This knife is razor sharp. We want no accidents, not here.'

'I... I don't understand. What do you want?'

'You got it wrong, Richard. Rebecca is away this weekend, at her mother's. Didn't she tell you? So I opened her mail... just in case.'

He manoeuvered Richard towards the car park and the old Ford Transit parked by the bushes.

Suddenly he gave a deep laugh.

'I sealed the letter back up, of course. So she'll know you've gone forever. But it's your own words I like best. No one will know where you've gone, you said. No one will ever find you. Will they?'

Alive and Dead

by

John R Mallon

Ivor stood broodingly at the centre of the numbingly cold room. His sore eyes expressionlessly examined Julia's rosy-cheeked, robust countenance. Cautiously he pushed aside the auburn hair strands that had somehow reached her crimson lips. Consequently his touch received her warmth.

The stout, bespectacled, balding, middle aged Dr Llewellyn puffed agitatedly at the long stemmed briar pipe, filling the cosy kitchen with a richness of smell as he rested against a large, black Welsh dresser whilst watching the three people at the fireside.

Muriel Jenkins, the mother of Julia, being a timid, God-fearing woman, looked anxiously to the other side of the great fireplace, to see her stern looking, bearded husband, Jenkin, remove the brass bellows from the ebony panelling, at his side, then give the lifeless fire several bursts of air. In between Julia's parents, her husband to be, Twm, silently glared at the fluttering orange flames as they danced up into the black chimney.

Mr Rhys, who had been premediating on the present quandary, decided to confront Jenkin, Muriel and Twm. The three turned to see the red-haired, youthful looking man leave his stool by the door and say, in a lucid, cheerless tone, 'He has been in there for two and a half days!' Muriel abruptly burst into tears. Twm lowered his head as streams of tears red-marked white bony cheeks as they rolled.

Jenkin Jenkins rose from his comfortless seat and left the room. As soon as the heavy, dark brown door had closed, Dr Llewellyn signalled Mr Rhys. Rhys, whilst clasping a dark blue bible approached the doctor, his long black robe brushed the heavily varnished floor as he moved. Once the priest had reached Llewellyn, the doctor whispered, 'The girl is as dead as dead! There's no indication of blood flow or reaction to pain, heat or light!'

The priest thoughtfully replied, 'She does not appear to be dead: her face shows health; her limbs are limp and are, therefore, different from those of a corpse!'

In a condescending tone, the doctor retorted, 'The eminent physician, Sir Geraint Owain has also examined her and his prognosis is no different from mine, you know!'

'What about her poor uncle?' retorted the priest emotionally. 'He cannot conceive that she's dead. He has not eaten or spoken to anyone in almost three days.'

Doctor Llewellyn replied impatiently, 'I can comprehend your contention, but if she isn't soon put to rest, her decomposition will become noticeable to all in this dwelling and all other homes within the Parish of Vaynor.'

In an understanding tone Mr Rhys retorted, 'Everyone in this family wants her buried, it's her stubborn uncle who is causing the delay.'

In a severe voice Dr Llewellyn added loudly, 'This man is illogical, in fact, he's probably insane. If he does not alter his tendencies... he may well end his life in Talgarth.'

'Talgarth,' retorted Mr Rhys. 'Ivor Roberts is the sanest, soberest churchgoer in the whole of Vaynor! Talgarth is only for the feeble-minded and the unwanted, is it not?'

Dr Llewellyn shook his head as he walked to the door. His parting words were, 'As a priest, Mr Rhys, you are concerned with the dead, whereas, being a doctor, the living, only, interests me? I must leave!'

For seven days and nights Julia lay in the open coffin. On the eighth morning, she was to be put into the earth. Ivor had finally conceded in his beloved's death. Yet before she was taken from her home, Julia looked alive: her cheeks still had colour; and her uncle could still feel warmth emanating from her. 'Maybe I am insane. Her heart still beats!' he said raising his head from her chest.

In disbelief, Jenkin, Muriel, Mr Rhys and Ebeneezer, the parish undertaker, in turn, put their heads to the young woman's chest; and each, after listening, said, 'There isn't a sound.' Ivor couldn't accept their observation, and quickly departed the room.

As he returned to the coffin, Ebeneezer spoke, 'Let him go. He's in shock. In a week's time, he will return to his normal self.' The undertaker subsequently closed the coffin, then hammered several nails through the coffin lid.

Julia had a large funeral. Ivor observed it... from the outside of Moriah church, but he didn't want to watch his niece lowered into her interminable pit. As he watched the crowd, Ivor became aware that Gladys, Julia's sister, wasn't present.

Even though it rained, he visited Julia's grave for the following fortnight - where he would place each of his ears against the soil that covered her; but not a sound was heard from below.

Ivor lived for another sixteen years, fifteen and a half of them were spent at Talgarth. Before he died his only request was to be buried with his niece. This was granted by Jenkin; but it involved the construction of a family vault, for there wasn't sufficient space in his daughter's grave. Less than a year later Jenkin, too, was buried with Julia and Ivor - two years later Muriel joined them.

Many years later Julia's sister, Gladys, returned home after spending much of her life abroad. At a very advanced age, her time to be buried arrived.

The horse and cart stopped outside the ivy covered vault on a summer's morning. The two undertakers named Gwyn and Emrys took an end of the coffin. As they transported

Gladys to the vault's door, Emrys said, 'Well, this is the last of them!' They lowered the coffin to the ground outside the wooden door, being reinforced by steel railings, intertwined with ivy branches that coiled around a huge corroded padlock.

As Gwyn utilized the key that had last been used forty years ago, he said, 'I cannot understand why the Jenkins built such a large tomb on the site of a used grave?'

Emrys responded, 'I remember our great uncle Ebeneezer saying that one of them was believed to have been buried alive,' as he pushed open the door that made an agonising sound, like a creature that had awoken from a timeless slumber, as it opened. 'I'm not going into the dark!'

Gwyn returned to the cart and retrieved a lantern and lit it. Once the small flame was produced, he stepped over the coffin and said, 'Come, Emrys.'

Emrys followed tentatively and said, 'This place scares me! I've heard so many stories about this family.'

As the darkness turned to a pale glow, the dampness touched their skin and the staleness entered their noses, Gwyn spoke, 'This Gladys is a strange one; being a spinster all these years, and requested that no funeral service be given at her burial.'

Through the depressing dimness, Emrys squinted at the brass plates on the two coffins, one stating Jenkin Jenkins; the other one read Muriel Jenkins. He turned to see his brother reading the coffin plate stating Ivor Roberts at the ledge opposite. They both curiously turned to see the coffin at the far end of the tomb. 'That's her!' whimpered Gwyn. 'Let's open her up and end all these old wives tales, about her being buried alive. I'll fetch a chisel.'

Once Gwyn had returned from the stonemason's shed, they both knocked upwards with their tools until the lid was prised off. Emrys grabbed the lantern and held it directly above the open coffin as its glow glimmered on the inside of the coffin lid.

The brothers stared in an hypnotic revulsion at the multiple scratch marks on the inside lid amongst several long stains of a dark red substance. The gravity of intrigue that permeated their fear, involuntarily forced them to view the contents in the coffin. The skeleton's hands were at its skull which had turned sideways.

Both screamed as they ran from the vault, tripping over the coffin outside. The brothers ran, and continued running, forgetting about their horse and cart and Gladys, but for the rest of their lives they would never forget Julia.

A Break in the Country

by

Ellen Whelan

'His mouth opened in a soundless scream as he saw the figure...'

'Naked. The naked figure.'

Liz considered. 'That's it, Trish! Brill! '... as he saw the naked figure, grotesque rubber-gloved hands clutching the knife...' Marvellous!'

'I just thought of it as you read it. Something had been nagging me about it.'

'And that finishes it. The end is self-evident now, we don't have to spell it out.'

Trish circled the ice-cooled lemonade jug with her beautiful tapering fingers, then absently pressed them to her brow.

'Headache again, Trish?'

'A bit. But it's this story - it's still not quite right.'

'Oh come on, Trish! it's the perfect ending. We don't have to say he killed the guy. Surely the reader can work that out for himself.'

Trish slowly shook her head. 'It's strange, Liz. I have this feeling that there's something more. The story's not finished yet.'

'No. If we add anything it will be too much. Leave it as it is.' She watched Trish with a slight frown. 'Tell you what. We've had enough for one day anyway. Let's sleep on it and look at it again tomorrow. The competition date is ten days off so we have plenty of time. How about a walk?'

They walked along the river bank. Lanky boys and elderly gentlemen fished. A few small boats made their leisurely way down river, one of them clearly rowed by a novice who happily splashed both himself and his laughing companion. A distant working tractor resolved itself into a remote hum.

The slight summer haze gently breathed its dimness on the water's edge, soothing the red earth's rim to a warm pink patched with moving green. The trodden path stretched ribbon-thin ahead as they strolled along.

'It's such a beautiful place. Right out of town, yet close. No neighbours. No telephone. Perfect.'

'It was a lovely idea, Trish. I'm so glad you asked me to come with you. Perhaps a week is long enough though. I don't think I'd have been bored with longer but you never know. Anyway it's back to work on Monday.'

'Shall we turn back?'

'Ok. Head better?'

'Much, thanks. Nearly gone.'

Slowly they returned. The cottage stood alone, back from the river. A wooden fence and a dog-rose hedge surrounded a lawn that in the spring would throw a carpet of buttercups and cowslips to the passing gaze. The hedge obscured the near view of the river from the cottage but the meadows on the far side ran down from the small grey church in a gentle slope.

They had made a rare visit to service on the Sunday and had been welcomed with friendly but not overwhelming courtesy. The organ and the singing had had the air of being unrehearsed and they had found it slightly amusing and rather charming. They were not surprised to learn that regular services were no longer held because the parish lacked a curate.

Liz slowed her energetic pace to that of her companion, whose mass of chestnut hair topped her own smooth dark cap by a good six inches.

'Who would ever have expected us to write a story?' Trish suddenly exclaimed.

'Well, pure chance, wasn't it? If I hadn't picked up that magazine and if you hadn't left your typewriter in the back of the car... Think what deathless prose the world might have missed.' They both laughed. 'Anyway, it's been great fun, hasn't it?'

'I still feel...'

'Rubbish! It's finished!'

Trish continued to look troubled.

Liz spoke firmly. 'It's only a story, Trish. What's more important is that you need to see a doctor. Those headaches are getting worse, aren't they; more frequent?'

'Yes. I'll make an appointment as soon as I get home. Promise.'

'Good.'

They sauntered on. After an evening meal they lay in garden chairs, reading and idly chatting, until the day grew dim.

The next morning they breakfasted in the garden, throwing toast crumbs to eager birds; watching the small signs of activity around the church. They completed their leisurely chores and began to prepare a light lunch.

'It's your turn to go for bread, Trish. Take your time. I'll finish up here. We can talk about the end of the story while we eat. Right?'

'Right.'

Trish walked slowly along the river bank, where mallards dipped and floating branches curtsied green skirts in the tranquil water. She leaned for a few minutes on the old stone bridge, watching two tiny cygnets chase after their drifting parents.

Her purchases were few and light and she carried them in a tote bag slung on her shoulder. She gazed up at the church clock and wondered if it would ever strike again, then turned for home.

As she looked at the cottage across the river the first faint, familiar pain began.

With resignation and a strange feeling of unreality, she crossed the bridge and trod the path with feet that seemed not to belong. She longed to stop yet felt compelled to continue. A sense almost of panic kept her moving doggedly on.

Thankfully, she reached the open door and leaned against it. Liz had evidently started the typing, she could hear the noise of the machine. Suddenly it stopped and Liz appeared.

'You look awful, Trish! Perhaps you walked too far. Look, go up and lie down quietly for a while. Can I get you some tablets or something?' She took the bag from Trish's shoulder.

Trish lifted a heavy hand. 'I think I'll go up and have a cool shower.'

'Good idea. Need any help?'

Trish shook her head, very carefully, and laboriously climbed the stairs. She stood for a moment at her open bedroom window, her head against the glass, before stripping and going into the bathroom.

As she leaned forward to switch on the shower she suddenly felt an overwhelming desire for a drink of cold water. Ice cold.

She reached the bottom of the stairs, where she could hear Liz busily typing once more. She turned into the kitchen.

Hearing her at the sitting room doorway Liz looked up.

Her mouth opened in a soundless scream as she saw the naked figure, grotesque rubber-gloved hands...

Losing

by

J D Gair

'Tampo' Talwyn Harris and 'Dagger' Dan Wynter sat quietly but alert on the steps to their pigeon lofts. They were waiting, watching the clear summer evening sky, tracing the horizon with narrowed eyes. They both sensed that their racing pigeons could appear any moment, and the result of the last race of the season meant more to them than the rest of the members of the Cymmer Valley Racing Pigeon Club.

It was a long way from Carlisle to South Wales but they expected a close finish, having trained their best birds with equal diligence. What made the race so important to them was the fact that whichever one clocked in the winter not only would he top the club point table, scoop a substantial amount of prize money and take the overall winner's cup, he would be ahead of the other in prestige after years of personal rivalry. Their personalities had always been in conflict, resulting in their rare verbal contact at the club where they could be guaranteed to express opposing viewpoints on any subject that arose during meetings. The atmosphere often became charged to the chairmans vexation.

Dagger had entered two birds in the race, Tampo one. All were blue pied in plumage - predominantly blue colouring suffusing white. Both men were well clear of all other racing club members in the points table but on an even score. So far as they were concerned the race was between their birds only to determine the overall winner of the season, an ambition either could achieve for the first time. Their lofts were just thirty yards apart a little way up the rather steep bank of a river. Dagger had painted his in black and white stripes, believing it would make his loft easier for his birds to see from a distance when returning at the end of a race. Tampo's was painted a light green, having learned and recognised that the colour of a loft made no difference to a pigeon's ability to home directly to it, so that it blended with the background.

A short distance away, lower down the valley, was their village, where other pigeon fanciers were manning their lofts with sweet anticipation, relaxed, intermittently calling and signalling to each other. A few were smoking pipes, a couple of younger ones slowly draining cans of lager. None felt the stomach tightening apprehension of the two men locked into hostile competition farther up the river. What they all had in common, though, was a love of pigeon racing, and it was customary - no - traditional to gave their best pigeons names.

Tampo suddenly stiffened and rose to his feet on the loft steps, his eyes fixed across the valley. Dagger gave a low whistle as he, too, looked in the same direction then stood up quickly. A pigeon had appeared on the skyline and was descending the far side of the valley, winging low towards the river. It was coming straight, not veering towards the village, becoming distinct as a blue pied as it neared. It could be either man's bird. They scrambled into their lofts, stood by the already open large entrance hatches and waited with drumming heartbeats.

On reaching the river, however, the bird did not make for either loft. In the middle of the river was a large rock that protruded from the water even when it was in flood. Wild ducks and the occasional heron rested on it when passing through the valley, and it was to this rock that the pigeon dropped and pitched well within sight of whichever loft it belonged to. It sometimes happens that a bird at the end of a race chooses to settle near its loft rather than fly straight in. The theory is that since it is probably not aware it's involved in a race it can take its time entering the hatch once the loft is within sight. The pigeon then has to be coaxed in by using various methods. Tampo and Dagger stuck their heads out of their hatches and looked at each other. Neither man could be sure whose bird it was and whereas any pigeon flyer claiming to be a sportsman would have coaxed the bird off the rock they felt disinclined to do each other a possibly good turn.

They looked down at the pigeon on the rock and Dagger shouted, 'c'mon, damn you! You're mine, I'm sure of it!' He was desperate to get his hands on the tall, most sought after, overall winner's cup, hear the rustle of the prize money - but sweetest of all to face Tampo down.

'C'mon, old son,' said Tampo quietly. 'You've made good time. Don't cheat yourself - go to your loft.' His attitude was more magnanimous, he simply admired the bird that had obviously flown its heart out. He reached for a tin half full of grain and rattled it. It was an old trick. At the end of a long race pigeons are usually hungry and the sound means there's food waiting for them. He rattled loud and long but the pigeon just shook its wing feathers and began to preen itself as precious seconds ticked by.

Dagger cried out as if in agony as he spotted another pigeon coming across the valley. Tampo stopped rattling and looked as the second bird, too, came straight on, also winging low. It was another blue pied. Tampo waited, frowning hard with tension, Dagger with clenched fists, grinding teeth and narrowed eyes. The unthinkable happened. The second pigeon saw the first pigeon on the rock, dropped down and settled alongside it. Dagger scowled at Tampo as thought it was his fault, and Tampo started rattling the tin again. They were both consumed with frustration and wondering the same things: whose birds were they?

Dagger cried out again and dashed out of his loft, shaking a fist. He picked up a stone and threw it to splash into the river behind the rock. Neither of the pigeons moved, nor did they move when he threw another one, nearer the rock, they must have felt more tired than frightened or hungry. Dagger picked up a bigger stone to make a bigger splash and lobbed that. Instead of splashing into the river, however, it fell short and came down on the first pigeon to have landed on the rock. It must have killed it instantly for it lay crumpled, unmoving. The other pigeon took to the air, circled, then flew in through the hatch of Tampo's loft. Tampo, of course, hurried to take off its rubber identification ring and clocked it in.

When Tampo came out of his loft Dagger was staring down at the pigeon dead on the rock, slowly blinking his eyes. Tampo took his shoes and trousers off, descended the bank and waded into the river to retrieve the unfortunate bird. After looking at its identity ring he climbed the bank, walked towards Dagger and held it out to him. Dagger, his eyes now vacant, took the lifeless pigeon, cupped it in his hands and muttered, 'it's Jackie Blue Wonder.' Then he shuffled into his loft.

Tampo, having dried himself in his loft, had put his trousers and shoes back on when he heard a flapping of many wings. He looked out of his hatch. All Dagger's pigeons where out of his loft and flying in a great circle.

Tampo, puzzled, locked up his loft and with timing in clock in hand was about to make the pigeon club when he saw smoke coming out of Dagger's loft. He hurried over as a crackling sound grew louder and bright yellow flames began licking through the still open hatch. Fearfully he opened the unclosed door wide and peered in. He only had a few seconds before the heat drove him away but he saw that the loft was empty. He looked about. Dagger was to be seen scuttling towards the village.

In the pigeon club that evening Tampo learned that Dagger had quickly packed a couple of bags and left the village. It seemed he could not go on living where people would know what had happened. He had killed his best pigeon which had been the first to return in the most prestigious race of the season, and in doing so sacrificed all he had worked for, helping the man he intensely disliked to win instead.

His other pigeons? Some went back to the wild but most were eventually coaxed into other lofts. They can be very adaptable creatures apparently.

Lucky Day

by

Graham Rouch

He read his horoscope again. The last couple of lines. 'Could be your lucky day. Great oaks from little acorns grow'. Christ, he could do with some luck. Not that he believed in horoscopes, load of rubbish. Didn't know why he read the damn things.

He'd been unemployed for what? seven, no eight months. Through no fault of his own; he'd been a bloody good salesman. His income had proved that. Never out of the top three in the list that his company had published every month. Five times, in the final twelve months of his working life, he'd headed the list. Not bad, considering there was always a minimum of seventeen salesmen on the pay-roll. Then the American parent company had decided to close down their UK operation, and he was out of a job.

It never occurred to him there would be any problem in getting another, and he set his sights high. Only top companies which offered a good basic wage; he knew he'd always be able to make his share of any commission. He never doubted his ability to sell, given the chance. The response from the top companies had been disappointing, considering his glowing references. It appeared, that in the current recession, they were, one and all, contracting their operations. When things improved, they would contact him, or invited him to contact them again. Until then, they wished him every success etc etc. He'd set his sights lower, then even lower. His last half dozen job applications had been for posts that, financially, would barely cover his obligations. All the replies had been the same. 'Sorry, but perhaps later on...' And now he was panicking.

Great oaks from little acorns. He emptied his pockets. Three one pound coins, and some small change. Perhaps he'd go to the club tonight. There was enough for two and a half pints. Have to make sure he didn't get into a school, or even get inveigled into buying bingo tickets. He had no desire to see people looking at him counting out coppers. He'd think about it. There was another unemployment giro due tomorrow. He whistled for the dog and called out to his wife upstairs.

'Taking the dog for a walk. Be about an hour.'

It was a blustery day and the park was deserted. He thought again of his horoscope 'Could be your lucky day, great oaks from...' The oaks would have to be great indeed. He owed five months on the mortgage. Call it two thousand. He owed about three thousand on hire purchase and various credit cards. When he was earning, he and his wife had lived high on the hog. Why not? He knew he could always earn good money. He laughed mirthlessly. There were bits and pieces of other things owing. Call it six hundred. Total, five thousand, six hundred. If he had just six thousand, he could pay it all off, have a few hundred in the bank and start anew. He was sure he'd never get into financial straits like this again. Six thousand. Twelve months ago he'd been making almost that in one of his good months.

He walked on, unseeing, and then some sixth sense, or something, he glanced down. A ten pound note. Nobody, but nobody in sight. Pull out a handkerchief, drop it, bend down nonchalantly, pick it up, together with the tenner. Put both into pocket. With hand still in pocket he fingered the note. Note? There was more than one. He walked briskly until he reached a bench and sat down. he surreptitiously extracted the money, and counted. Five brand new ten pound notes. Fifty pounds. An hour ago it would have been a godsend. Now he thought of the six thousand he really needed. The words returned, 'Great oaks from little acorns...'

He took the dog back home; the house was empty, his wife was out. Picking up his morning paper he went out again, and walked the mile or so to the shopping precinct. The words kept running through his mind. 'Great oaks'. An hour ago he hadn't had the fifty pounds. If, in an hours time, he'd parted with it, was he any worse off. He went into the betting office, took a seat in the corner and opened his paper at the racing page. There were four meetings and racing was about to commence.

The first race had nine runners. The favourite was forecast odds on. He didn't particularly fancy it. The only thing in its favour was the trainer, a man at the top of his profession. On the other hand, its form on the prevailing soft was definitely suspect. He opted for the horse that according to the TV screen was on offer at five to one. This horse had been running consistently well for some time, without actually winning; but he'd always performed best on soft going. He wrote out his bet. Forty pounds win - no tax. As a saver, with the remaining ten pounds he wrote out a bet, the favourite first to beat his selection, ten pound forecast. As he had suspected, the favourite tired on the sticky ground and his selection won by a very easy five lengths. Returned odds of eleven to two. Amount due two hundred and twenty pounds, plus stake, less ten percent tax. Total two hundred and thirty four pounds.

He held the money in his hand. Little acorns he thought. A race at another meeting was almost due off. There were nineteen runners and the favourite was even money. The old racing adage came to mind. The bigger the field, the better the favourite. He pocketed four pounds and wrote his bet of two hundred and thirty pounds. In the two minutes before the off the horse drifted out to odds of six to four. It made no difference, it won pulling up. Returning five hundred and seventy five pounds, less tax. Net return five hundred and seventeen pounds, fifty pence. An hour later, he was sitting in the shop with over four thousand pounds in his pocket.

George came into the shop. He knew George fairly well; only because they both bet there quite often. George was a shrewd character, well dressed, certainly won more than he lost, and was rumoured to know people who knew people in the racing world. He came across and produced a betting slip, already made out for one hundred pounds win on a horse in the next race. 'I've been told this one's trying,' he said. 'Take the opening price because it's going to be well backed.'

'Thanks George.'

The horse in question had been forecast in his paper at eight to one, and nobody had tipped it. It opened up at six to four. God, the information must be hot.

He counted his money and wrote out his bet. Three thousand, seven hundred pounds win. This time pay tax of three hundred and seventy pounds. Total four thousand and seventy pounds. He placed the bet and requested the current odds of six to four. In the next betting show the horse was even money. At the off it was seven to four on. Put on seven to win four. He wasn't concerned; he'd taken odds of six to four against. The horse seemed to struggle in the middle part of the race, but then got its act together and was always going to win in the final furlong. Returns nine thousand, two hundred and fifty pounds.

Suddenly he felt physically drained, and stood up, ready to go home. A voice impinged on his consciousness. 'The favourite at... is Lucky Fellow at six to four. Lucky Fellow.' He looked at his newspaper, then counted his money. Nine thousand, two hundred and sixty pounds. He wrote out his bet. Lucky Fellow, eight thousand, four hundred pounds win, tax eight hundred and forty, total nine thousand, two hundred and forty pounds. He put twenty pounds into his back pocket and handed the rest to the cashier, taking a price of six to four. He worked it out. There would be returns of twenty one thousand exactly. It was a two mile hurdle race. Lucky Fellow fell at the first hurdle.

When he got home, his wife had returned. 'What's it cost to have your hair set?' he asked.

'About a fiver, why?'

He handed her the twenty pounds. 'Get it done and hang on to the change. We'll use it to go to the club this evening. Have a couple of drinks and a game of bingo. It could be our lucky night.'

Stranger than Fiction

by

Hannah Morris

It was while she was spending a weekend alone, away from home, that it had happened she remembered. It had been a painful year for her, full of unfamiliar emotions, questioning herself as to why this or that, what if, when had and so on until she had felt a stranger to herself and those overwhelming feelings that possessed her unceasingly. They were all the more bewildering because all her life until then she had been a 'practical' woman, organised and full of 'common-sense'. (Why was it called that? she wondered. It wasn't very common at all). Or had she really been forced into that role by circumstances, by other people's lack of order, their irresponsibility? Too easy to blame others she had admitted to herself. Finally, after months of indecision, despair, fruitless exchanges of words with her husband (one could not call them discussions), she at last decided that she had to get away for a while; somewhere new, somewhere where she could look at her life from a distance, with some perspective and realism.

So, she booked a small cottage in a busy but cultural town, where she could be both anonymous and yet able to partake of the feast of theatrical experiences possible if she felt so inclined. She *had* visited the large, professional theatre one evening she remembered and had enjoyed the visit, delighting in the excellence of the performances and forgetting for a brief time her own problems.

Remembering that time now, she recalled how hot that summer had been. For weeks on end, the sun had blazed down relentlessly and everyone had basked in the unusual experiences of long, sun-kissed days. As she had walked slowly along the dusty pavements of the unfamiliar town, thronged with tourists, she had not felt lonely although she knew no one; alone, yes, but not lonely; just apart, detached, observing. Apart from observing others, the way they spoke to one another, their expressions, she was even more aware of observing herself... a middle-aged woman who did not feel middle-aged inside her head but who had come to some sort of crossroads in her life and who was trying to unravel the tangled thoughts that perpetually wove themselves painfully through her mind.

Perhaps it had been because of the heat, but she had slept restlessly alone in the strange bed. One night, in particular, it had been impossible to sleep and she had tossed and turned, getting up to drink and then returned to thoughts of her children, her husband, her marriage, problems, endless problems. She was getting nowhere.

And then, finally, she fell into a deep slumber, as one often does at the end of a restless night, and it was in that deep slumber that she had had *the* dream. What was so surprising was that she was able to recall it so vividly afterwards, because, unlike many people she knew, she had never before been able to retell a dream she had experienced. But this one was different...

In her dream, it seemed as if she was walking alone along a place where walking was not easy: it felt as if she trudged on loose sand, on uneven ground, sand-dunes possibly, and her walking was extremely arduous. It was made more so because she was carrying something very heavy; something very heavy indeed; something big and very cumbersome which was difficult to hold onto but which she felt she could not put down. It was a living creature she had carried in her dream but, at the time, she could not easily identify it. All she knew for certain was that it was alive, very heavy, very still and that the creature had large, trusting eyes and definite, large whiskers! She was sure of that. Thinking about it now, it seemed such an insignificant dream and not one to recall so vividly. But she had, later. She had considered her animal to be a cat and her dream had not gone further... she had not known what had happened after her struggle to carry her burden...

The next day, dream momentarily forgotten, she had walked into the town and decided to buy herself some reading matter. Browsing through the paperbacks in a quiet bookshop, she came across titles by a well-known authoress which she had always meant to read but had never had the time. Now was her chance! She selected one, purely at random, knowing nothing about it whatsoever and flicked over the pages. It seemed very well-written and also appropriate, as it was about a middle-aged woman much as herself. As she turned the pages dipping into the book, she came to a part which made the hair on the back of her neck rise and her heart thud; it was uncanny! The fictional woman had had a dream: she was carrying a heavy creature which she could not put down; it had large eyes and large whiskers; it was *her* dream! She could not believe what she was reading. The dream in the book was the same as hers in all respects except that in the book the creature had been a seal, not a cat. Of course! she realised... a seal has large eyes and whiskers... what did it mean? She felt a cold chill as she read on and found that the significance of the burden was the woman's family and in the dream, the woman had finally put her burden down to care for itself.

As she thought about it now, years later and living alone, busy, but more sure of herself, she still marvelled at the fact that she had dreamed her dream a day before reading it in a work of fiction. How could such an unusual coincidence happen? Had it been just a coincidence or something even stranger? Had her 'burden' signified her family as in the book? Had it influenced her? Who could tell? She had loved her family and had not thought of them as a 'burden'. Her life had certainly changed drastically in the years that followed that time. That time of endless thinking had been unfamiliar to her, a luxury, for all her life she had, like all women with a family she supposed, been too busy with their needs and wants to question where she was going. No wonder that at a certain age such women may feel as she did, although not all were as fortunate as she had been, to have had the time to reflect, that thought made her feel guilty, had she been selfish? Maybe, but then perhaps she needed to be; she'd felt guilt often enough.

On occasions when she had cautiously related the dream incident to a trusted friend or two, she could tell that, although expressing wonder and surprise, they secretly suspected that she had read the book *before* the dream. But *she* knew the truth; she knew she hadn't. Truth could certainly be stranger than fiction.

Bouquet of Heather

by

Shirley Silman

Danny Kent, breathed in the fresh air of the mountain top, hugging the peace and solitude to him as though a garment.

Below in the valley lay the village of Cwm-Eira; situated between the reservoir at one end and at the other, by the great wheels of the pit cage dominating the skyline. Behind rows of small whitewashed houses were miniature mountains of slag; which deprived the inhabitants of the sun's warmth by casting long fingers of shadow upon the streets below.

Amidst the grazing sheep, that bleated and stared before running away, Danny made his way down the mountain to the village.

Walking up the main street, he saw a scattering of shops with a pub, or two, alongside a small mission hut and a chapel that dwarfed its surroundings. Children playing hopscotch in the road afforded him a brief glance, while the women chatting on their doorsteps, gave the stranger a smiling welcome.

At the end of the street, Danny pushed open the doors of the 'Morning Star'. Wall lamps gave a warm glow to the dark wood panelling and high backed settles against the walls. Wrought iron tables and polished chairs occupied the centre of the room. Everywhere was gleaming brass, giving a homely feel of comfort. Danny moved towards the bar where the landlord waited with hands resting on the counter. 'Good evening, sir,' he said. 'You're a stranger around these parts.'

'Just passing through,' Danny answered.

'Been walking along the mountain top, I'll be bound.' The landlord beamed a smile. 'We get quite a few hikers this way. Well now! How can I help you?'

'A pint of beer and a plate of sandwiches, please.'

While attending to his order, the man chatted amiably. 'My name is Isaac. I'm landlord here, as my father was before me. Nice people in this village, most of the men work in the pit of course! Are you planning on staying long?'

'Just tonight if I can find a place to sleep. Do you know of anywhere, Isaac?'

'Lizzie Price takes in lodgers now her husband has passed on. Her two sons, Morgan and Richard, work down the pit. Morgan and our Bethan are getting married in a number of weeks. Lovely is our Bethan! She teaches the infants in our local school.'

'Do you think Mrs Price will put me up?'

'No doubt about it! What's your name, lad? I'll send a message right now!'

'Danny Kent.'

He went to the door leading upstairs. 'Joe! Joe! Can you hear me?'

A voice answered.

'Run down to Lizzie Price, and tell her she's got a lodger tonight. His name is Danny, and he'll be down later. Off you go now, and no dawdling mind!'

The bang of the door announced the message was on its way.

Isaac served some customers between chatting to Danny. 'It's choir practice at the chapel tonight, so things will be quiet for a bit. Later on, they'll all come here and even a speck of dust won't find a place to settle. Morgan is in the choir, so you'll be able to meet him before you go to Lizzie's. He and our Bethan make a lovely couple, everyone says so! They've been sweethearts since childhood. Made for each other, those two!'

Pride rode on every word as Isaac spoke of his daughter and future son-in-law. Danny hitched himself further onto the stool by the bar and prepared to enjoy his evening.

The door suddenly opened and a crowd of men swarmed in. Choir practice was over. The pub was now both busy and noisy. With pints on the table, a hum of voices spiralled into singing as regulars and choir members lifted the rafters in song. Danny revelled in this atmosphere; this new experience of man's joy.

'Morgan! Morgan!' called Isaac. 'Come and meet Danny. He's lodging with you tonight. Doing a walking tour, he is, before going into the air force.'

A smiling giant gripped Danny's hand in greeting. A shock of black curls tumbled over his forehead and the brightness of eye showed a zest for living.

'Hallo there! Been along the mountain top, have you?'

'Yes. Lovely views!' Danny answered.

'Aye! You had the weather for it, too! Lucky there! So... you're going in the air force, then?'

'Yes. A trainee pilot.'

'Good for you! Mam expecting you, is she?'

'Isaac sent a message.'

'That's good! Come and meet some of the chaps, then.' His voice lifted. 'Tom! Idris! Come and meet Danny. He's going to be a pilot with the air force!'

For the rest of the evening Danny felt one of them. He had walked in a stranger, and now he couldn't remember when he had ever felt happier.

At closing time, Danny walked home with Morgan and received a warm welcome from Mrs Price.

'Your bed is nicely aired, Danny. I put plenty of hot water bottles in it as soon as I got Isaac's message. Come and have some supper now, it's all ready! Richard is working the night shift. Now Morgan! Stop talking or else it'll go cold.' And she busied herself cutting bread, while ensuring her men folk did justice to her cooking.

Danny stayed on with Morgan and his family. He met Richard and Bethan, and made a number of friends. When he could stay no longer, he bade a tearful farewell.

'If you can make it to our wedding, Danny, we'd love you to be there,' invited Morgan. Bethan smiled and nodded.

'I'll make it,' vowed Danny. 'Somehow.'

It was dry and sunny the day of the wedding, and a purple blanket of heather clothed the mountainside. It looked as though the whole of Cwm-Eira had turned out as the chapel filled. The minister was proud to unite in marriage these two people that he had baptised and watched grow into adults. Mrs Williams, the emporium, waited at the organ for the arrival of the bride. It was her pleasure to provide the music.

The strains of the wedding march peeled out, and Morgan saw his lovely Bethan, a vision of white, walking towards him on her father's arm. He loved her so. He knew he was a lucky man and therefore, he could feel pity for the one whose love had lost. His Bethan. His adored Bethan, would soon belong to him forever.

As the minister began, 'Dearly Beloved', Bethan heard faint sobs. Tears at a wedding; happy tears.

Flying low over the mountain appeared a plane. Suddenly, the engine spluttered forcing it to earth. From the reservoir flames followed an explosion.

Inside the chapel the choir was singing with gusto.

Danny, distraught, dishevelled and dragging an injured leg, came down the street clutching a bunch of heather he'd plucked from the mountainside. His bouquet for the bride.

He turned as he heard it... stared in horror then tried to run faster. Behind him the reservoir broke its banks and water poured in torrents down the valley.

Weak from loss of blood, Danny banged on the oak doors of the chapel but no one was listening; his cries of danger went unheard. As the voices swelled in praise, Danny collapsed unconscious.

The swirling waters took the heather from his fingers and he was swept to oblivion.

On a hillside above a lake stands a monument. A man reading the epitaph, stood with tears falling down his weatherbeaten face. 'Oh! My Bethan.' He moaned, and sobs racked his body.

'Morgan, can you forgive me? I'm sorry, Morgan, so very, very sorry. I never meant to bring the black omen to your wedding. I loved you both, you know that. Can you hear me, Morgan? I couldn't go through watching the woman I loved marry another man. I knew I'd hate you for it. You, my own brother! I left a note. Did you read it, Morgan? I couldn't stay and face your happiness. I went away and signed on the first ship I could. I signed on for each trip and it was years before I learnt of the tragedy. Learnt that I had lost all my loved ones. The guilt lays heavy on my heart, my mind in torment. And poor Danny, that Fate should have been so cruel to use him to condemn my sins.'

Richard plucked from the mountainside a bunch of heather and laid it on the monument. 'My precious Bethan,' he whispered. He turned to look at what was once Cwm-Eira, his home. In the waters he saw again the people of the village. He saw them smiling at him and there was Morgan, Bethan and Isaac.

'Forgive me,' whispered Richard. And there he was, walking along the village street and his mother coming to meet him, a smile of love on her lips. And as the reservoir of his heart broke its banks, Richard found peace in the arms of his loved ones; while the evening light mirrored a sea of purple heather.

Cai

by

John Williams

Coming to North Wales from the Midlands is a move we have not regretted making. Mind you, I'm inclined to agree with my wife. She maintains that many incomers try too hard to integrate. Their efforts in rural areas tend to be misconstrued as patronage. I think it's best to allow the community to absorb one gradually, like a mollusc.

Simon our eldest was just at the right age to start at the local primary school, and in no time he was prattling Welsh like a native. What's more; we like Mrs Roberts the headmistress, and her balanced approach to bilingual education. I had the occasional informal chat with her when I took turns with Joan to fetch Simon at the end of the day.

Mrs Roberts laid great stress on this duty, and she was able to impress upon the children the need not to talk to strangers, nor accept lifts in cars, without frightening them unduly. We in our turn were naive enough to think that we had left the evil of child snatching far behind when we came to this backwater.

There is no doubt that a father's social horizons are widened when he becomes involved in a school's parental swim. I was drawn into the inevitable exchanges with those - mainly women at that hour - who waited at the school gates at three o'clock, and I learned from such interludes, that the prevailing problems of the day were shared very much in common.

In time however, I noticed that there was one lady who kept well apart from the rest. She sat on a bench under the rowan at the far end of the playground.

The others took scant notice of her. I guessed that she would be in her thirties, although it was hard to tell. She seemed to be the kind who could have made much more out of her appearance if she made the effort, but she seemed to have an air of indifference about her. Yet, she was intriguing.

So intriguing in fact, that some days later, I found myself, by accident and design, sharing the bench with her. This went on for a day or two without any word being exchanged. Eventually, one afternoon I ventured the usual opening:

'Who have you here?'

'Cai,' she said without preamble, and that single name seemed to open the floodgates of her mind. She began to regale me with a detailed description of her son - how well behaved he was, how good looking - and clever, and all the virtues under the sun.

After that, whenever I went near her, she would acquaint me with her case history in the most intimate manner. For the most part the details washed over me, but I do remember she was a single parent.

I got so much of it however, that I began to avoid her too, but I became very curious about that paragon child of hers, if only to compare him with my own product. But he seemed to be a dilatory little chap. He didn't seem to materialise with the rest. And then of course I was in a hurry to get away out of the pell-mell.

I asked Simon in the end whether there was anyone called Cai in his class, but evidently he had never heard the name, and the whole business mystified me - that is - until I spoke to Mrs Roberts soon after. Of her own volition she said:

'I see you've beaten us all. You've made contact with Mrs Owen.'

'Oh - the lonely lady,' I said. 'The usual talk you know; comparing offspring and all that. As a matter of fact, I've been trying to make out which is her's. Er... Cai isn't it?'

The headmistress realised by then that I was completely in the dark.

'He used to come to school you know,' she said in the end. 'But he was snatched one Saturday afternoon when his mother was shopping in Chester. He's not been seen since.'

She knew of course what I was going to ask next, but she saved me the effort.

'She keeps coming here every day like this,' she said. 'And she stays until everyone has gone. No one can persuade her otherwise. We can't ban her of course.'

And come she did in all weathers. But blame me or not, I wasn't keen on having her company either, after that.

Windfall

by

Betty Lucking

The fifty thousand pounds was packed neatly into a cardboard box. Laura's tiny kitten crept to the back of the cupboard under the stairs, and there it was. Laura stared in disbelief. She'd never imagined so much money. But it wasn't hers. Or was it? Only Jack could have left it there. Had he meant her to have it? He'd never said anything, but then, their marriage had been brief, with no time to arrange anything much. After thirty years of loving him they'd had three years and three days of pure joy before Jack died. Laura had wallowed in every precious second. Both in their sixties, their marriage had caused little sensation although Jack's daughter Maxine didn't approve, she'd made that plain. When they insisted they loved one another she'd raised her eyes to heaven, making some spiteful remark about going daft in their old age. That was all she'd ever said but the resentment was always there in her eyes. Laura, dear friend to her parents, and 'Auntie' to Maxine became an interloper. Laura made excuses for her, knowing she was upset over her mother's death.

Laura pushed the box back into the cupboard and stood up, her back aching through kneeling too long in one spot. Her first instinct was to tell Maxine but that would only bring more accusations and bitterness. Perhaps they could share the money. No, that was a silly idea. Laura knew Maxine would claim the lot and she didn't want her to have anything after the way she'd behaved when Jack died. She'd left Laura nothing to remember him by - not things anyway.

Laura sank wearily into the armchair, remembering that dreary rainy Saturday afternoon when Maxine and her loud-mouthed husband had forced their way into her home. Laura realised now she shouldn't have let them in, but there was little she could have done to stop them. They'd taken away all Jack's belongings - his clothes, cassettes, all his personal things. They'd even snatched the photograph of him from Laura's bedside table.

'Please leave me that,' she'd pleaded.

'It belonged to my mother just as Jack belonged to her.' Maxines small dark eyes were wild with spite as she ransacked the bureau for private papers. She still believed Laura was hiding something despite having benefited from her father's will.

They'd called Laura a gold-digger and accused her of frittering away Jack's money. They'd blamed her for his death. Why hadn't she left the old man in peace? Questions flew at her one after another. So many questions and insults in raised voices. Maxine had lumbered across the room, pushing Laura roughly into the armchair.

'I see it all now. My father was a womanizer and you his whore.' Her huge frame leaned over Laura as she spat out those never to be forgotten words. 'Carrying on behind Dolly's back,' she'd screamed, 'while all the time pretending to be her friend. That's the ugliest part - pretending to be her friend.'

'It wasn't like that Maxine. We did nothing wrong. Your father was faithful to Dolly, faithful to the end.'

'Wicked lying old woman.'

'It's true. Jack and I were never together in that way. We respected Dolly.'

'That's a joke.'

'Please Maxine, don't think of your father as a...'

'Shut up.'

Laura had desperately wanted to explain, but neither Maxine nor her awful husband would listen. They wouldn't believe it had been an affair of the mind and the soul, and all those years she and Jack had stayed silent for Dolly's sake. Dolly was Laura's closest friend and like Jack she would do nothing to hurt her.

They'd piled everything into their car, throwing things one on top of another. Jack's little radio lay smashed beneath a pile of heavy books. Laura's heart turned over as the diary he had written so beautifully fell into the gutter into a pool of dirty water. They didn't care. They valued nothing. They'd torn Laura's life apart that afternoon. Laura had watched them drive away, their two confused little white-faced children plonked on top of Jack's things in the back of the car. Sadly she'd turned away from the window to clean up the mess they'd made in their frenzy to clear Jack out of her life. So that was that, she had thought. The terrible business was over and she would hear no more.

Now there was the money. Laura rose from the chair, drawing her cardigan across her thin shoulders. She closed the curtains and switched on the light. She'd pack the money in her zip bag tonight and deposit the lot in a bank account tomorrow. She needed time to think.

She found the note at the bottom of the box. A simple note from Jack, addressed to her. 'Thank you Laura for giving me your life.' That's all it said, but it was enough. It gave her the right to the money. Laura smiled. She could take a holiday, buy clothes, refurbish the house. Her imagination ran riot for a few minutes, she felt a sense of excitement, until those wicked words came flooding back yet again.

'My father was a womanizer and you his whore.'

Tears sprang into Laura's eyes as she made her decision. She would leave the money in trust for Maxine's children, together with her story. Whatever poison their parents laid they would come to know that she was no gold-digger and their grandfather was an honourable man.

'That's the best I can do for you now Jack,' whispered Laura.

There were raised eyebrows at the bank, but they were only too pleased to open Laura's account with no questions asked. Feeling rather important she was escorted to the manager's office where the money was carefully counted.

'Can't bank this,' smiled the manager, handing Laura a folded piece of paper which fluttered to the floor from between the bundles of notes. Laura pushed it quickly into her pocket, curious but in no hurry to discover the contents.

It was late afternoon when she remembered the yellowing newspaper cutting from 1955. There was no mistaking the photograph of a smiling young Dolly holding a tiny baby, and the tall upright figure of Jack wearing his Hong Kong police uniform. They'd never talked about their short time abroad and Laura felt she was intruding on a part of Jack's life that wasn't her concern. But, her curiosity aroused, she began to read details of the story.

The childless couple had adopted the baby of a convicted murderess who having killed her boyfriend in cold blood, died while giving birth in prison. Jack, instrumental in the woman's arrest had felt pity for the tiny orphan. Their immediate return to Britain protected the child from any stigma in later years. She would know nothing of her real parents, the murder, or the adoption.

Laura's excitement rose. Jack and Dolly had meant to take their secret to the grave, but now she knew. She had the power to spoil Maxine's life, pay her back for the shabby way she herself had been treated. Revenge would be sweet. As for the money, she could without guilt keep it for herself. After all, the children were nothing to do with Jack and she didn't care now what they thought of her.

She made plans to send the cutting through the post, but quickly changed her mind. Far more satisfying to hand it to Maxine herself and enjoy the reaction, see the wounding. Laura picked up the telephone. Maxine would soon come running if Laura told her something important had turned up. No reply. Laura would have to be patient. She cleared her tea tray and turned on the television, watching without seeing, pre-occupied with what she intended to do, anticipating the can of worms she was about to open.

Later that evening Maxine's husband answered the telephone, his gruff voice raised above those of his noisy children.

'Hello, yes?'

Laura stood silent as her eyes fell again on the scrap of paper. The photograph leapt out, Jack and Dolly, her dearest friends, kind trustworthy people. She began to tremble, feeling the full impact of what she was about to do. Her head swam. The triumph of revenge would never outweigh the pain of betrayal. How could she do that to Jack and Dolly? How could she live with it?

'Who is that?' he sounded impatient.

Slowly Laura replaced the receiver. Still trembling, she picked up the cutting, snipped out the photograph and placed it on the mantelpiece. Carefully she dropped the text on the back of the fire, watching as it curled, blackened and finally turned to ashes.

Bonding

by

Ceri Vale

Mathew Thomas was a foul mouthed, overweight, bigoted slob. Such was the judgement of Carla Samuels. As she sat in the office, she watched his great bulk move slowly around the showroom. His shirt, the buttons straining against his waist, seemed to ripple as it undulated on the fat it encased. She grimaced and blushed as her judgement of the man flew through her mind once again, her hand instinctively moving downwards to finger the string of beads in her pocket. As her probing fingers moved, they came to the small crucifix. She relaxed.

Suddenly the door opened and she found herself staring into the wobbling face of her boss.

'Carla?' His voice was surprisingly high for one of such bulk.

'Yes Mr Thomas?' Her voice was steady.

'Can you do an extra few hours tonight?'

The question was inevitable, an integral part of Mathew Thomas' grand plan.

Horrified at the idea of spending an evening with the man, she muttered a feeble excuse about meeting someone then stared at the Amstrad's screen, her face expressionless. She could sense him entering the room and circulating the desk until he stood beside her. Bending forward, he seemed to reach for one of the drawers. She could smell garlic on his breath.

She fought the urge to shrink away until his reaching hand stroked her leg. Her stomach lurched as she swung them away, only to find that his great bulk was pressed into her back. Then his mouth was at her ear, whispering, suggesting, threatening. She engulfed the wooden beads in her sweating hand, unspoken pleas and prayers filling her mind. But the voice insisted, would not be blocked. Then he was gone.

Her reflection in the computer's screen seemed bleak, empty, though at no time in her life had she ever felt alone. Faith held no questions for her, no complications, no conditions; it was simply there. Night and day it had comforted and caressed her with an unblemished touch, filling her life with a joy that she saw in few others. She seldom considered herself to be a fanatic. She felt proud that despite her school title of 'Bible Basher', she'd always striven to avoid invading the privacy of others with her beliefs. Now she found her faith stretched to the limit.

She knew she was pretty. Not beautiful, but she was, she thought, quite presentable. Dark hair and darker eyes, a well proportioned face and neck that continued downwards to an equally well proportioned, virginal body. Yes, she'd often thought, she was desirable. Yet it was her Faith that had really shone, providing her with unshakeable self confidence and poise. Now the obscene mating rituals of her boss were waging war against her entire spirit. She sighed, pulling the beads from her pocket. Staring at the image of Christ in his torment, she prayed for strength.

St David's church was empty but warm, despite the winter wind that howled beyond its portals. Carla knelt before the altar, her mumbled prayers seeming loud to her ears. The Book had replaced the beads as her torments and fears poured forth, her tears wrinkling the thin, hallowed pages. Darkness fell slowly beyond the stained glass but Carla cared little. She felt protected from the shades and hidden forms of the night.

Mathew Thomas was in an unsavoury mood. A meticulous man, he hated anything that proved to be less than straightforward. Right now he hated Carla Samuels. He'd been certain that the threat of the sack would have had the desired effect on the Ice Queen. He found it hard to believe that one so timid could resist the threat, especially after searching long and hard for work.

'Ungrateful bitch,' he muttered as he walked from the showroom towards his office. As he decided to sack his secretary the following day, he noticed the light that emanated from the small, glass encased room. Stepping inside, he saw that it was the secretary's Word Processor. Turning on the light, he stared at it, puzzled. On the screen glowed one word.

Repent

Frowning, he sat facing the screen and his eyes caught sight of something on the monitor. Closer examination found it to be a rosary. Swearing, he reached forward for the power button, but his hand remained in mid air as he realised that in its present position, the system should not have been in operation. His heart seemed to skip a beat as his finger pressed the button again and again, with no result. Believing the fault to be with the switch, he reached under the desk for the socket. Impatiently he pawed blindly for the plug before glancing under the desk.

'Christ,' he muttered as his mind registered the sight before him. He could clearly see the socket, and to its left lay the plug. His heart pumping, he snapped himself upright, his heavy breasts jiggling violently. The word continued to glow, with a single addition.

Repent!!!

Suddenly, filled with anger for the religious bitch who had somehow left this insubordinate message for him, he hammered the keyboard, typing

Fuck You!!!

beneath the first message. A smile of pleasure spread over his face as he stared at his words, a short and sweet message for her when she came in the next day. Then the smile fell as words appeared slowly under his own, typed by an unseen hand.

Come then, and be judged , Mathew Thomas

As the last letters of his name appeared on the screen the rosary, still lying on the monitor, began to tremble, then rise. He stared, mouth open, as it hovered above the computer, the crucifix swaying slightly. Then it parted. Bead after bead slipped its leash until they all hovered freely and the string that had once held them fell to the desk. The fat man managed a single exclamation of 'Jesus,' before they came for him, holy projectiles guided by a celestial hand.

His body stiffened as they penetrated chest and stomach, their paths unhindered by neither fat nor bone. Thomas could feel them within his carcass, moving and probing at will. Then, as if in answer to a silent command, atom left atom in a silent explosion as, for a split second, they found themselves freed from the bonds of attraction that give form to the Universe. Twinkling particles of dust filled the air and where Mathew Thomas had sat, there now lay several beads and a small crucifix. Silently the computer switched itself off.

Carla Samuels sat at her desk, phone in hand. Her eyebrows lifted further and further as she learnt the details of her previous boss' resignation due to ill health, and her temporary promotion to the vacant position. In her hand she held her newly repaired rosary.

Galt Yr Ancr

by

Gerald Shew

It was Richard's bright idea, well the bit about the impersonation of the hermit was, though of course, that could not have happened had I not told him the hermit story in the first place, and, if you are completely on Richard's side, it could be claimed that the whole incident only happened because I invited him to come and stay for the weekend in the first place.

We have this tradition you see, whereby once a year, my friend Richard, together with a colleague of his, Ted, and I, would go off walking together. Nothing very strenuous, just a day out on some fell or mountain and back in the evening was the usual pattern. So when my wife and I moved house and went to live in a rather remote valley in Mid-Wales, it made sense to invite them both to come and stay for the weekend, it would be an opportunity to show off our new home and at the same time do some walking over the bare expanses of the local Berwyn range.

'By the way, Ted's keen to come but cannot get away 'til Saturday afternoon, will that be alright?' asked Richard on the phone.

'Sure,' I answered, 'I've got two walks planned, you and I will do the easy one on Saturday and I'll leave the nasty one for Sunday when Ted is with us, how's that?'

The walk I had selected for our Saturday jaunt started from a point about five miles from my house and as we drove off Richard remarked upon our local hill, which, though not particularly high seemed somehow to dominate the village. 'Galt-Yr-Ancr is its name' I told him, 'Hill of the Anchorite -' so called because way back in the seventh century, one of our local saints is reputed to have lived out a life of solitude and self-denial up there on the top, if you like we can go up one evening, it affords a splendid view of the valley, in fact, we could take Ted up with us tonight; just to break him in like!'

I don't remember where the idea of having a midnight feast up on Galt Yr Ancr came from, it was a warm day as we trudged in and out of valleys and along forestry tracks, the prospect of a cool evening walk became particularly appealing, especially one that could be complimented by a chilled bottle of wine and something tasty to eat.

'We might even meet the ghost of the hermit,' I remarked at one stage as we squelched over a bleak bit of boggy upland. This seemed to set Richard off on one of his more outlandish ideas, he wanted to 'stage' a sight of the hermit for Ted's benefit. At first he thought we could smuggle a sheet with the food and drink, to be draped over some suitable bush, but all that seemed a bit tame, Richard wanted more of an impact!

'What we really need is someone to walk across the skyline, someone dressed to look like a hermit,' said Richard, warming to his theme, after all he was in advertising wasn't he?

'Who do you know in the Village who might do it for us?'

'Well,' I answered, 'there's Ivor Griffiths, he's in the local operatic society, and he does happen to have a splendid full beard, you may be able to persuade him.'

We called at Ivor's house on our way to collect Ted from the station later that day, and Richard with his well practiced charm soon had Ivor prepared to climb up the hill sometime around midnight, to patrol backwards and forwards on the highest point of the ridge until he was sure that we had seen him, and then swiftly fade out of sight down the far side of the hill.

Ted's train was on time and on the way back we prepared him for the night hike and outdoor supper. He wasn't enthusiastic at first, expecting preparations for the next day's walk to involve sitting before a map in some bar, with pints of ale to help with considerations of contours and map references. But when we told him of the wine and food waiting to be collected from my fridge, he came round a bit.

'Anyway,' I said, 'we can call at the 'Crosskeys' for a drink before we make the ascent.'

All went according to plan, we arrived at the top of Galt Yr Ancr about eleven thirty. In the pub and during the climb, Richard had been careful to entertain Ted with the story of the hermit, adding his own personal variations which included an account of how, during the period of the full moon, a number of villagers claimed to have seen a monk like figure, walking backwards and forwards on the hill top.

We were quite ready for the refreshments by the time we reached the summit, and had just started on the second bottle of wine when Richard abruptly halted his rather involved story about one of his clients, to point to something that had just appeared on the skyline to our left.

I was very impressed by Ivor's performance, the figure that we three watched in silence walked slowly along the ridge, he wore a long robe - a dressing gown I expect - and used a long staff to assist his old man's shambling gait. When he got to the end of the ridge, he slowly turned and made his way back until he came to a path leading down to where we three were seated, and started to descend it.

At this Ted jumped to his feet, 'I don't know what that is but I'm certainly not staying to find out,' he cried, and made off at a fast run in the direction of the path leading down the hill. I don't know if Richard had anticipated such a dramatic reaction on Ted's part; anyway all we could do was to forget about Ivor and take off after him. We could hear him crashing through the undergrowth some way ahead as we ran to catch him, when suddenly we heard the thud of a body falling and a sharp cry from Ted. He was obviously in pain when we reached him, in the dark he had missed the path and found a badger's hole instead, he thought that his ankle was broken.

Somehow we got him down to the road and I dashed off to fetch a car. In the local hospital they set and plastered Ted's ankle, and decided that it would be best if he stayed there for the night to keep him under observation. Next day, instead of fell walking Richard and I visited the hospital, we found Ted much recovered and the doctor agreed that it would be Ok for Richard to drive him back to London that day. I managed to ask Richard, while we waited for Ted to get dressed and discharged, if he intended to tell him the truth about the phoney ghost?

'Well I suppose I've got to, haven't I?' he answered, 'but not just yet, I know he'll give me hell when I do.'

Several days elapsed before I rang Richard, mainly to check upon Ted's progress, I also asked how he had taken the news about the ghost hoax?

'It looks as though we were the ones being hoaxed,' said Richard, 'Ted says he knew it was a put up job the moment he spotted the 'apparition', much too solid to be a ghost, and he just thought he'd play along and pretend to be scared. So the fall was as much his fault as ours thank goodness, anyway, the ankle is mending nicely and he is enjoying the enforced idleness.'

Well, I certainly had been feeling quite uncomfortable about my part in the somewhat childish event, and this bit of news took a load off my mind - until I went to see Ivor Griffiths about a week later to thank him for his star performance on the hill.

He was digging in his garden when I arrived, and before I got the chance to bring up the purpose of my visit, he started to apologise,

'I'm sorry I let you down the other night, I was just getting ready to start out when we had a bit of a family crisis see, Gwen's mother had one of her turns and we had to dash off to Aberystwyth, by the time we got home again it was too late, pity - perhaps I could do it next time your friends visit you instead?'

The Peach

by

Anna Jones

She remembered the ribbons. There were white ones and velvety pink ones and some the colour of delicious peaches that curled like the dying leaves of that plant with the long name. She remembered how they had pulled at her hair and how she had rubbed and rubbed at the tightness on her head until it was quite sore. Mummy would tut and pull at an end and the whole lot would come tumbling down so that there was hair in her ears and eyes and mouth. Mummy thought that looked messy.

One day in the park she and Mummy and the dog had been looking at the little snowdrops. She loved the way they frosted the park like a Christmas cake and was proud because she remembered that last year they had been here too and had been followed by oceans of blue flowers weeks later. She remembered a whole year!

A shadow had fallen onto the flowers. She heard a deep phlegmy cough and then a big, knobbly hand grabbed at a pigtail and another was on her neck, the dirty thumb in her mouth. She could not cry out. She froze like a frightened rabbit as the man pulled her away into the trees. The dog must have heard her thumping heart. It barked. The man pulled her hair and hit her, hard. The white ribbon tumbled to the ground. Then Mummy turned back to see why the dog was running into the trees, and the man fled.

Mummy carried home the trembling little bundle and tucked her into bed. The police came and Eva was excited to see the uniforms and the car, but she didn't like telling them about the man. She was so scared that he might take her away next time.

The years brought change. Eva, her education complete, spent her days typing letters at *Jackson, Selby, Marks & Co* assisted by Marie, a tall girl with curly dark hair who liked to read the private files.

'Would you believe it of old Carson! Whatever does she see in him?' Eva shrugged. 'He's old enough to be her... grandfather even! And Liz Carson is the dearest lady. There's only one reason isn't there?'

Eva knew what the reason was and smiled to herself.

'All these divorce cases boil down to it. But Carson... now he doesn't know what he's doing I'm sure!' Marie tugged at drawers in the filing cabinet, pulled out buff files and flipped through them, chuckling. It had been a quiet morning. Mr Jackson was in court, Mr Marks was on holiday and Mr Selby and Mr Arthur were with clients.

Eva understood Marie. Sex. That was why all these strange things happened. She laughed at the stupidity of it all. Sex was a pleasant experience, she had found that out, but so was eating a juicy peach. She smiled as the thought of top shelf magazines full of pictures of succulent, smooth peaches. Men in dark pubs boasting to their comrades about the peach they ate after tea. Would Carson have left his wife for a woman who always kept a fruit bowl topped up? In his position, Eva certainly would.

She was dragged from her reverie by Jackson. He strode in without glancing at either Eva or Marie. His brow was furrowed. Eva politely enquired about the case.

'Guilty,' frowned Jackson, and slammed his door behind him.

'Guilty as hell,' Marie echoed. 'These perverts should be castrated.'

There it was again. A man had lost his freedom because of his insatiable appetite. Eva laughed out loud and tossed her hair out of her eyes. How weak men were! How stupid, to be ruled by their passions. There had been a man like that in her past, she remembered. Where was he now? Women were in control of their hunger. Women were the masters. She reached into her bag, found her lunch box and took out a velvet globe, radiant in colour, warm and soft in her hand. She had a red silk ribbon in her hair, decorating a neat plait. She pulled it out and tied it round the peach finishing off with a pretty bow held in place with a map pin through the knot.

'A little present' she said proudly, 'for Mr Jackson.' She tossed it to Marie. 'Take it to him. It might cheer him up.'

Loop

by

Steven Meredith

The kids scuttled into the shadows like cockroaches escaping a shaft of light. The last was carrying a machete, dragging the point along the pavement, pin-shaped sparks flying up around his Nike sneakers as he ran for cover. He was eight, maybe, but life had made him older.

Cameron eased the car towards the pavement and came to a stop. He drove a battered old Citroen with temperamental gears and a bronchial sounding engine. Nobody would give it a second glance but he was in Loopsville and here sense did not matter. He glanced back towards the alley where the kids had disappeared. Nothing but shadows there. The single lamp that was working on the street cast a yellowish glow across some of the alley but its warm, protective web could only stretch so far.

Cameron waited to see if the kids were going to come back and then, satisfied that they weren't, got out of the car. The air was crisp and cold. Clouds of breath billowed from his thin lips. He reached inside his leather jacket and pressed a hand to the comforting butt of his Colt .22 Repeater.

Just you and me now, boy, he mused. Don't let me down.

He stepped away from the car and started walking down the street. At the end stood a prostitute, barely out of puberty but made up so that she looked a woman of the world. She said she could give him pleasure beyond his wildest dreams. Forty quid. A bargain. He flashed his police ID at her and she scowled, called him 'limpdick,' and moved away into the shadows.

He watched her go.

They all wanted the safety of the shadows. Sometimes, more often recently, Cameron wished he could join them.

At the end of the road, he checked the street sign to make sure he was on the right track. This was not a place to get lost - not for a city boy and certainly not for a cop. He was looking for a dealer who had gunned down two people during a raid on a bank in Hammersmith. He'd got away with three thousand pounds most of which was probably used up by now.

Crack addicts had a habit of soaking up the readies.

Ever since the price had gone up.

Red was one of those dealers that Cameron almost felt sorry for. He was ten years old and was born in a time when most of the world had given up hope of stopping the drugs war. Cameron remembered days when you could safely walk down a street and not expect to get mugged or murdered or raped. He was older than most. Red didn't have that advantage. The best he could hope for was to read about it in history books but then, Cameron guessed, the kid never learned how to read.

Red had nothing but the need. The need for his fix and the need to destroy the ones who stopped him getting it. When he was born it was estimated that there were under two million addicts in Britain alone. Now, ten years on, the figure had gone off the scale. No one could even hazard a guess. Statistics were a thing of the past. Red saw nothing wrong in what he did. Why should he? He was just one side of a very dirty coin.

The Gentry were on the other.

The time had come when the world split quite definitely into two. There were those who took drugs and those who didn't. The war wasn't as clear cut as others that had gone before. The Gentry, the ones who were supposedly pure of mind and body, who got high on Alf-Alpha and bran flakes, had devised a solution that was barbaric. In the context of the situation there wasn't much else that they could do. Life had become a question of survival. It had been that way since the mid-nineties when the crack epidemic exploded.

Loops were to be shot on sight. Some were even burned at the stake like witches.

In a way, Loops were a helpless breed, driven by the compulsion to snort or smoke or inject. The young ones, those who had known no difference, like Red, were addicts before they were born, victims of wayward mothers and pimp fathers. In another way, they were a violent, basic breed, unable to control their vicious urges, unable to prevent the violent intent that erupted from their drug-addled brains.

Gentries would kill Loops to protect their houses and their non-arterio-sclerotic arteries.

Loops would kill Gentries to get their hourly fix. Loops would just as easily kill each other for that matter.

The split grew because people didn't want to face the truth. That was why they elected politicians who were good at talking without actually saying anything. By the time the situation had reached a crisis point, TV had joined the bandwagon, heavy on denial, low on truth.

Crack problem? There's no problem. Don't be silly!

TV did what it was good at - promoting an image - and politicians did what politicians are good at. They combed their hair and smiled their collective smile and spilled poetic words onto a video sound-track. They were words that melted musically together but then, when you examined them closely, had as much substance as a Guns n' Roses song. They could have recited Humpty Dumpty for all the sense that it made.

At the time, Cameron had seen the problem but he, like millions of other people - frozen by some cosmic game of musical statues. There he was, standing as still as possible, waiting for the music to start again, and out of the corner of his eye he could see someone free-basing but he wasn't going to do anything, because he didn't want to break the rules of the game.

Soon, it seemed, he was the only one around who wasn't injecting something into his veins or feasting on yogurt and muesli.

The crack epidemic seeped like a bad sewerage leak into the neighbourhoods and streets of every respectable town and village. Wars were breaking out all over and there was no way to stop it. Cops like Cameron did their best while feeling as if time and events had left them as far behind as the dinosaurs.

Loops.

They got their name in the mid-nineties from the things that they did, like cutting off their own hands and laughing, eating dog meat because the crack had made them so hungry and there was nothing left in the cupboard, like shooting strangers in broad daylight on a crowded street all for the sake of a fiver. Loops. Loopies. Nuts. That's what they were. At least, that was how drugs made them.

Red was no different. Cameron knew he had wasted a family in Woodford, sneaking into their neat semi at the dead of night. The man had been a broker, the woman had owned a clothes store, the kids were just setting out on their education. Red had ripped out their hearts and painted the walls with their blood. No witnesses. No evidence. But Cameron knew that Red had been responsible.

He recognised Red's house instantly. He'd been here before, a while back, to question the dealer about another, equally gruesome crime. There was a white picket fence that was cleaner than any other thing in this land of the dead. There was a smell to the place like a giant had taken a dump over the roof. It clung to the walls, seeped into the ground and played kiss n' chase with the ice cold air. Reds, house. Reds, kingdom. A ten year old boy who should have been starting elementary school. A ten year old boy who knew more about death than God himself. How to deliver it and how, maybe, to accept that it was always a shadow, tapping you on the shoulder and whispering sweet nothings in your ear.

Cameron walked up the path to the door. The grass was littered with creased cans and old hamburger containers. Where the gate had been pristine white and proud, the door was plastered with graffiti that would have made the devil blush.

Cameron felt the fear uncurl in his stomach. Acrid bile squeezed its way up into his tongue and he swallowed it back. He gritted his teeth and reached for the .22.

He pushed at the door. It opened with an eerie creak.

The stench rallied and then charged over him like a living thing. He forced himself not to turn away as tears welled up and burned onto his cheeks. It was death, waste and excrement. It was failure, despondency and disease. It was everything Cameron had come to hate, but it was also everything he had become used to.

Norms were mans worst enemies. It was amazing what he could learn to accept.

We made this, he thought.

We all made this. Through our blindness, we made this place.

We created Hell on earth because we couldn't find the courage to face it head on.

Red, who in another world, another time, would have gone on to be a university graduate, lay crumpled like an old rag against the hall wall. Above his head was a splash of crimson - a surreal bunch of flowers knitted to his blond hair. Above that was a slogan daubed in luminous green paint.

'He who fucks with God, fucks with me.'

Cameron didn't know what it meant. All he knew was that Red's brain was plastered all over the hallway. He tried to see a ten year old kid but all he could see was something abhorrent, something they all had made. A kid who killed his first man at the age of six and who had nowhere else to go but down. Things were all a matter of time for people like Red.

In his left fist was a crumpled bouquet of notes.

Cameron let the door swing shut and turned away.

Loops and Gentry.

Two sides of the same coin. He guessed that the loops would blow themselves out, kill each other or just plain OD. But people had been saying that for the last ten years.

Sooner or later, one side had to win.

He stepped back to the path. Something scuttled in the shadows to his right. He thought he heard a whisper. Another day, another time, he would have gone to investigate.

Not now.

He moved away from the house, sneaking a last look at Red's mausoleum. He kept his hand buried in his coat, resting on the butt of the gun.

Case solved. Go home. Try to get some sleep.

When he got back to his car, his wheels had been stolen and someone had daubed a fresh slogan across the paintwork.

'Welcome to Hell!'

Night Mist

by

David K Wharfe

Gradually the screaming subsided, and was replaced instead by the rhythmic ticking of the clock at his side.

'Nightmare!' he thought. 'It was only a nightmare!' Then he shuffled out from beneath the damp covers and sat on the edge of the bed, his head in his hands.

It was the same every night! The mist. The barking dogs. The stranger with his gun. And the fatal shot which ripped through his heart, bringing the dream to an end and flinging him back to the drab security of his lonely wood-chipped room.

He let out a deep sigh before rising and stumbling over to the sink for a glass of cold water, but he stopped in his tracks as a dog barked outside his window, and he turned slowly, half expecting to see the stranger from his dreams, but seeing only the moonlit shapes of his room. He looked at the mirror above the sink, shaking his head at his own stupidity as he whispered,

'Pull yourself together Nick!'

It was five forty five, two and a quarter hours before he had to be in work, so he glanced back at the bed, wishing forlornly for another hour of sleep. But he knew he couldn't risk it, he would only have the nightmare again, and once a day was quite enough! Instead, he decided to clear his mind with an early morning stroll by the sea, so he dressed quickly, leaving the room and its nightmares behind.

The sun had barely cleared the horizon when Nick arrived at the beach, and he watched for a while as it rose into the cool blue sky, pulling away from an early morning sea mist which capped the waves in the distance. It should have been a glorious sight, but he couldn't help feeling that there was something wrong with it all! Something slightly amiss in the shades of the sea and the sky, and the texture of the sand beneath his feet, everything in fact seemed strange! It was nothing definable, yet somehow it all seemed slightly 'wrong!' He shook his head and tried to ignore it all as he walked on. Perhaps he'd needed the fresh air more than he'd thought!

Further along the beach, where the sand gave way to pebbles, he stopped to skim a stone on the water. It only bounced three times. So he skimmed another which bounced eight. And he spent the next half hour trying to beat the eight, but never getting past a six. His game was cut short however, when his stones began to disappear within the mist that had crept unnoticed across the waves.

Memories of his nightmare came flooding back and the fine hair on the back of his neck began to bristle. It was silly he knew, but he just couldn't help feeling that right now would be a good time to turn around and go home. He didn't of course, he had more sense than to be scared of a little mist! So he tried to take his mind off it all by swapping his smooth, flat stones for small boulders which disappeared into the white oblivion with a satisfying 'splosh!' But he'd only thrown a couple when he heard the dogs!

He stopped in mid throw, a large rock held in his upraised hand as the faint sound of barking echoed across the beach.

'It's just a coincidence!' he told himself. But the fact remained that this was exactly as it happened in his dream! The mist! The barking dogs! And then the stranger!

He spun around with the rock still clasped tightly in his palm, no longer afraid of being foolish, just afraid of being right! And sure enough, through the mist ahead, a figure approached!

Nick still held the rock above his head; and as the stranger from his dreams stepped into view, he brought it crashing down on his skull, striking before the man could fire his gun.

The side of the stranger's head exploded outward with the force of the blow, and he fell to the floor, twitching violently for a moment, before his entire body fell still. Only then did Nick notice that the stranger didn't even have a gun, and he stared down on the lifeless body at his feet, struggling with the realisation that he had just murdered a completely innocent passer-by! And then he screamed, he screamed until his head swam, and the world grew black.

Gradually the screaming subsided, and was replaced instead by the rhythmic ticking of the clock at his side.

'Nightmare!' thought the stranger. 'It was only a nightmare!' Then he shuffled out from beneath the damp covers and sat on the edge of the bed, his head in his hands.

It was the same every night! The mist, the barking dogs, the stranger with his rock. And the fatal blow which ripped through his skull, bringing his dream to an end and flinging him back to the drab security of his lonely wood-chipped room.

A Day at the Races

by

Susan Holbeche

Entering the lounge bar of the Fox and Goose, Alan saw that his three regular drinking pals were already ensconced in their usual corner of the bar, where they were likely to remain until well after closing time, resolutely defying the efforts of less experienced drinkers to push their way through in an effort to get served. The other regulars didn't even try, resigning themselves to patiently waiting at the other end of the bar until they could catch the eye of one of the bar staff.

'The usual, Alan?' said Morris, the eldest of the group, as Alan pushed his way through, 'we were just discussing next week's race meeting at Inkborough. John thought it might be an idea for us to go down for the day next Wednesday. What do you think?'

'Great idea,' responded Alan, 'it's about time we had a day out. I'm sure I can organise a day off. After all, what's the point in being self-employed if you can't please yourself occasionally?'

'That's settled then,' said Morris, passing Alan a pint of bitter, and handing a fistful of loose change to the barman, 'John and Emrys reckon they should be able to take a day's holiday, so we can make it a foursome. Bring plenty of cash in case you want to bet on the gee-gees.'

'Well, we all know you're the expert,' interjected Emrys, 'you'd better give us some tips.'

'Right you are,' Morris replied, 'stick with me, you guys, and you won't go far wrong.' This brought a wry smile to Alan's face who was only too well aware that although Morris fancied himself as an expert, his regular dealings with the bookies were generally far from successful.

Wednesday morning dawned, if not bright and clear, at least with the promise of becoming so as the day progressed. A slight misty haze lingered in the cool morning air as Alan made his way to the Fox and Goose car park, where the four had arranged to meet. They were journeying down to Inkborough in Morris' Rover as that was the largest car owned by the various members of the party, although Alan had valiantly volunteered to drive, to enable the others to imbibe copious quantities of liquid refreshment. This was not quite the self-sacrificing gesture that it might at first sight appear, as Alan had decided to devote his efforts to investing in the turf, and wanted to keep a clear head in order to study both form and the odds. With two hundred pounds bursting to get out of his wallet, Alan was determined to invest it wisely.

'Told ya so!' gloated Morris as the first race drew to its end, 'you should have bet on Mother's Boy as I told you. Not on that three-legged apology for cat's meat that you were determined to chuck your money away on. How much did you lose?'

'Twenty five quid,' replied Alan. 'Ok big head, what do you recommend for the next race then?'

'Put your money on Plantagenet,' said Morris, 'the odds are pretty good. Five to two, and his form's good too, especially in hard conditions like today.'

So Alan accepted the proffered advice, and made his way to the nearest bookie to place a fifty pound bet. Alan never did things by halves, and by doubling up on his previous wager hoped to not only win, but also to make good his earlier losses. Needless to say he was also the eternal optimist.

The four friends stood in the refreshment marquee, eating sandwiches and recapping on the mornings racing. Alan was beginning to regret volunteering to drive. He felt he could do with a stiff drink. Several stiff drinks in fact. He still hadn't a winner, and his original two hundred pound investment had now dwindled to seventy pounds. It wasn't that he couldn't afford to lose, he was quite comfortably off by normal standards. It was just that the day seemed to be falling a little flat all of a sudden, and his three companions' merry bandinage, with his gambling losses being the main butt of their humour, was really getting to be too much for a sober mind to take.

'Just off to visit the little boys room,' said Alan to his friends, as he pointed himself in the direction of the gents, 'see you in a bit.'

He didn't really want to go to the gents, he just wanted to be on his own for a while, so instead of going into the toilet block he walked around the back towards the car park where there was another refreshment tent. He'd have himself a quick pint where the others wouldn't see, and then rejoin them.

Unfortunately, he didn't get his drink. He was midway between the toilets and refreshment tent when he suddenly felt a splitting pain in the back of his head, and everything went black.

Morris, John and Emrys were just beginning to wonder, via an alcoholic haze where Alan had got to, when the announcement came over the public address system. 'Would Mr Morris Jones, Mr John Greening, and Mr Emrys Evans, please make their way to the police office in the main stand.'

As they entered the office, they saw Alan being tended to by a St John's Ambulance volunteer, and looking rather the worse for wear. 'What on earth's happened,' said Emrys, as Alan looked up rather sheepishly.

'I'm afraid your friend's been mugged,' said a police officer. 'There doesn't seem to be any serious damage, but you'd better take him to the local casualty department for a check up.'

'How much have you lost?' asked Morris, as he helped Alan rather shakily to his feet.

'Just my wallet,' Alan replied. 'Seventy quid left in it. Still, it could be worse,' he continued, with a wry grin. 'If it had happened this morning, I might have lost two hundred pounds.'

Bare Bones

by

Susan M Anderson

Eve got up from the homemade table with the crystal ball on it. She walked barefoot across the sandy cave floor and stood looking down at him, naked and beautiful.

'They'll never believe this, you know.'

'What?' He looked up at her from his seat on the rock.

'Us. You and me.'

'Why on earth not?' Adam was puzzled. His dark, simple face creased in a frown. 'We're here, aren't we? There's you and there's me. Who could possibly find that difficult to swallow?' He rose, walked to the mouth of the cave and looked out at the elegant and luxurious garden beyond, teeming with life of every shape and size.

'Now that,' he said, incorporating it all with a wave of his hand, 'that's incredible if you like. How He managed it all in the time beats me.'

'I know.' Eve was troubled, trying to find words to describe what she had seen. She came and stood beside him, leaning her head on his shoulder where it fitted. Her long hair tickled his chest. He liked it. 'I know Adam. It's all very natural to us, even out there. But there will come a time, believe me...' The words sounded wrong for a normal conversation, too heavy. She hesitated, then made up her mind and carried on with a rush. 'They'll say we're just a story, a myth. That there never were just two of us. That we were many. That we're half something else. That we were thought up just to keep people quiet, to make them stick to the rules. They'll say all that. Then they'll use it as an excuse to do whatever they want.'

He didn't understand. 'Who are they, anyway?'

'The ones who come after us.' You sweet, simple man, she thought.

'You mean He'll make some more?' His face brightened. Sometimes it was lonely, even with her.

She snuggled into his chest. 'Of course He will. Or rather... we will.'

'Us? How?'

'Tell you later. I must go and change.' She winked at the bright green snake which was slithering into the undergrowth, bent down and picked something from a basket on the floor.

'Have one of these. I found them this morning, growing on one of the trees. I think you'll like them.'

A Spark of Life

by

Andrew Hodson

'So what are you going to do now then?' enquired Aunty Meg in her usual manner. More nosey than concerned, and more intrusive, than polite, observed Harold McNulty, but at least she did have the decency to ask.

'Start to live, I think,' were the words he found that took her aback, and left her looking - er - gobsmacked! Yes, that was the word, gobsmacked. 'Living' was something he had never really done. Up 'til now, he decided, all he had ever done, was exist. 'Mind your 'P's' and 'Q's', 'Oh you can't go out looking like that' and 'We'll have no swearing in this house'.

A lifetime, nay an eternity of having to conform had stamped itself upon him, and he felt stifled. Now, yes, from this minute on, he was going to live, do what he wanted to do, do it when he wanted, and do it how he wanted.

A feeling that life had in some way entered a second springtime crept over him, and he smiled. There, in that moment, the decision had been made, and the feet had been firmly planted down the first steps on a new road. Staid ways, though, can take a lot of shaking off, and life can be a funny thing, especially when you are not very experienced at living! Take for instance, the very first question he now encountered - 'How do you go about it?'

Mr McNulty hadn't got a clue. Mind you, he did have some ideas on how *not* to proceed. He was most definitely not going to buy a medallion, nor a tacky two seater sports car, and neither was he going to go in for a Neo teenager type wardrobe of new clothes. There had to be a better way. A man still has to have standards.

In the event, his first purchases to assist this new life were bought more on impulse than anything else. He saw them in the shop, and bought them; just like that! A new tie, and a cushion that he would put in the lounge. Back at home later that afternoon, the more mundane aspects of change came under consideration, like what colours should be used to replace the dowdy greens and browns his home had been full of for so long. With pencil in hand he sat preparing a scheme, when looking up his eyes caught sight of his new cushion.

'Bah - I'm at it again,' he mused to himself as he thrust the paper away 'back to the old ways.'

He looked again at the cushion, which was a kind of reddish colour. He smiled, but he couldn't leave it on display, it would have to go under one of the other ones.

'No time like the present,' he murmured, and with a quick flick the job was done.

He was still admiring his new tie in the mirror when the doorbell rang. It was Peabody from next door:-

'Hello Harold, have you by any chance got a pair of pliers I could possibly borrow, I've er - oh I say! - that's a bit er' he spluttered rubbing his face in absolute astonishment that Mr McNulty could ever wear such a thing.

'I bought it today,' beamed Harold, 'what do you think?'

'Well, - I - er' but that was as far as Peabody got with his response, because Harold continued:

'I got it for the sake of Aunty Meg really, - on a bit of an impulse, do you like the design on the big flower in the middle?'

Peabody leaned forward, only to jerk backwards rubbing his face for the second time.

Now he couldn't wait to test Aunty Meg's reaction, but wait he must, all day Sunday, all day Monday and all day Tuesday. Wednesday would be the day. He knew Wednesday would be the day, as Aunty Meg always did her mid-week shopping on a Wednesday, and she invariably called in to 'catch her breath', have a cup of coffee and almost talk poor Harold to death. He found himself always having to convince himself that 'she means well' - or she gets very lonely on her own, or - oh I don't know.

True to form, at about midday, the doorbell rang, followed by the unmistakable she let herself in.

'Coo eee - good morning Harold.' The voice then usually continued with such an unterrupted flow of verbiage, that it left Mr McNulty wondering if maybe she had some alternative breathing system. This morning, however, it was different. As Harold emerged from his lounge, Aunty Meg's bottom jaw dropped open, quivered, closed, dropped open again, several times, but there was no sound. She staggered forward a few more steps, her eyes wide in disbelief. Harold grinned:

'What's the matter with you?'

'What's the matter with me?' spluttered, 'nothing's the matter with me, but I sometimes get very worried about you, - what on earth do you call that?'

'There's no need to be rude, Aunty Meg, it's a very good tie, just have a feel.' As Aunty Meg bent forwards, Harold squeezed the plastic bulb hidden in his pocket.

'Argh!' gasped Aunty Meg, wiping the water from her face as she leaped backwards.

'Oh Harold,' she began to scold as she lowered herself onto the settee.

PFARRRP!

Harold giggled, but Aunty Meg was not amused, yet the cushion had worked a treat.

'Well you silly Bu----.'

Harold delighted for once to butt in:

'Ah - ah! We'll have no swearing in this house,' he beamed and thought to himself - 'I could quite get into this 'living' business.'

A Day at the Seaside

by

Betty Peacock

Sylvia would have preferred to spend the Bank holiday the way they usually spent it. Having a lovely lazy morning , then taking the children to the nearby park, with it's large boating lake and children's playground. However George had insisted that this bank holiday they would have a 'proper day out'. 'Besides' he had said, 'the man from the Weekly Gazette is at the seaside this weekend, giving five pounds to anyone who recognises and challenges him.'

So it was, that Monday morning found them at the railway station, waiting with what seemed to Sylvia, half the town's population, for the 8.30 train to the seaside.

By the time they had arrived at their destination, her nerves were already frayed. They had stood, for over two hours, packed like sardines, in the corridor of the crowded train, she, trying to pacify Janet who always panicked in crowds, and listening to Richard complaining loudly that he wanted to be sick. To make matters worse, she was feeling decidedly squeamish herself. That made it four mornings in a row. She determined to see Doctor Parry tomorrow.

At last, outside the seaside station, they waited while George consulted his copy of the Weekly Gazette to read yet again the description of his prey, and the area where he could most likely be spotted. He need not have bothered about the latter. The throng of people streaming out of the station were all shuffling purposefully in the direction of the pier. The men all clutching their copies of this popular paper of the day.

'Come on dad,' cried Richard, his sickness completely forgotten, 'I want to build a sand castle.'

'I want to paddle in the sea,' said his sister from her safe perch on her father's shoulders.

'Later,' replied George, 'this fellow is somewhere in the vicinity of the pier about now until noon. If we spot him we could have five pounds to spend this afternoon.

'Ooh, that means lots of rides on everything on the fair,' said Richard extravagantly.

'I don't want to go on everything,' put in Janet, 'I like the Helter Skelter best.'

So on they trudged, following the prescribed route, and peering hard at every man bearing even the slightest resemblance to their quarry, until at last they reached the entrance to the pier. Sylvia looked with dismay at the crowds teeming on to the pier and decided that all she wanted to do was find a quiet spot to sit down and eat some of the sandwiches she had packed. George however, had other ideas. 'The WGM must be here somewhere and I am determined to have a go at finding him,' he declared.

'What's a WGM, daddy?' enquired young Janet.

'He means the weekly gazette man, silly,' piped Richard, who was a very quick-witted lad.

'I'm not silly, and I bet you only guessed it, and you are horrid, you're always calling me silly,' Janet was beginning to cry. Turning to Sylvia she pleaded, 'mummy, tell him he is not to call me silly.'

'Now then, you two, don't start quarrelling,' put in George.

'I'm not quarrelling,' said Richard, 'anyway, can't we look for the WGM after we have had something to eat. I'm starving.'

'Me too,' announced Janet, her hurt feelings already healed. 'The children are right George,' said Sylvia, 'I think we should try to find a quieter spot and have some of the sandwiches we have brought. I don't know about you, but I feel hungry too.'

George looked at his little family, then at the milling crowds on the pier. 'Tell you what,' he began, 'how about you three going to sit on the sands just by those steps over there,' he pointed to a spot on the beach, not too many yards away from the pier. 'You can all have something to eat, and I will come and join you. Hopefully with an extra five pounds in my pocket,' he added as he lowered Janet to the ground. Sylvia thought this was a good idea. Secretly she was feeling ravenous, having returned what little breakfast she had eaten, less than five minutes after eating it.

Taking hold of Janet's hand she said, 'I think that is a good idea George, come on children the tide is out so we can find a nice little space for ourselves.'

A few minutes later and they were all tucking into the lovely egg sandwiches and fruit from the picnic basket she had borrowed from her sister-in-law.

'We had better save some for daddy,' she said at last. Reluctantly packing away the few remaining sandwiches. The next hour passed happily enough. The children busying themselves building an enormous sand castle and moat, joined in their labours by two young children from the family a few yards away from themselves.

George had still not returned however when the other family packed their belongings together and left to go back to their hotel for lunch.

'Look how far the tide has come in,' exclaimed Richard.

'Can we take our buckets and get some water for the moat?' he asked. Sylvia viewed the short distance left between them and the waters edge. 'If George isn't here very soon, we shall have to go up onto the promenade' she thought. Aloud she said, 'alright but only go to the edge. Don't paddle right into the sea.'

Another fifteen minutes went by, and she was considering calling the children to come and prepare to leave the shore. Suddenly Janet, who until that moment had been happily splashing about at the waters edge, began screaming hysterically. Almost immediately a tall young man, who had himself been walking along the beach close to the incoming tide, rushed to her and lifting her up, carried her the few yards to her mother.

'There was a horrible big thing grabbing my foot,' sobbed the child as Sylvia took her into her arms.

'It was only a large chunk of seaweed,' said the young man smiling broadly.

Sylvia smiled back and was just about to thank him, when Richard pushed himself forward, brandishing the copy of the Weekly Gazette, left behind by the family who had recently left the beach.

'You are the man from the Weekly Gazette, and I challenge you to pay me five pounds as my reward for finding you,' he shouted.

The young man turned to Sylvia, 'you have got a smart young lad here,' he said, taking five pounds from his pocket and handing them over to Richard. 'That's the first time I've been challenged by a youngster. You were only just in time though,' he remarked looking at his watch. It is just one minute to twelve o'clock and the time the project finishes.

Sylvia could hardly find the words to thank him and bid him goodbye, before he had walked on in the direction of the steps.

'Here you are mummy,' said Richard holding out the unexpected windfall, 'now we can go and have a lovely time on the fair this afternoon with daddy.'

They were just moving towards the steps when George returned. 'Not a sign of the fellow anywhere,' he grumbled, 'and now the time is up. Mind you I wouldn't be surprised if it was all a ruse to sell more papers.'

Sylvia shot a warning look at the children, who were just about to blurt out the story of their small fortune.

'Well never mind,' she said. 'Let's just sit on the sea wall while you eat the sandwiches we have saved you.'

'I don't need any just now, I had a pie and a pint in the bar at the end of the pier. I thought the chap could have been in there - a sheer waste of time,' he finished gloomily. Actually he was beginning to feel guilty about neglecting his family all the morning. He supposed he had been a bit obsessed with finding this man.

'Well buck up love,' smiled Sylvia taking a sandwich for herself, 'the children have some news for you. Tell your dad what you have just accomplished, Richard.'

The rest of the day was spent enjoying the delights of the fairground, before setting off once more for the station and home each tucking into a bag of luscious hot chips.

'It's been a jolly good day, after all,' remarked George.

'I'm sorry if I neglected you for an hour or so this morning, and as far as I was concerned it was wasted.'

'But I had good news for you dad, didn't I?' said Richard.

'You did that, son,' answered George, 'I always enjoy hearing good news, and what could be better news than you had to tell.'

Sylvia smiled to herself. 'Just wait until I've seen Doctor Parry tomorrow and you may hear some even better news,' she thought.

Combat

by

George Rodgers

This morning I woke with a fire in my heart, dreams of destiny still playing around the edges of my sleep-clouded mind. Today would be a day like no other. This was the day of the ultimate combat.

Rising from my bed I ate lightly for I had no wish to dull my senses through gluttony. Having eaten I returned to the still silence of my room and meditated alone within myself. This was as it must be. I could little afford to waste my thoughts on others, not on this day of all days. For thoughts are energy and I would need all my strength for what lay ahead.

Today I would be Swordmaster. The path would not be easy, that I knew, but I had within me the quiet easy confidence of one trained long and well in the arts of Combat.

To be Swordmaster had long been my ambition and the road to this, the ultimate combat, had been gruelling and precarious. Indeed, I had seen off some twenty opponents to reach this stage and today I knew, if I could maintain complete control over mind and body, the sweet taste of victory would be mine to savour. How I longed for it.

For a moment, on the way to the Arena, I lost the fierce concentration I had built to block out the hustle and bustle of the milling crowds who filled the city streets. For a moment, just a moment, I thought of the girl. But this was not the time and, silently cursing my lapse, I exorcized her from mind. With victory she would be mine.

Entering the Arena I felt the change begin. My chest filled with indrawn breath as it expanded to more than twice its normal size. My hitherto skinny arms now became great pulsing masses of muscle and sinew and I felt the hair, long and blonde, tumbling down between my shoulders. Around each of my huge biceps, a thong of leather, symbol of the warrior. The metamorphosis was complete. The warrior was here.

Until now, caught up in my own adrenalin-charged psyche, I had not registered the large, noisy crowd come to witness the great event. Secure now in the absolute certainty of destiny fulfilled I could watch, detached, the sea of excited faces around me.

In some quarters money was changing hands and I afforded myself a grin at the thought of those poor fools who would be placing hard-earned coin on the future of my doomed opponent. His head would be mine.

The thought of the final cut, as the broadsword cleft his head from mighty shoulders, filled me with a primitive excitement. True, he had been a good Swordmaster in his prime but my day was dawning and with my dawn came his dusk.

The crowd were cheering now as the Swordmaster entered the Arena. All around him people clamoured to pat his broad back and to shout words of encouragement. But, while all other eyes were on him, mine were not.

My gaze rested on the thing of pure beauty that clung to his arm as he pushed his way forward through the baying crowd. Red hair that turned copper under the artificial light framed a face both sensual and innocent at one and the same time. My body ached for her and I averted my eyes for fear of losing the total control so essential to my victory.

I must win. I had to win! For she was with him I knew, only because he was who he was. Swordmaster. Well, tonight when the sun went down, she would still be on the Swordmaster's arm. But this time the arm would be mine.

And so, to Combat. There was no going back now. The officiator brought us together but his words went unheard as we stared icily into each other's eyes, the drone of his voice ignored as he repeated the rules we both knew so well. The few rules that ended with the words 'one winner'.

He stepped back, allowing us to move into position, each with our arms folded neatly behind our backs and eyes on the broadswords that lay gleaming on the floor in front of us.

The crowd were silent now, mindful of the rules that governed the match. Suddenly, the officiator's voice, cracking like a whip through the electric air.

'Combat.'

We sprang forward together, reaching for our swords. Big though my opponent was he was fast and agile and his speed caught me unawares. As I clutched at the hilt of my weapon a blur of distorted light on my right warned me of danger and I rolled instinctively to my left, his great blade swinging through the space that seconds before had been me. The blade struck the stone floor with a scream and sparks flew up around the off-balance swordsman. Taking advantage, I leapt to my feet and swung double-handed at the exposed back of his neck only to see the blade pass over him in a hollow 'whoosh' of wind as he bent at the knees.

In one movement he bounced back up and arced his sword upwards in a curve of gleaming metal aimed at my right hip. The muscles stood rigid on my shoulders as I pulled back my sword, point to the floor, to block the attack. The two great weapons met in another shower of sparks, the air alive with the sounds of tortured metal.

Ready now to take the initiative I was too slow and could only stand and watch as my opponent leapt back out of the range of my sword to stand gloating upon a stone ramp.

Taller now than me by a head he stood patiently awaiting my attack. I moved cautiously towards him, two hands on the hilt, and tip of the sword pointing upwards to fend off a thrust or swing from above.

Suddenly, sword raised, I lunged towards his left side.

Stepping back slightly he countered with a swing at my head, surprised by the rashness of my move. But there was method in my madness and, as he swung, I pulled out of the lunge and dropped to my knees away from his weapon and, in so doing, brought my blade down hard into the side of his lower left leg.

Shocked and in pain but still on his feet he pulled back immediately as blood welled brightly in the wound.

I was aware now of the shouts from the crowd, their primitive passions aroused by the sight of his blood running freely. Chasing him up the ramp I could see he was frightened, knowing I now held the upper hand.

Confident in my approaching victory I moved forward swinging the great sword in front of me, first one way then the other, taunting him in his suffering.

Trapped in front of me his head was mine for the taking and I could almost smell his fear.

In obvious desperation he lunged at my right side but I stepped back slightly and swung at his exposed flank. As I did so he began to drop and I realised in that instant what he was doing.

He was using my trick. Just in time I pulled out of the swing and turned the sword down to cover my vulnerable legs. I saw too late the change in direction as he rose up and drove the point of his sword under my chin in an explosion of scarlet.

I lay dead and the crowd were cheering, hailing their champion confirmed. Swordmaster again for another year. Looking at my lifeless body I can't tell you how upset I felt.

As the words 'Eliminated - please try again' lit up the giant screen I stood up and looked imploringly at the girl of my dreams, the girl I knew should be mine.

'Next year?' I mumbled at her.

'Get lost creep,' replied the vision of loveliness before blowing a bubble in her gum.

'Come on Eric, let's go out and celebrate luv.'

Oh well, dream dead, back to reality. No more Arena arcade.

Work tomorrow.

Nobody Told Me

by

Florence Feasey

If you are sitting comfortably and not wanting to go anywhere special-like, I mean personal to your requirements, I will tell you how I got Evan Preece for my lawful wedded husband. What helped of course, were my conversations with God.

I was brought up to Chapel, three times on Sunday, and two meetings of the Band of Hope every Tuesday and Thursday. So you see, my training was pure as a snowdrop.

Well, after our old minister was gathered to his Fathers, Evan Preece came to our village like a Bomb from the Bible. A bachelor he was, not strictly handsome you understand, but O Duw, a beautiful speaker, and no spit over the pulpit like the old one.

All the women cast their nets for Evan Preece. Ceinwen Roberts, Gwyneth Thomas and Olwen Rees were the worst, but I had a trump card in my pack - my conversations with God! These had taken place since I was eight years old. Granted they were a bit one-sided, these little chats, well, I would have dropped dead if I had been answered verbally. No, the answers always came in signs.

The fourth Sunday after Evan Preece descended upon us (like manna from Heaven I may say) I mentioned to God casual-like, that I wouldn't mind having Evan Preece for my lawful-wedded in the near future.

The next day, I looked for a favourable sign or special word from Evan Preece - after all, I was getting on a bit, and had a good double bed at home doing nothing, feather it is too. Well, nothing happened out of the ordinary that day, but we all know God helps those who help themselves.

The following Sunday I stayed behind after Chapel and waylaid Mr Preece as he was coming down the aisle. I was full of confidence as God was on my side see. Smiling like the whale that swallowed Jonah, I said,

'Good sermon you preached this morning Mr Preece, da iawn.'

'Oh thank you Miss Morgan,' he said, putting a rather heavy hand on my shoulder (nothing intimate intended you understand, just a sign from God). Very encouraged I felt.

'Yes, Mr Preece,' then I plunged. 'Do you know I have had chats with God for many years?'

Mr Preece stopped dead in his tracks. 'Anwyl mawr, Miss Morgan, is it blaspheming you are? No one but men of the cloth are allowed to talk with our Maker on equal footing.'

'Well,' I said bold-like, 'I am always answered with a sign of 'yes' or 'no', never indefinite.'

Mr Preece looked hard at me, and I was glad I'd had my hair crimped the day before.

'Dear dear,' he said, and I knew he was impressed, 'sit down Miss Morgan, or Megan isn't it, and tell me more.

So we sat on the hard Chapel seat, fourth row from the back, and we weren't there ten minutes before Mr Preece knew that I owned my own cottage, and was a dab hand at bara brith and Welsh cakes, as well as communing with the Deity.

Well, to cut a long story short, I got Evan Preece for my lawful wedded, not so much struggle either. But what disillusion!

For nigh on twenty years I have had to listen to Evan Preece's sanctimonious mutterings, and oh! Mam Fach, how boring they are. What with them and his everlasting sermons, home and in the pulpit, all boring, boring. Well, he never stops talking. I tell you, his teeth still chatter in the glass at night. And his wig he treats like a pet rabbit, smoothing and brushing it every night on the brass knob of the bed with the best brush from Boots. I never watch when he unscrews his leg, though solid oak it is mind. That leg has always been a bone of contention between us. Well, all this gets you down after a while.

I'm beginning to wonder if I might have read a sign wrongly all those years ago. That hand on my shoulder could have been a warning! The real crux of the matter is, that so many people knew of Evan Preece before he came to the village. They attend Chapel as often as their patience and purses allow, but they must have had a good laugh at the whole situation at times - that's what gets me: nobody told me in time. Nobody told me.

Untitled

by

Alan Chappell

George stood in the garden, looking in desperation at the jungle which surrounded him. Moving house was upsetting enough, he hadn't wanted to go anyway, and if the bank hadn't called in his mortgage, he would have been quite happy to have stayed in his old home. The new property was rented, there was no money for another house. And besides, if there had been any money available, it would've had to go towards paying off the credit card company - another debt that George could see no way of clearing. He turned to face the house, and saw Diane looking at him through the lounge window. George eyed the property from roof to ground. It was one of those large Victorian houses, imposing, even slightly depressing, but, it was in good condition. And it was a home, there were plenty of people in his position, living in bed and breakfast accommodation, or worse still, in a cardboard box on the street. He should have counted himself lucky, he still had a roof over his head, even if it wasn't his own, but he didn't. Luck was something he felt he'd run out of. George sighed, and walked back towards the house.

The lounge, like the rest of the house, was spartan. The carpet, which was threadbare, didn't quite cover all of the floor, leaving an area around the edges of exposed floorboards. The three piece suite was second-hand, and invariably had a certain shabby look. And apart from a battered teak veneer coffee table, the room was empty. Neither George or Diane were used to living in these conditions, it was depressing.

Diane turned to face George, as he entered the room.

'It looks like you've got your work cut out,' she remarked.

'You know how I hate gardening!' George cried anxiously.

'Yes I know,' Diane replied in a low voice, 'but at least it'll keep you busy, now that you're unemployed.'

'Huh!' George grunted resentfully.

'Never mind, eh?' Diane said sympathetically.

'If we had the money, I'd employ someone to tidy it up for me.'

'Well we haven't got the money!'

George turned away from her, sat in a chair, and buried his face in his hands.

'Oh God, what a mess!' he groaned.

Diane said nothing, and stared out of the window again.

Some weeks later, on a bright autumn day, George finally got round to tackling the garden. He'd got up early that morning, cleared the tangled web of brambles and weeds which had overrun the flowerbeds, and then cut the grass. Already the garden was starting to look shipshape, and by the end of the following day, he reckoned that he should have finished it. He had only to clear away the weeds under the fruit trees, prune them, and cut the grass, and the job would be done - the sooner the better, as far as George was concerned.

The following day, George was up early again, and had soon started the final leg of the task. It was as he was chopping at the weeds, with a pair of hedge clippers that he noticed something under the trees. It caught his eyes, in much the same way a glimmer from a diamond in the sunlight would. At first he thought it was litter, spread out on the ground, but then on closer inspection, he realised what he had seen. There, just a little way in front of him, on the ground, were laid five, ten, and fifty pound notes. He picked one up, and looked at it closely, it felt crisp between his fingers, he held it up to the sky, it was genuine alright, it had a watermark. He scratched his head, and looked down at the pile of money. He was bewildered, and questions began to go through his mind. He looked around the garden, and wondered where the money could possibly have come from? He supposed that it could have been thrown over the hedge. Perhaps it was stolen - hot money? There had been a spate of hold ups in banks and building societies in the area, recently. Maybe the thieves had got the wind up, and dumped their haul? Thrown the money over the hedge in the heat of the moment?

George didn't know what to do. Should he take the money along to the police station? Of course, that would be the right thing to do, and there might be a reward as well. But then George had second thoughts. He needed money, and as he stood looking at it, laid invitingly on the ground, he calculated that there must be several thousand pounds. For a reward, he'd only get a percentage, perhaps ten percent? He'd be lucky if he ended up with more than a few hundred pounds. And anyway, the bank, or building society wouldn't miss it, they were always being robbed, and they were bound to be insured against that kind of thing. With these thoughts in mind, he walked back towards the house, torn between honesty and deceit.

He entered the kitchen, Diane was preparing breakfast, he sat down at the table, staring thoughtfully into space. Diane looked at him.

'Anything wrong dear?' she asked.

'If I told you that I'd just found a load of money in the garden, what would you say?'

She paused thoughtfully for a moment. 'I'd say brilliant! Why, have you?'

George looked at her somberly. 'Yes,' he said.

Diane burst out laughing, and poked him playfully on the shoulder. 'Oh you are a case!'

George stood up, and took hold of her wrist, leading her out of the house.

'Come with me, I've got something to show you.'

He took her to the fruit trees at the end of the garden. 'Look,' he said pointing at the money on the ground.

'My God!' Diane gasped, staring in disbelief at the notes laid on the ground.

She picked up one and held it to the sky.

'I've already done that, they've got watermarks, so they're genuine,' George informed her.

'Where did it all come from?' Diane asked searchingly.

'I don't know,' George replied.

'Well don't just leave it laying there, let's pick it up, and take it indoors!' she squawked, bending down and gathering up a handful. 'There must be four or five thousand pounds here, at least!'

George hesitated. 'I was wondering, perhaps we should hand it in to the police?'

Diane turned to him, 'you what?'

'Well, it might be stolen or something? From one of those robberies we've been hearing so much about.'

'You are joking?'

'It was just a thought.'

'We're going to keep it!' Diane said resolutely. 'This is like a Godsend! We can't hand it in to the police, we would be fools! So what if it is stolen? Finders keepers!'

Clearly there was no point in arguing with her. And it was quite true, they did need money. They were at the bottom of the pile, and although the prospect of ending up in court, and possibly going to prison, for handling stolen money, wasn't one George relished. It would only really be the final humiliation in a catalogue of recent personal disasters.

They kept the money, and they spent it, over a period of months. They used it to furnish the house, and have proper carpets laid. Some was spent on luxuries - jewellery, clothes, champagne and so forth. Time went by, and they heard nothing about any stolen money turning up in shops. The following autumn came round, and to George and Diane's amazement, the same thing happened again. They found a pile of money under the trees, in almost exactly the same place as before. They were perplexed. They gathered it up, took it indoors, and stashed it away, just as before, and eventually spent it. They went on holiday to the Bahamas. George would have liked a new car, but that would have been too conspicuous, and he still owed the credit card company. He didn't want to swank with the money, both he and Diane wanted to keep their good fortune secret. The same thing happened again, and kept on occurring, over a period of three or four years. Once every autumn, around the time when the apples fell, there would be a pile of money under the trees. George finally concluded that they must have a secret benefactor.

'Oh yes, the tooth fairy keeps leaving it,' Diane said sarcastically.

Finally one autumn, the money stopped coming. It was the autumn after the spring, when George had decided to cut all the fruit trees down - to help minimise the work. After he'd cut them down, he'd thought to himself, how strange it was that one of them never came into bud or flower. It looked, to all intents and purposes to be dead, but it wasn't, it grew a little bigger every year, one or two new shoots. And strangely enough, that was the tree that the money had always been under. George had cut that one down first.

Incident in Panama

by

Ernest Gibson

Had it not been for my friend Huilio's attentiveness since my arrival, I would not have entertained his request to help him in his crack-brained scheme; but I owed him a favour - after his selflessly showing me around all those places of historical interest in the locality, during my stay in Nombre de Dios.

Nombre de Dios. Not a Spanish oath but once the northern Atlantic terminus - on the Spanish Main - of the land route from Panama; by which trail the gold and silver from the Peruvian mines started a journey which would end eventually at King Philip's treasury in Seville.

Huilio had reminded me of this and related how his own 'treasure' was being kept from him by his tight-fisted mother. However, he had a plan by which he hoped to prise his patrimony from her and, hopefully, escape her matriarchal influence forever.

On one of our trips of historical interest, we had journeyed to the heights of Darien (where his ancestor - Vasco Balboa - had stood in 1513 to become the first European to see the Pacific Ocean). He had commented on the terrain - explaining that it used to be the lair of bandits in the past and was reputedly used still by characters who, for one reason or another fought shy of the law - then shook me completely by saying that he intended pretending that the youngest of his three brothers had been kidnapped by some such characters and a ransom demanded. Rodrigo - the 'kidnappee' - would be deposited at a friend's house until the 'ransom' had changed hands.

Well, much to my surprise, mama fell for the ruse and made the necessary withdrawal from the bank. In true Hollywood fashion, she had bought a briefcase and dramatically placed the wads of the American dollars asked for, in it.

The rest of the scenario followed like an old 'B' movie, with mama tearfully exhorting Huilio to bring back her baby; until, just as our hero was about to take the briefcase from her, it changed into a horror film - when his younger brother Emilio burst in with 'mama, mama, Rodrigo is at the house of Alphonso Valasquez!'

Had Huilio grasped the briefcase, he would have been minus a hand from the force with which his mother pulled it to her bosom. As it was, his ears took a pounding from the abuse she hurled at him until, white with anger, he turned and stalked from the room. I was surmising whether or not the gleam that came into her eye was an appreciation of what she detected to be a touch of the 'hidalgo' in her firstborn, when her wrath was turned on me. Opening the briefcase, she extracted a wad of bills therefrom and flung it on the table in front of me. 'Leave my house!' Dramatic pause. 'There's your fare, go back to your own country!' She closed the case and left me standing there stupefied.

I picked up the money and called Huilio - turning to see young 'blabbermouth' Emilio's head disappearing from the window. I thought nothing of it and, getting no reply from Huilio, made my way outside to where the second of his siblings was playing. Giving Lazaro the money, I asked him to take it to Huilio and tell him I'd see him in town the following day.

He scampered into the house and I made my way to the gate. On an impulse, I picked up the thick multi-coloured plate which I assumed was meant to keep the gate open and scraped the earth from it the better to see the design which had caught my eye some days ago.

Suddenly, 'Hey gringo!'

For some unaccountable reason, I held the plate against my chest as I turned to face a very angry Huilio. As the shotgun in his hand exploded, I felt as though I had been kicked in my chest - rather absurdly wondering why this should have resulted in the pain I felt in my head, before lapsing into oblivion.

I returned to consciousness to find my recumbent form surrounded by the family and, from the hysterical conversation that ensued, it appeared that 'blabbermouth' had been busy again. He had raced upstairs to tell Huilio exactly what he had seen through the window - my collecting the money from the table (this lad, though not a liar, was a bit too honest for comfort!) - and it had been too much for Huilio. In the state of mind his mother's outburst had engendered, this had been the last straw - his friend making off with his birthright (dramatic, I agree, but the fellow is full of Spanish blood remember).

I pushed a contrite Huilio away from me as he made as if to embrace me. 'It's a damn good job I had that cast-iron plate in front of me,' I gritted.

Huilio laughed uproariously. 'Look again at that cast-iron my friend.'

As my eyes focused on it, I could see that the colours which had caught them originally had all but been blasted off, leaving a shiny gold middle with speckles of gold radiating out to its circumference. 'Is it...?'

He nodded. 'It's gold!'

Explanations followed.

It seems that all those years ago, families like Huilio's had buried their gold and silver; only to have their rascally Cimarron slaves reveal its whereabouts to the Elizabethan arch-rascal Francis Drake and his band of privateers. This had prompted Huilio's forebears to resort to the stratagem of painting such gold treasures in the multi-coloured Inca style, then leaving them lying about the house before fleeing into the surrounding countryside (the Spanish colonists were in absolute terror of Drake - in fact, families still threaten naughty children thereabouts with such a bogey-man to this day).

Unfortunately, the ruse was so successful that, while Drake's men contented themselves with the silver rewards available, their simple Cimarron allies had helped themselves to those of the attractively-painted plates which had taken their eye.

However, no doubt finding on their return journeys to their hideouts that such 'pottery' weighed more like pieces of iron, it must be assumed that such items were soon tired of and jettisoned - as evidenced by the amount found by the returning Spaniards later on - but not all were recovered and over the years, first one and then another would be found. The one before me was obviously one such itinerant piece; but how had it ended up by the front gate?

'Honest Joe' Emilo provided the answer. He admitted to having found it in the woods some weeks before, had tired of playing 'hoop' with such a heavy disc and had left it where I found it. Emilio's title as the 'saviour' of the Vallejo family's fortune was assured - after all, might he not be able to lead them to where he had found the plate. And might there not be some more thereabouts...?

'And but for you my friend, we might never have known of the good fortune which lay at our very gate!' Huilio was almost waxing lyrical.

'You could have been minus one friend in the bargain!' I was waxing very emotional.

'Oh, you were in no danger - I never meant to kill you, just to teach you a lesson,' he said airily. 'I am, after all, an acknowledged marksman.'

'With a rifle no doubt!' I expostulated.

He dismissed my observation with a shrug of his shoulders. 'You were only ten metres from me and the plate is twenty five centimetres in diameter. In fact, had you not hit your head against the gatepost, there would have been no need of your lying here now.'

His arrogance grated on me and he needed to be brought down a peg or two. 'Well, 'William Tell', remember this maxim in future - it may help save someone's life, should you want to indulge in another such whim.'

The family had caught the ambience between us and gone silent.

I felt like a pedant but the point had to be made. 'Unlike a rifle bullet, shotgun pellets disperse radially at a rate of one inch per yard of linear travel. I'll leave you to work out the metric conversion, but believe me, had your assessment of the distance between us been correct, they would have been picking a ring of pellets out of my chest - and you would have been picking oakum in the 'calabozo'.'

His mute consternation was a joy to behold. The look his mother treated him to bespoke volumes as to his imminent chance of becoming the 'Don' Huilio which her earlier look of pride might have implied.

It looked as if he would be spending some years more in his 'apprenticeship'.

I, on the other hand, from the way she crushed me against her ample bosom, had suddenly acquired a new mama - an enriched one who had apparently forgiven my earlier 'pecadillo'!'

Wisp of Smoke

by

Geoff Ransford

Carol felt the tiny hairs on her neck spring erect like the hackles of a dog.

He must be here again.

She turned. There he was, that damned pipe in his hand, those eloquent dark eyes fixed on her in mute appeal.

'What do you want of me?' she asked helplessly. 'Tell me, please.'

His eyes poured out their earnest plea but he remained silent, sucking on his pipe and sending smoke eddying round the gallery.

The sound of a car brought Carol to the window, desperately hoping it would be David. But an old Austin drove past. She swung round to find Owen was gone. All that remained was a wisp of smoke caught in the rays of the sun.

Carol braced herself. Despite her love for David she could not escape the effect Owen had on her. Her mind went back to her first glimpse of the cottage. There was nothing to warn her then.

When he had seen the state of the cottage, David snorted in disgust. But Carol was entranced.

She climbed up to what the house details described as a 'minstrel gallery'.

'David, David! Come and look!'

His mutinous expression clearly showed what he thought of the ruin, but as Carol drew him to the rail, his scowl softened. Interest came alive as he saw the square room below, rising in graceful lines to the arches of the roof. There was a splendid fireplace just made for a blazing log fire.

'You like it, don't you?' Carol was positively willing him to say yes.

David gave a stage groan ruefully signalling his defeat.

Carol jumped into his arms and they capered round the gallery in a wild dance that sent dust spurting into the air. Her feet caught a huge clay pot and David nearly dropped her, trying to stop it falling over.

'What an ugly thing,' said Carol.

'Oh, I don't know,' protested David. 'I rather like it.'

The pot resembled an enormous vase but the blank top with no mouth spoilt its looks.

Carol had had enough of the peculiar pot. She grabbed David's hand and said, 'Let's inspect the rest of our cottage.'

They had gone straight to the estate agent and to their delight their offer was accepted. Then followed the endless hours of cleaning and restoring. Each day they worked side by side until dropping exhausted into bed.

Then Owen appeared.

David had gone into town and Carol was working on the wood in the lounge. Suddenly she had the oddest feeling she was no longer alone. She spun round but there was no one there. Yet she could feel eyes on her.

She looked upwards and screamed.

Leaning on the balustrade of the minstrel gallery was an odd young man, staring down at her. Thick black hair curled down to his shoulders. He was wearing serge trousers and a rough-spun sweater. In his hand was a pipe with blue smoke curling upwards.

'How did you get in? What are you doing here?' Carol quavered.

There was no reply.

Carol pulled herself together. She shouted, 'Get out of here! Go on, get out and don't come back!'

The figure didn't move other than to draw on his pipe. But those intense dark eyes bored into hers, asking for something.

Anger bubbled up and Carol tore through the door and up the stairs only to halt, perplexed, on the gallery.

It was empty.

Frantically she searched the bedroom, the only other upstairs room.

No one.

The windows were still on the first latch. There was no other way out. He could not have swung over the balustrade to drop down into the lounge - she would have heard him.

Had she imagined the whole thing?

Then her nose twitched at the acrid smell of pipe tobacco.

She reeled as she reached the only possible conclusion.

She was still a bit shaky when David returned. She caught hold of him and said, 'David, it sounds stupid, but I've seen a ghost!'

He burst out laughing. 'What? A woman going upstairs with her head under her arm?'

'No. A man dressed in clothes from the last century. Very handsome as a matter of fact.'

David gave a disbelieving snort and looked at her pityingly. 'Look, love, you need a break. We've worked on the cottage non-stop. Come out and we'll climb the mountain.'

A week later when David had gone for more paint, the ghost appeared again. Still he did not utter a word. Still he puffed on his pipe. Still his eyes pleaded with her. He seemed to get right inside her mind, yet she had no idea what he wanted. She cast around for a name for him and picked on Owen.

Owen only appeared when David was out. His visits were making her nervy and irritable. For the first time she was having rows with David. The rows focussed on that ugly pot. He spent hours scraping off the white rime and rubbing in tile polish. Carol hated it and she nagged him about the time he was wasting instead of getting on with the house.

Then this morning they had had their worst bust-up when David installed the finished pot at the edge of the hearth.

Carol had screamed that she loathed the pot. She was not having an ugly Grecian urn in the house.

David had bawled that it was staying there whether she liked it or not.

Carol shrieked she would smash it.

David had stepped back and said quietly, which made it all the worse, 'Perhaps you would be better off without me, never mind the pot.'

The door had slammed behind him with finality.

Now Carol leaned on the balustrade, tears coursing down her cheeks. She loved David but she had ruined their marriage and now he had left her. It was all her fault.

Then something caught at her mind, forcing itself through her veil of misery. It was something to do with this morning's row.

She tried to remember every word. Then she clapped her hand to her brow. That was it! 'Grecian urn'. An urn contains the ashes of the dead - or their soul!

Carol leaned over the balustrade, staring with wide eyes at the pot by the fireside. That was what Owen wanted. His soul must be imprisoned in the urn. If she opened it up he would be free. No more would he haunt her.

Feverishly she ran down the stairs and knelt in front of the pot. She fetched a mallet and chisel and with infinite care she tapped the blade into the seal.

The pot clanged resonantly.

She tapped again, praying it would not shatter.

A flake flew out, revealing a joint line beneath.

Carol worked her way round then, summoning all her courage, she put the chisel into the gap and levered it backwards.

With a grating snarl, the cap came loose.

A spiralling wraith of pink mist billowed out. Then Carol saw Owen at the rail. There was something different about him. His eyes were shining. His lips were parted in expectancy.

The pink mist swirled upwards taking on a solid form, until standing at the gallery rail was the most lovely girl, her hair a golden halo. Her cheeks were pink with excitement and she hurled herself into Owen's waiting arms.

Carol found her eyes misting with emotion as she watched the reunited lovers.

They each raised a hand in farewell and disappeared in a shimmer of blue light.

Carol looked down at the pot. Now the top was open, it was transformed into a beautiful vase.

From outside came the crunch of the car on the gravel and Carol dashed to the door.

There was David, his arms full of gladioli. His face lit up as he saw her and he said, 'I'm sorry, love. Here's a peace offering. All that fuss over an old pot. Tell you what, we'll smash it together this afternoon.'

Carol rushed to him, all but demolishing the flowers, and kissed him deliriously.

'Hey!' he gasped after a moment. 'Hey!'

Carol disengaged herself and commanded him, 'Wait here.'

The flowers went perfectly into the vase, the flaming colours complemented by the warm tones of the pot.

'Now you can come in,' she called.

David gazed open-mouthed at the vase. 'You've made it perfect, love. You're a genius.'

Carol smiled modestly. If only he knew how it had come about.

David grabbed her by the hand and headed for the stairs, saying mischievously, 'Now you can have your reward.'

Carol pulled back, her hand slipping from his, her eyes sparkling.

'Come on,' he grinned enticingly.

Carol glanced up at the gallery. There was no wisp of smoke.

An impatient growl came from the top of the stairs.

A low, excited laugh gurgled in Carol's throat and she bounded after him.

A Right Lovin' Family

by

Grace Goodwin

Beneath the glittering chandeliers, the reception had been a haze of faces, of courteously extended hands. Practically all those there were strangers to me, but my long-dreaded speech had been warmly applauded. Now the dinner was over and silent-footed waiters were clearing away to make room for the dancing to follow.

I moved across to the table beneath one of the panoramic windows, to where I was to autograph copies of my latest novel. I had been born in this dour old town, but now there were new roads, new blocks of flats and offices. Even this tall hotel, built high above a multi-storied car-park was new to me.

Ironic, I thought, to be tonight's guest of honour, and to look down to the very spot where I was born! To where once there had been narrow, mean streets... but Tarratt's Terrace was no more...

We lived just inside the Terrace in a two-up and two-down, with an entry and a back-yard to each half dozen houses. God knows it was a squeeze for our family, but what it was like for the Peggs, heaven knows. The Peggs...

All my childhood memories are coloured by the comings and goings of the Pegg family. A cobbled cul-de-sac with a high wall on the closed end, the Peggs lived in the last house on the left of Tarratt's Terrace. On the wall, a bracket held the one gas lamp, and beneath its light, in the pavement outside their door, we kids had our best 'chocks' for marbles.

The wall served as a goal for football, had chalked stumps for cricket. It was a perfect backdrop for ball games; the den for 'tin-lurky' and 'weak hosses are coming' games. The feeble glow of the lamp drew us there in the winter evenings as we swung the tins of burning rags called Winter Warmers.

But it was the excitement of the Saturday night rows at the Peggs' house that lit up our otherwise drab existence, although it was mostly in the Summer that *I* saw these at first hand. It was hard to get children to sleep in those hot stuffy little rooms; the men and women used to take their seats outside on the pavement to gossip with neighbours, trying to capture any cool breeze that might find its way up the street. A closely-knit little community, joined closer by mutual hardship and poverty, they found Saturday night special. A drink at the Black Swan in the next street (the Dirty Duck, we called it!). Or a pint of ale in a jug from the off-license. Best suits out of pawn till Monday; pictures or the

Palais for the courting couples; the barrow boys still calling their wares at ten o'clock at night...

And then the pubs turned out - no discreet closing here! No - a real chucking-out, especially of Dan Pegg. He really got drunk every Saturday night. We would watch with eager anticipation as Dan staggered the length of the Terrace, usually singing a hymn at the top of his voice.

With difficulty he'd find his own door, and then the fun would start. I can hear the din now... the clamour that always heralded his return. The front door would be violently flung open, out would come Dan, followed by pots and pans - anything Mrs Pegg could lay hands on. He'd lie there cursing; getting up enough courage for another attack on the door.

'A fine way to treat yer 'usband when 'e comes 'ome,' he'd yell, 'an' me with a bottle of stout in me pocket for yer...'

The next morning Mrs Pegg would be sporting a beautiful black eye, but she'd airily tell all and sundry.

'Sure, m'dear, I walked into a lamp-post. Fighting? Not on your life - we're a right lovin' family, we are...'

If ever we saw a policeman, you could be sure he was on his way to the Peggs, and that Dan would soon be absent again for a few months. Even the youngest kids knew he'd gone up the road to jail - and peace would reign for a while. But oh, the wonderful bust-up on the day he was released. This time they would both stagger home from the pub, arms fondly entwined, and sure enough, another little Pegg would arrive nine months later.

Although the neighbours grumbled about the shiftless Peggs, as soon as another confinement was imminent, they would all rally round. My mother, too. How she would sermonize every Saturday night, trying to keep the scandal from us kids, and yet her best sheet and honeycomb quilt always adorned every Pegg accouchement!

I forget just how many children they did have; I lost count of the babies that came along. But it was Billy, the eldest, that we kids laughed at the most. A great lummox of a lad, he was harmless enough if left alone, but frightening if plagued too much. His one pride and joy was his bike, for in those days, possessing a cycle was like owning a Rolls today.

Admittedly, his had no mudguards, the pedals were without treads, but it had two wheels, hadn't it? How Billy loved that bike. Then one day , he disappeared, only to return unannounced a week later. Unannounced did I saw? All the kids of the Terrace were following him... jeering, laughing, shouting. For Billy was *carrying* his cycle across his great shoulders; a bundle tied with string round his waist. I edged carefully near to ask.

'What're carrying it for, Billy? Is it broken?'

'Naw!' He shook his head. 'It's tired.'

We howled with laughter, careful not to get too near as we did; one swipe from his huge fist could knock your head off your shoulders, I reckoned. Poor Billy - it wasn't long before the Saturday night fights included him, too.

One thing irked my mother about the Peggs - the Christmas dinners. Years before, a rich old man in our town had left a sum of money to provide Christmas dinners for the poor. The Peggs always got one! I can picture it now - Mrs Pegg, for once in a clean apron, collecting it from the nearby bake-house. Hot from the oven, in a brand-new baking tin, the succulent, steaming roast was borne home with all speed. If it was a particularly bad year for us, mother would mutter.

'Well, that lot'll fare better than us this Christmas.' But she soon forgot her bitterness, and the next time a little Pegg came asking.

'Please, can yer lend me mum a penny for the gas.' she would hand over the precious coin, knowing full well she'd never see its return.

One Summer, the Peggs came into money! At first no one would believe it, and heaven knows the amount grew with each telling - from five pounds to fifty. Anyway, it seemed that a relative of Dan's had made good in Australia and sent them some cash. He must have had more brains that our branch of the Pegg family!

But a cheque, after much folding and unfolding, was duly cashed at the corner shop.

'Now Dan'll be drunk for a month.' We all thought we knew what would become of the money, but we were wrong.

Mrs Pegg proudly announced that she was giving a tea-party for everyone in Tarratt's Terrace! We were all agog - treats were few and far between. Besides, didn't the Peggs need new furniture and clothes? But no - a tea-party for all it was to be.

How well I remember the meetings the women had: the many lists drawn up and consulted anxiously; who could lend tablecloths, crockery and spoons? My mother had just acquired the first gas copper in the street - that was to serve for brewing the tea. The men helped organise the trestle tables, with many stopovers for a pint, from the Black Swan. Banners were hung from bedroom windows, all taking turns to borrow the window-cleaner's ladder.

The women vied with each other to produce more and more colourful garlands, as well as crepe-paper fancy dresses for their offspring. Shopkeepers supplied the food at wholesale prices, and seeing that the Peggs owed most of them money, it was only fair that they should get some of the trade.

What a Saturday that was! All that lovely food; the banners flapping in the wind; the long tables almost the full length of Tarratt's Terrace. Mothers, clean aprons over best frocks, urging their kids to eat up whilst they had the chance! Dan Pegg at a table on one side doling out ale to all the men.

As night fell, the party got livelier; paper dresses fell apart; young children packed off to bed, the older ones allowed to stay up. Tables were cleared away and we danced and sang long into the night. The beer-stained old piano, willingly hauled from the Black Swan, had been pressed into service, front doors propped open and living-room lights shone out over the crowded street.

I remember the local paper sent a photographer, and full of importance, we all crowded round trying to get into the paper. The next day, we found they'd got all the principals' names wrong, but that night no one cared. Finally, we all sang 'For He's a Jolly Good Fellow' round Dan Pegg and his brood, and for once they did look a right loving family.

Of course, the money didn't last a week, but we talked of the party for a long time after. I was growing up, and the Pegg family's affairs affected me less and less as other interests grew more important to me. I did notice that Mrs Pegg was getting quite peaky-looking. She had always been a small, wiry woman, but then she seemed to get smaller and paler. I thought no more of this because we moved away from Tarratt's Terrace; my sister and I started work and dad decided we could finally afford to rent a bigger house.

It was a shock to us when we heard the news that Mrs Pegg had died that morning... somehow we couldn't imagine Tarratt's Terrace without her! We sent a wreath and went back to see the funeral. It was the custom then for all the neighbours to turn out and watch a funeral in respectful silence... mostly in genuine sorrow. As I've said - we were a close-knit community. That day, the whole street turned out; curtains were drawn at every window, with a black baize-covered board nailed to the Peggs window-sill.

I can still hear the muffled stamping of the two great black horses pulling the hearse, and never had I seen so many flowers; every one of those little houses must have sent a wreath. I hardly recognised the Peggs - subdued, red-eyed, snivelling, according to their age, and dressed in an assortment of borrowed black clothes. Some with just a black arm-band - they all followed the hearse - for the centre of this loving family was dead, and I, too, mourned her passing.

From time to time, scraps of news drifted back to us. An aunt in North Wales had taken Jackie Pegg, the one really bright boy of the family. Some of the other little ones were sent to Children's Homes; others were in the care of neighbours. Maggie, the eldest daughter, a pretty, blue-eyed girl, went off to live with some rich chap - without the benefit of the clergy they said, but I never knew if this was true or not.

As for Dan, he sat in his customary corner of the Black Swan, telling anyone who'd listen of his right lovin' family. And that's how I was remembering them - the whole caboodle of Peggs... and Tarratt's Terrace. And now it had been demolished, and along with it, a piece of my childhood.

A rustle of silk, the faint perfume from the bouquet she still held, brought me back from the past with a jerk, and I turned to see the wife of the Chairman - a bluff, self-made man with a blunt turn of phrase, and I smiled as she stood beside me.

'A beautiful view from up here...' she mused softly, and I quietly agreed. And we both looked down to where the broad road ran past the hotel; the passing cars looked like beetles; the lights like a coloured necklace. 'It's so changed, you can hardly remember what it was like before...' She paused, and something in her voice made me turn away from the window and look at her - really look at her, for the first time tonight.

Instead of just another face in a sea of faces, I now saw that blue-black hair, those dark violet-blue eyes of...

'Yes,' she said quietly, 'you're right. You *do* remember me - I was Maggie Pegg. It seems we've both gone up in the world, love...'

No Harm in Asking

by

Joan Beale

The first hymn was just finishing, as the Reverend Reginald Smithers made his dignified way to the pulpit for the sermon. He glanced at the beautiful stained glass windows, the morning sunlight enhancing the colourful religious figures depicted there.

Then his eyes strayed upwards. Strong oak beams, supporting the now, brand new roof, brought a smile to his lips. At long last, his seemingly endless striving for money, to pay for replacement of old crumbling tiles, was finally over. His congregation could now worship in a dry, if not warm church.

As he patiently waited for the crop of nose blowing and coughs, which usually arose between hymns and prayers, he couldn't help but think back, to the first time the sorry state of the roof had been brought to his attention. He'd just said,

'Oh Lord above, give us a sign of your love,' when suddenly old Annie Cox screamed triumphantly,

'He's answered... he's answered,' as she wiped away a large blob of water, which had splashed down on her rather bulbous nose.

All eyes strained upwards, his included, and as if on cue a whole bombardment of drops and spurting jets of water, gushed down on everyone's faces and Sunday best clothes.

Needless to say, the service had to be abandoned, as parishioners, looking more like drowned rats than people, hurried home to dry off. Poor old Annie still maintained it was a sign, and if that belief assured her regular attendance, Reginald was quite content to agree with her.

Now he was faced with an apparently unsurmountable problem. Where was the money coming from to pay for the damaged roof. He asked his flock if they could spare just a little extra in the collection plate. And that's what it was... very little.

The 'extra' turned out to be pennies not notes, and the usual assortment of foreign coins, still kept appearing. So he craftily began to draft his sermons towards the joy of giving, hoping for a better response. He tried the 'widow's mite', 'better to give than receive', and other thought provoking quotations, but the results were poor. He appealed to the WI, Mothers Union, and other church gatherings, but still the incoming money was pitiful.

So the roof continued to drip and pour over everyone. Annie alone was pleased. Every time she got wet, she knew her prayers had been answered.

Then Reginald had a brain-wave. Something that might do the trick. So for his next sermon, he tried, 'be sure you sins will find you out', and 'God knows everything.'

Well, that really put the wind up everybody, much to his delight. As he looked at the expressions on the peoples faces, he knew he'd found a weak spot in their armour. He could almost hear the thoughts running through their heads.

'I've been a fool', 'I wish I hadn't done it', 'what if he or she should find out', among other guilty misgivings.

The collection plate that Sunday, was practically overflowing. No foreign coins, not much copper or silver, but plenty of pound coins, five pound notes, and even a few ten pound ones. It was evident his shamefaced parishioners, were willing to part with cash, in the hope that previous hidden departures from the straight and narrow path, would not be revealed.

Every Sunday from then on, Reginald reaped the rewards of that sermon. Even Church Guilds and Unions played a part. Bring and Buy sales, Coffee Mornings and other activities were arranged. All of which greatly increased the ever growing fund for the roof.

Then the day arrived when he decided there was enough money to make a start. Ringing up a firm of Surveyors and explaining the situation, he was informed a Francis Benton would come and make an inspection of the now more 'holey' than 'righteous' roof.

At ten o'clock precisely the next morning, the Reverend Smithers stood awaiting his arrival.

'Thank goodness it's dry,' he thought, 'I don't want him slipping on wet tiles,' but as it happened there was no risk at all of 'him' slipping, because 'he' turned out to be a 'she'... and what a she.

Around five feet, four inches tall, slimly built, with shoulder length blonde hair and lovely blue eyes.

Reginald extended his hand and stammered, 'I thought a Mr Benton was coming... a Mr Francis Benton.'

The vision, because that's how she seemed to him, laughed.

'Easy enough mistake to make. I'm Frances with an E, not an I.'

'But surely you're not going to climb up there?' he asked apprehensively.

'Of course I am... I've never been afraid of heights.'

'Well, if you're sure,' he hesitated, then said, 'I wouldn't want a pretty little thing like you having an accident.'

She blushed becomingly, and he gulped self-consciously, as he realised what he'd just said.

'Don't misunderstand me,' he began in embarrassment, 'I don't usually speak li...'

'That's alright,' she cut in, 'no offence taken. Now let's get started shall we?' Signalling to the workmen who had followed her in a van, she called, 'I'm ready for the ladders now.'

'Right you are Miss,' they shouted back, and started unloading them. Within minutes they had them secured together, and propped up against the outer wall of the Church. Frances slipped off her high heeled shoes, and put on a pair of plimsolls, much to Reginald's relief. He hadn't fancied her climbing in those stiletto heels.

He felt a tinge of shame as he thought, 'I'm glad she's not wearing slacks.' His neck ached as he watched her upward progress, and his heart jumped, as he caught a glimpse of her pink frilly petticoat and shapely nylon clad legs. He hadn't felt this way since he was in his twenties, and that was a long time ago. He'd almost forgotten how light headed he used to feel at the sight of a pair of neat ankles, and a pretty face. Now it all came rushing back, and the sensation was most enjoyable. 'Oh to be young again,' he thought, 'I'd give her a run for her money.' He just couldn't take his eyes off the tantalizing sight of the young woman perched above him. He greedily assessed every curve and line of her attractive form.

How long he would have stood in his dream world, nobody knows. It was only when a sharp voice cut through his pink cloud of fantasy, that he jerked back to reality.

'Is that all you've got to do?' asked his wife peevishly. 'Have you forgotten the Christening service?'

'No dear,' he murmured, as he looked into her insipid brown eyes and noted her straight mousey brown hair, and overweight body. Before moving away, his eyes strayed upward once more. A final picture to store in his mind. One he could recall and savour anytime he wished.

He never did see Frances again. She phoned her report in, and the actual replacement was contracted out to a local firm. As for Reginald, he began to have pangs of guilt. Remorse for the lustful longings that young lady had aroused in him. In his mind he had been unfaithful to Angela, his wife. She'd been young and pretty once, and she'd been faithful. Still was, in fact.

'Yes, I've harboured sinful thoughts over another woman,' he censured himself. 'She'll never know though,' but his conscience did, and that bothered him. So perhaps that was why, the following Sunday he meekly slipped twenty pounds into the collection plate.

As the congregation fell silent, Reginald's voice, firm and strong addressed the worshippers.

'Blessed are they who repent, for they shall inherit the earth,' and under his breath added, 'and a new Church roof.'

('Now what can I ask for next?')

Taboo

by

Abbie Ross

Everyone thought Mum was coping really well with Dad leaving. She was going out even more than before, and she still roared with laughter at the slightest thing.

But then her friends had never seen her mask slip, not even for an instant. That was something only I saw.

The first time was a week after Dad went. He just left one night, leaving a telephone number by my bed. We're eating breakfast and I tell Mum that it's probably time I rang Dad.

I say this and she crashes her fists down on the table, milk dribbling down her chin. Then she starts screaming, her mouth still full of cornflakes. This is really not my mother's style.

'Don't you *ever* mention him again, he's *taboo* in this house!' she yells. She carries on about him never coming back and how he's out of our lives now. Very dramatic. I thought people only spoke like that in soap operas. Then she crumples in her chair, looking like the lead singer of The Cure, her make-up all smudge and wonky.

I'm a bit knocked out by this, although I try to be cool. I hand her some tissues for her streaming nose, and point out the cornflake on her chin. We both laugh and she hugs me, pressing her soggy face against mine. She tells me that I'm quite sweet really, for a boy.

After that we didn't mention him again. I suppose he was taboo - though I wasn't exactly sure what it meant. The dictionary said it was something forbidden, but my mate Lenny said that it was an African curse or something, too dreadful even to think about. I just didn't get it - that wasn't my Dad! - and we agreed that it was a stupid way to carry on. Afterwards I think: she's just upset and can't think straight yet. I decided to be extra nice to her.

The phone often rang, but I wasn't to answer it. He did write to me - really nice letters - and I hid them carefully. I sometimes wrote back telling him I missed him too, and agreeing to meet when things calmed down. I was a real 'tug of love' child! What would happen if Dad turned up one day to take me away? I imagined them tugging me really hard, Mum trying to drag me inside and Dad trying to pull me out. I could see the headlines: *Tug of Love Leaves 15-Year Old Boy Armless! Will Never Play His Gameboy Again!*

Mum started spending hours trying to give herself a new look. Make-up, haircut - the works. I told her she looked great just as she was. She would just laugh and kiss me, leaving a lipstick print of Max Factor's latest shade on my forehead.

We were really skint, but she still went shopping. She's never buy anything, but she loved to try on really bright, flashy outfits. She's feel them and sigh in an 'if only' sort of way. I'd sigh too; Mum had definitely had a taste by-pass recently, and a style transplant operation was urgently needed. Someone call the Fashion Police! If this was where her image was heading I prayed we stayed skint a bit longer.

The second time her mask slips, we're out shopping again. She's parading in front of a shop mirror in an outfit that looked like someone's sick after overdosing on Smarties. I mean, 'busy' was an understatement, this gear was *frantic.* I suggest - tactfully - that she tries something in just one colour. I say what about green? Dad always said green suited her best, I tell her.

As soon as I say it I want to suck the words back into my mouth. I really didn't mean to mention him, but it's harder remembering this taboo thing when you're out of the house.

And she's off again. The shop is full of people, but there's no stopping her. She's yelling that she doesn't give a shit what colour my father likes best! Then she runs into the changing rooms, and everyone can hear her sobbing. I feel gutted of course, but I'm really embarrassed too. Everyone's looking at me. They must think Dad's a real bastard to make her go all hysterical like that. I want to tell them that he's a great Dad really, and he writes to me loads. But it would take ages to explain, and I'd probably make a real prat of myself. Besides, if I tried that, the men in the white coats would probably take us both away, one nutty woman and her gibbering son. Even now, I go hot and prickly when I think of it.

When she eventually comes out, her face all red and blotchy, the assistant doesn't ask her how she liked the suit, lying in a rumpled heap in the cubicle.

After that, things were ok for a while. Mum was really nice to me, saying she didn't know what she'd do without me. I could get quite used to this adoration. When she was out I'd often rearrange the place, so that she'd return and shriek with delight at the new-look sitting room or cutlery drawer or whatever. She was out a lot these days.

Then she brought Roger home. I didn't know what to say. I'd thought I was doing ok, but she must have thought I'd lost my rearranging flair or something.

Roger was a tiny, balding man, smaller than me even, and would have looked like a dwarf next to Dad. When he spoke he had this nasal whine, but he must have found long sentences difficult, because he grunted a lot.

He was arrogant, too. He really thought he was being helpful by watching telly with us, eating our food, using up our electricity. I wanted to tell him we didn't need him, but he wasn't that open to suggestion. His curl-up-and-die stares at me were full of loathing. Well, what I felt for him was way beyond that.

Mum seemed to like him. I couldn't believe it! How could she fancy such a pigeon of a man? But he made her go all giggly and pathetic. I didn't like to see her like that, so I stayed in my room more.

I worked out from one of her magazines that she was probably 'on the rebound'. From then on I renamed him Roger Rebound, and hoped he'd boomerang back to where he came from.

One afternoon Roger Rebound starts chatting to me. He'd stopped trying to be nice to me after about a week, and only spoke to me if I was blocking his view of the telly, or to ask me to go and get him something, and so leave him alone with Mum. Besides, Grandstand was on the telly, and he hated anyone talking when that was on. Something weird was up.

Anyway, he's making smalltalk about football, and then he asks me if I didn't think she'd been much happier recently. I just smile in a non-committal sort of way, but I'm thinking: bastard! He thinks it's all down to him! He doesn't know my Mum. Just because she laughs it doesn't mean she's happy.

Then he finally says what he's been leading up to. Perhaps - he whines - I should get used to the idea of calling him Dad.

What happened next is still a blur. I hurl abuse, and then myself, at him. Full force.

It turns out that Roger is not the pigeon I took him for. His eyes go all bulgy, and after I hit him a few times he suddenly snaps and lets fly. His iron fists pummel into my head, and eventually I black out...

Roger had rebounded now. He's out of the picture. Mum is sitting on the edge of my bed. She says I showed her the monster in Roger and she's sorry she ever met him. I'm glad he's gone, of course, but I feel really funny inside my head. It's as if Roger Rebound brought some forgotten thoughts back to me. Now they're slotted back into place, like a jigsaw.

I tell her that I think we've probably had enough of monsters. She kisses me tenderly on my ear - the one I liked to hide under my hair. Not that the scars look like cigarette burns anymore, but somehow when they're hidden, it's like Dad never burnt me in the first place, never 'hallmarked' me, as he put it.

I got another letter from him today, and this time I don't hide it or even open it. I cut it into tiny pieces with the scissors Mum's brought upstairs to cut my hair. I've asked her to give me a short back and sides, to get my hair away from my ears. Because I don't want my scars to be taboo anymore. Just the person who did them.

The Visitor

by

Jack Thomas

'Well, well, come in, come in; fancy you coming all this way, it is good of you. Sit there, yes, that's right, that was Doris' favourite chair, most comfortable in the house she reckoned. She used to sit there by the fire, with her knitting or bit of mending, watching the telly and dozing for hours. Bit chilly in here at the moment I know, I was just about to light the fire. I leave it till about now - saves on the coal. It's not too bad usually, but the weather's been a bit nippy all day today. Never mind, we'll be as warm as toast once it gets going.'

'Been a good while since you were in this house last isn't it. Let me see now, you were over for our Jessie's wedding weren't you, yes that's right, seven, no... more like ten years now, eh? You know, time seems to go by quicker when you get older... funny that.'

'How are you keeping now, you're looking well. We did hear, some time ago now it must be, you had to go into hospital. I remember Doris reading the letter out, sitting in that chair she was then... you had to go in for some tests or other, ay, that's right, I remember now, you'd been in for the tests, but everything was all right... yes that was it.'

'Doris had them tests too you know... I don't mean exactly the same as you had but the same sort of thing like, you know.'

'Must be nearly six months ago now...'

'We didn't hear anything for a few weeks, then they wanted her in again, for further tests they said... I never dreamt it was as bad as it was. You don't do you... I didn't think then she wouldn't be coming out again...'

'They did the operation. The doctor said he was hopeful, and she did seem to improve for a while.'

'She was always cheerful you know, but she was worried about me, here on my own like. Forever asking me if I was getting proper food, and was I taking my vitamins... she did worry about that. 'A proper balanced diet is important' she'd say, 'not enough goodness in the food these days, not like years ago.' I told her not to worry, she knew I could do a bit of cooking myself... Jessie called in when she could, and the neighbours were very good. She still worried about me though. Natural enough I suppose, that was the first time we'd been apart since Jessie was born... 'Make sure your clothes are properly aired before you put them on'... that was another thing that bothered her...'

'She was older than me you know, yes, we used to joke about it, two days older she was. We used to have our cards an' that on the proper day like, but if we had a bit of a celebration; you know, a couple of drinks down the pub. They money wouldn't run to a proper meal out or anything like that, not like the youngsters do these days. No, we never had that sort of money to spare, not in recent years anyway... but when we did go out it was always on the day between. You know, she was on the ninth, and I was on the eleventh, so we always went out on the tenth...'

'Daft I suppose, but she always wanted it that way, 'sharing our birthday' she'd say...'

'I should have realised something was wrong a long time ago you know. She used to wince from the pain from time to time, and she'd have to lie down for a couple of hours... 'just my age' she'd say, 'bit of a funny turn that's all, be all right in a minute.'

'It got so she used to go into the spare room some nights. I'd wake up and she'd be gone... 'Didn't want to wake you' she'd say, 'just wanted something for my indigestion'... that's what she said was the trouble, 'just indigestion.'

'Of course in the end she went to see old Doctor Davies. You remember him, been our doctor for donkey's years...'

'Always used to be on his own, but there's a few of 'em up there now. She wouldn't see any of the others though, even the lady doctor, nor the young Indian doctor they got up there now. Brilliant lad they say, diagnosed some outlandish disease in young Timothy Waters, when everybody else said there was nothing wrong with him. Saved the little lad's life you know... but no, it had to be old Doctor Davies for Doris... 'Got nothing against the others' she said, 'but he's always served us well over the years.'

'He sent her in for the tests straight away...'

'Shall I make you a cup of tea, or coffee perhaps, I've got nothing stronger at the minute. I'm a bit afraid to keep anything in the house right now, might get a bit too fond of it; you know. I could easily, but it doesn't help anyway, I've tried.'

'We always used to keep a bottle or two. Doris liked a glass of port now and again, and I'd have a tot of whisky with her... we kept it mostly for visitors though...'

'I never missed a night you know, visiting that is. I'm glad now of course, but it was a bit of a bother I can tell you... I got the bus at the end of the road here into town, got off at the supermarket, then had to walk to the station. You'll remember where that is, must be half a mile; then the bus to the hospital...'

'No, never missed once. There was visiting in the afternoon too, but well, I just couldn't manage it all. She wouldn't hear of it anyway. 'You must get your rest' she'd say, 'can't have you knocking yourself up, or you'll be in here as well. Come when you can in the evening, that will do fine...'

'I wish sometimes they would cart me off too,... but no, I know, that's no way to talk, she'd give me a right telling off if she could hear me sometimes...'

'I would have loved to have visited her in the afternoons as well though, especially if I'd known...'

'We did have a little car for a while you know, yes, her father left it to her when he... er, when he passed on, a few years after the war.'

'I was driving in the army so that was no problem... I did try to teach Doris, but it was no good, we always ended up rowing...'

'We had to get rid of it in the end, couldn't afford to run it. I remember we got sixty quid for it. Lot of money in those days. We sold it to that chap who had the smallholding by the vicarage; you remember him, used to come around with a hand cart in the old days, with fresh veg and eggs and that, that's why he wanted the car; for his round. Kept it going for years. Had a little van later on. Never see him now, supplying the supermarket I expect...'

'We had a good holiday with that sixty quid, went to Bournemouth for a week. Nice little boarding house, not far from the front. Bed was a bit too soft for us I remember, but the food was good. They said that week was the best weather they'd had for years... She did enjoy that holiday, 'so nice to be waited on' she said. But you know, by the end of the week she was helping the landlady with the washing up and that... she never could stand idle when others were struggling to keep up, well, you know what she was like...'

'They sent for me, the hospital I mean... in the end... middle of the day it was... it will be a month now come Friday... I was just sitting down to the fish and chips I'd bought. Only been back from the shop a few minutes, then young Jimmy Wilson was at the door. You know the Wilsons; two doors away, I'd given their telephone number to the hospital, for emergencies like, they were the nearest telephone, and they'd said they would be glad to help; they're very good. Me and old Tom, his father, were mates for years, what with the allotments and that... he's gone now, couple of years ago...'

'Well anyway I was between buses and they'd said it was sort of urgent so I got young Jimmy to phone me a taxi. I was there in half an hour... took me nearly two hours on the bus...'

'She wasn't conscious when I got there. The doctor, very nice young woman, said she'd been talking to her only a couple of hours before, but this wasn't unexpected, often happened in these cases she said... She didn't think she'd come around again... I could wait in the waiting room if I liked, and they would let me know when... when the end was near.'

'They brought me umpteen cups of tea and sandwiches, they were very kind... I'd never liked hospitals, I suppose nobody does really, and until Doris went in I'd never been in this one... I was glad of the tea but I couldn't face the sandwiches.'

'The doctor came to see me about six o'clock, she said I could wait at her bedside... There was nothing more they could do... and it wouldn't be long now...'

'I was sitting at her bedside holding her hand when she finally went... must have been about ten o'clock... funny, I didn't feel a bit tired, just sort of numb... I hadn't slept much for weeks, not since they'd taken her into hospital, but I didn't feel tired... just sat there holding her hand, she looked so peaceful... I couldn't cry... not then anyway, I just felt this numbness, like all this wasn't really happening... I couldn't believe she was gone...'

'I just wish we could have had a last few words... you know, just to say goodbye like...'

'They were very kind at the hospital, took me home with her things, in the ambulance...'

'Pity you couldn't have made it for the funeral... you were one of her favourites you know.'

'Your tea all right, sorry there's no coffee, I'll have to get some in...'

'I've started making lists of things I need, as I think of 'em, like she used to... I'll get used to it soon...'

'I'll never get used to being without her, but, well, lots of people live on their own these days don't they...'

'Jessie said I could move in with them, but I didn't fancy that. Too bloody independent I suppose... Doris always told me so...'

'No. They've got their own lives to lead, haven't they, don't want an awkward old sod like me about the place... no, never could play the beggar at the feast like...'

'Anyway I can manage fine here on my own, Jessie comes over twice a week to do a bit of washing and cleaning, and the neighbours are very good.'

'Can I get you another cup of tea before you go, it won't take a minute...'

'I'm glad you came, it's painful to talk about it, but I know I've got to face the fact that Doris is gone...'

'You will come again I hope; soon...'

'Have a safe journey home... and... thanks.'

The Dishonourable Retirement

by

Eric Morgan

Jack Wilson leaned back in his comfortable leather chair, his hands clasped behind his head and contemplated his position in life.

He hadn't done so badly, he'd had a fairly eventful Army career, ending up as a Captain with an MC and various other gongs, an impressive report from his Regiment, and was well respected as a pillar of local society, and as Chairman of the Community Council.

Now, here he was, Manager of a fairly large Bank in a prosperous market town, very much part of the local business and social scene, and with quite a few local ladies being very interested in what the Mothers Union regarded as a distinctly eligible bachelor.

For bachelor he was, and for the time being quite content to remain so. True he did permit himself a discreet dalliance occasionally when the opportunity presented itself.

You see he had big plans, plans for the future and his present status was just one more step towards his ultimate goal, to rob his own Bank.

Just then there was a sharp rat tat on the door and a head crowned with a mop of bright red hair insinuated itself round the door, it was Tom, Tom Dempsey in fact, his Deputy Manager, an exuberant character, full of life, and a very capable Deputy and personal friend, although outside of business hours they had little in common.

Tom indicated with thumbs up that all was ready to lock up for the long holiday weekend, a normal procedure, and he departed slamming the door behind him.

Jack smiled to himself, he had always wondered why Tom bothered with a wig, everyone knew it was false, but they just accepted it.

Jack himself had been almost bald for years and it didn't concern him one bit.

Poor old Tom he thought, if my plan works out he won't worry for much longer either.

He stood up, straightened his shoulders and walked with a determined stride out into the trading area of the bank, checked that the guard had locked the outer doors securely and gone home, then went down the steps at the rear to where the main gates of the vaults filled the passage from floor to ceiling.

Tom was already standing alongside the huge door waiting for Jack to check that all was well, and to satisfy himself that normal procedure had been observed, they would then close the doors, set the time locks, check the intruder alarms, and finally double lock the steel gates, each with his own special key.

Later that evening the local Constable was patrolling the High Street and as he passed the Bank he noticed that lights were still burning in the main offices.

He was just considering whether he should investigate further when he heard the door being unfastened from inside, for a moment he thought that some intruder had gained entry but he relaxed when he saw the familiar figure of an old friend emerging, carrying a large suitcase.

His old pal turned and saw the Constable and, after a little hesitation said loudly 'Good God it's only you Charles, you scared the wits out of me for a moment, I thought I was being mugged, anyway now you are here you can give me a hand with my luggage, I should have been halfway to the Lake District by now.'

He indicated the car parked nearby and together they loaded the luggage and various obvious holiday gear into the boot.

As the boot lid slammed shut the Constable said with a laugh 'you're not robbing the Bank are you?'

'Of course I am' was the reply, 'but I've left the safe open so that you can help yourself after I go?'

After the car had left the Constable tried the door, found it securely locked and resumed his lonely vigil.

The following day in a small seaside village in Brittany a man alighted from the Paris train and waved to the solitary taxi standing near the exit. He was evidently expected and, after a familiar exchange of pleasantries the man settled down on the back seat while the taxi took him a short distance to a small cottage overlooking the harbour.

On arrival the driver helped his passenger carry his luggage into the hall then departed with his usual large tip.

The man closed the door, looked around him, then breathing a sigh of relief he mopped his bald pate and said to himself, 'I've done it, no more worries now, just a long happy retirement with all the money I shall ever need, and, who knows now that he was living in the village permanently he might be able to persuade the young widow at the Boulangerie to marry him.'

He had already told her he was taking early retirement from his position as Liaison Officer with a large International Organisation and she, and her family seemed to be all in favour of such an alliance.

For a moment he had a qualm of pity for the man lying dead in that vault in England but then he thought 'ce la vie, it was him or me after all was said and done.'

Tuesday morning came and a small crowd of people, mostly members of the staff had gathered outside the Bank waiting to get inside and they were loudly discussing the situation.

The Security Guard was explaining that he had arrived at the usual time but he had seen or heard no sign of life inside.

Someone suggested they called the Police, this was agreed and shortly afterwards a patrol car drew up with a Sergeant and a young policeman inside.

After a brief discussion the Security Guard gave the Sergeant the telephone numbers of the Manager and his Deputy.

When the Police failed to get any answer at either of the numbers the Head Office of the Bank was notified, and soon two Senior Officers arrived with duplicate keys and they entered the Bank, followed by the puzzled staff.

By this time the timing mechanism had activated and they were able to enter the vault without further delay.

The door was opened wide by the visiting officials and as everyone peered through the doorway a gasp of surprise was heard. There in the corner was the body of a man, a man with a ginger wig half off his head, and with an obviously fatal wound.

Someone said, 'it's the Deputy Manager, he's been murdered and the Bank has been robbed.'

But as the Murder Squad carried out body past the waiting staff the blanket covering his face slipped and revealed the face of the Manager, Mr John Charles Wilson.

Sarah's Story

by

M E Carnac

'I've left him, after thirty years. He doesn't care, he comes in late never speaks to me. I've tried so hard, sacrifices, so many of them...'

On and on she went, words tumbling out of her. Words of anger, words she'd dammed for so many years. Did I want to listen? Did I have any choice! She'd turned up on my doorstep in such a state I'd had to let her in. I really wanted a quiet night, I'd had a hard day in work listening to similar problems, I didn't want to be an unpaid social worker at night as well.

Back I came to the monologue, my professional, caring stance suddenly shaken by her words 'I got the farm for him you see - I got it on my back.' I looked at my neighbour in amazement. She had always struck me as an ordinary, homely little woman. I tried not to show my surprise. I must admit that I was now intrigued, but knew that I must not interrupt if I were to know what she was talking about and by now I was very interested indeed.

'Before our Steve was born, it was. Haydn was just the workman then at Maes-y-Parc and we were living in a tied cottage. I was happy then, no real worries - we were pretty hard up but I was used to that. My dad never earned much money, well nobody did then, did they? Well we didn't anyway. I used to help out at Maes-y-Parc quite a bit and enjoyed it. Old Bill, the farmer, was a lot older than us, he must have been well into his fifties. He was a funny sort of man a bit short tempered at times, but he seemed to like me. He'd never married and I thought of him as a confirmed bachelor. In the back of my mind, I thought at first that he was not interested in women - you know what I mean.

She said no more, looking at me briefly then studying the floor. 'I remember Bill,' I said eventually, 'he used to go to the village whist drives when I was young.'

'Did he?' Sarah said, 'that must have been before we came here. He didn't go out much when I knew him. Bill only went to market on Fridays and that was it.' She stopped again.

'Look,' I said, 'I don't want to pry but if it would help to tell me I'll listen. It is my job, I listen to peoples' problems all the time.' Not usually as intriguing as this though, I thought.

Sarah said, 'I forgot that you're a social worker. You must have heard much worse stories than mine, so you won't be shocked.'

'Well, it soon became clear that Bill fancied me. He used to come into the dairy when I was working and accidentally on purpose brush against me. His eyes used to always be on my boobs. You know what it's like. I didn't know what to do, I didn't want to make a fuss, jobs were hard to find and Haydn and me just wanted to get settled. I'd got the cottage coming on nice and wanted to stay there. I didn't say anything to Haydn because I was frightened. But I did sort of drop hints and try to keep near him when Bill was around. I think now he must have realized, must have had some sort of inkling, but we never talked about it. Looking back now, now that I know Haydn so much better, I wonder if he knew all along.'

I said nothing, she was in full flow now and didn't need even an encouraging nod from me.

'Anyway, one day Haydn had gone to get the tractor seen to and Bill and me were alone at the farm. I was in the kitchen making dinner when he came in. I felt myself go all cold but just carried on as usual, hoping he'd just come in for something and would go out again quickly, but he didn't. He just hung around, ruffling through some old papers on the window sill. I thought I'd try to make a bit of conversation, I can't remember what I said, but all of a sudden he came right up to me and grabbed me. I froze, honestly that's the only way I can describe it, I just froze - I couldn't speak, struggle or anything. Bill didn't say anything either. There isn't much to tell, it was over in a couple of minutes. All the time it was happening, I was looking at the bluebottle caught in a web on the beam. It had only just got stuck and was trying so hard to get away. I remember thinking - how sad, it has not got a chance. When he'd finished, he just buttoned up his trousers and left. He didn't say a word. The top button of his trousers was missing, it's funny how little things stick on you mind, isn't it? God, I was so upset, it was awful, like animals. I couldn't understand why I hadn't stopped him. I could have screamed, struggled, anything.'

I couldn't resist interrupting, 'You know, don't you that what you're describing is quite a normal reaction to rape?'

Sarah stared at me. 'Rape,' she said, 'how could that be rape, he didn't force me, I just let him do it?'

'Did you want him to?' I asked quietly.

'No, of course not,' Sarah replied, 'but I was frightened that Haydn and me would lose our house and jobs.'

'Then it was rape, it truly was,' I said, 'because you were forced against your will. Submission doesn't mean consent. He did not ask you if you wanted to have sexual intercourse with him; for whatever reason, he just went ahead. Perhaps he knew that you would be too frightened to make a fuss or perhaps he had such a strong impulse that he did not know how to control it.'

I tried to recall what I knew about Bill Spencer, he had been much older than I and was just a sort of shadowy figure. In fact, from what I could recall he seemed to have very little personality. His conversational skills were very poor and the only time I could remember talking to him was about the weather or something equally innocuous. Even then it had been hard work. I had formed the impression of a man who would have liked to have been sociable but who did not know how. His dress had been consistently drab, rather an unattractive little man. I should think his experience with women had been extremely limited, that is to say non-existent, before Sarah came into his life. Sarah could well have been his first love and his feelings for her too powerful for him to control.

'What would you have said if Bill had asked you?'

Sarah looked at me and I honestly thought that I saw some light dawning on her. 'I expect you've been blaming yourself all these years' I said 'women do, you know. We've been conditioned to feel guilt much more than men.'

'Oh, I've been blaming myself for more than that - what's happened since has been worse. It didn't end there. You see, I was pregnant with Stephen when it happened. I was pretty sure, but I hadn't said anything to anyone. Well a couple of weeks went by with Bill avoiding me like the plague. He looked awful, he'd aged ten years or more overnight. Even Haydn, who wasn't the best at noticing people, remarked on it. He thought Bill must be ill or something and asked what I thought. I didn't say anything. I couldn't - Oh God I wanted to.' Sarah was sobbing now, rubbing her eyes and nose with a tattered tissue. I went upstairs and fetched a box of Kleenex.

'Well, eventually, I had to go to the doctor about the baby. I put it off for weeks because I couldn't bear the thought of a man touching me. I hadn't let Haydn near me either and he was getting very wound up about it. Dr Phillips was a really nice old boy though and he told me straight away that I was four months or more gone. He seemed surprised that I'd left it so long, but I just said I'd missed periods before and he was OK I knew he was right about the four months though and knew that the baby was definitely Haydn's.'

Sarah looked at me, expecting a comment I suppose, so I said 'Well that must have been a relief' knowing full well that there must be more to come.

'Haydn was thrilled - he couldn't contain himself. I begged him not to say anything yet, but he went straight over and told Bill. I stayed at home - I just wanted to hide away. I made the pregnancy an excuse for not going to the farm, saying I felt faint, sick, anything and then one Friday, Bill came to the cottage. I wasn't going to let him in, but the neighbours were in the garden, so I had to. He came, with his cap clutched in his hands. He couldn't look me in the eyes, he just stood there in the hall. I asked him what he wanted, I was so scared. All he said was 'I've left the farm to you and Haydn' and he left.

Well, again I was stuck. I couldn't tell Haydn, so I just kept it to myself. I had two huge secrets burning inside me now.'

Sarah looked at me and I found myself thinking - how would I have coped in her situation? I felt such sympathy for her and now regretted my resentment at her unannounced visit.

She went on in a flat voice 'and then he hanged himself.'

'What' I said 'I mean who? Do you mean Bill?' Why hadn't I known that, it must have happened when I was living in London.

'Yes, he went straight back and did it. Haydn found him in the barn when he went to get some feed for the sheep. I've thought about it so much. I think he must have thought that he was the father of my baby. Do you think he did?'

'Yes, it's quite feasible or maybe it was guilt. No-one will ever know. Had he left the farm to you and Haydn?'

'Yes, he'd been to his solicitor that morning and changed his will. There was a terrible fuss with Bill's family, especially his two nephews, because they'd been expecting the farm. They tried to say he'd been of unsound mind when he changed the will but his solicitor would not have it. They did talk about going to Court, but they never did.'

'And you and Haydn?' I asked.

'Haydn was flabbergasted, but over the moon at getting the farm. He kept saying - why did he do it? and things like that. But do you know, I think he knew. All along I think he knew because ever since he's been queer with me. I don't know how to describe it, but sort of suspicious. When Steve was born he took ages before he would hold him and do you know, I don't think he ever took to him. Steve's gone now, I expect you know that as soon as he was sixteen, he was off.'

'Where is he now?'

'I wish I knew, I think he's living up North, but he never writes. It breaks my heart. Andrew is different mind, he's the apple of his father's eye and so is Alice.'

I'd seen Haydn with Andrew and Alice many times and often been struck by the strong family bond between them. I'd always thought the Taylors a very close family but realized now that I had never seen Stephen with his father. Haydn had always seemed a capable, astute person, who without the benefit of much education could hold his own in any company. He had always seemed devoted to his plump little wife. Perhaps he had depths I had never suspected, obviously he must be a natural actor. I began to wonder what lay behind his good humoured stance. Was he capable of using his wife in such a cynical way or had he just, like Sarah, been carried along by events?

'What are you going to do now?' I asked Sarah.

'I think I'll go to my Mum's for a while, she's nearly eighty but she's very fit. She'll be very upset though at my leaving Haydn, because I am sure she thinks we're OK.'

'Yes, well that's often the way. But I've been wondering, why did you decide to leave today?'

'It's the anniversary of Bill's death tomorrow and Haydn started talking about him, going over and over it as if he wanted me to confess, but I just couldn't. I've never told anyone 'til now, I was just so ashamed. Then he started calling me a slut and a whore and I just ran out of the house. But he was right wasn't he, that's what I am?'

Sarah looked up at me, tears pouring down her cheeks. I just felt angry.

Caroline

by

Beverley Warren

All important people have friends and enemies. The song goes that, after life, only love remains, but Caroline couldn't believe that this is the whole truth. There is hatred too.

She stocked shelves in the local supermarket (not a fun job at the best of times, but there had been nothing else). Caroline knew she was more than that.

I think it's true to say that all children, at some time, have fantasies of being important - a prince or princess kidnapped by the local tinkers and adopted by an unwitting childless couple. Caroline was adopted. Her real mother, coincidentally, also worked in a supermarket; she was thirty five, Caroline was twenty. Caroline's father had died in a car crash soon after Caroline was conceived - at a party; both of her parents were drunk, Caroline's mother so much so that she wasn't absolutely sure who Caroline's father was, but the guy in the accident was as likely as any, if anybody had *really* wanted to know, which they hadn't.

Caroline's adoptive parents were a good ten years older than her mother, and they loved her, but didn't really know her. Nobody really knew Caroline. Nobody really had much chance to. They didn't seem to want to, anyway.

This paints rather a dismal picture of her, but I must stress that she was popular, went out a lot with the people she worked with: danced, drank wine (though she never got as drunk as her mother had - it didn't appeal to her - she knew her limit and stuck to it).

Caroline was a fairly ordinary looking girl: shoulder length brown hair, brown eyes, a smile, really similar to any number of girls you might pass in the street. But one thing separated her from the crowd - she had been a queen, or rather the Empress of Byzantium.

She had read Yeats' poem in school when she was about twelve and had equated her already present feelings with it. She knew that the reason why she wasn't mentioned was because she'd been unfaithful to the Emperor. To her, the poem was a sort of narrative, almost a piece of history. She was Queen of the Birds, Empress of Art and Nature, and the patron of everything pure and beautiful.

Sometimes, when she thought she was alone, Caroline could be observed, walking in a stately manner, nodding and smiling to her courtiers, taking the hand of the Emperor - who, for some reason, bore a remarkable resemblance, in her mind, to Oliver Reed. And sometimes, when even the Emperor and the courtiers weren't there, she flirted with her lover. She didn't have a face for him, except that of an intangible filigreed mask of beauty, and a smile much like her own. He was King of Music and Song, and he was the only person she had ever loved.

As with all tragic queens, her love had been her downfall. The Emperor had had an adviser - more of a spy than an adviser, she reflected bitterly. He was dry and harsh, she had always feared him. He had denounced her and her lover. They had been pierced through the heart on the same spear and died in their last embrace in the tauntingly passionate fire at the stake.

But now, in the returning gyre, she was back to finish what she had started. A dream is only badly-formed reality, life was beginning to start again. The characters were gravitating towards her and, any day, she anticipated their arrival.

The first person to appear on the scene was the Emperor's adviser. On seeing him, she felt a piece of the jigsaw falling into place in her mind. He was the new store detective: Mr P Jones. Jones, when applied to him, became a jarring sound which rattled through the brain hoping for escape. Shoplifting tolls dropped considerably after his arrival.

Caroline could be sure that, whenever she looked over her shoulder, Mr P Jones would be there, with a cruel smile on his face, watching her. The other staff reported similar occurrences, and even the bravest of them couldn't stare him down - one of the check-out boys swore he had, but nobody believed him. However, Caroline also experienced joy at his arrival: the machinery was starting to move.

She started praying at nights, and wore earrings with birds on them for luck - although she was told by the supervisor to take these off because they weren't suitable for work. Hidden under her overall, she still wore her nightingale pendant, and when Mr P Jones was around, she held it tightly in her hand and closed her eyes, her pulse racing.

These days, when she thought about Byzantium, she seemed to be warmed and comforted by a golden haze. Mr P Jones was watching her more.

Work at the supermarket became more and more tiresome, several of her friends left in close succession for other, better jobs. She had given up looking for other work, married, temporarily, to the supermarket because of the omen of Mr P Jones, who seemed to watch her all the time: never criticizing, never smiling, only musing with a frown on his face. Sometimes, she even considered asking him whether he didn't have anything better to do with his time.

One day, she noticed him talking to the supervisor, they were both looking at her, then they looked away. Soon afterwards, the supervisor told her that she was spending too much time day-dreaming, and if she didn't wake her ideas up, then she'd get the sack. The supervisor asked her if she was in love, or something. Caroline smiled and shook her head.

It got to the stage where Mr P Jones could not have watched her any more.

Caroline realised that this time the Emperor was the supermarket. She yearned for her lover to take her away. Her work didn't matter to her at all anymore, the one thing that she cared about was turning over her memories of Byzantium, trying to find out what she'd forgotten to do to set the final wheel in motion. The last piece of the jigsaw was missing.

Sometimes, she almost screamed out loud, 'there's something more, something's missing!'

Then one day, Mr P Jones shattered her life again. He and the supervisor told her that since she was obviously far more fond of daydreaming than of working for the supermarket, they intended to give her more time with her deepest passion. She was sacked.

Caroline walked home, and slowly the golden haze departed.

In Loving Memory

by

Paul Lewis

Frank felt heat beating down on him, but when he looked up he realised the sun cast no shadows in the graveyard.

He straightened painfully, old joints clicking and popping as he used the headstone to lever himself upright. He shrugged his shoulders to ease some of the kinks, and glanced at the sky.

Clouds obscured the sun. No, not clouds... some kind of heavy mist, hanging in the air like smoke. Strange weather for August, Frank thought, glad at least it was dry. And warm - perhaps too warm. He had read that enough exercise to build up a sweat was good for a man; he wondered if the same held true at his age.

'Get on with you, daft bugger,' he said aloud. He looked around quickly, partly out of guilt because he had sworn in a churchyard, mainly out of worry that Vicar Michaels might have passed by just then and overheard his profanity. The coast, thankfully, was clear.

Frank had lost track of how long he had been working on the grave, but if the way he felt was anything to go by, it must have been hours. Time for lunch soon, he told himself, then realised he did not feel hungry. Must be the weather.

Deciding he deserved at least a break, Frank lowered himself to the grass. He sprawled out alongside his wife's grave, resting on one elbow. He ached all over. His doctor told him he should take it easy, but what did doctors know? They had not been able to help Daphne, only diagnose the cancer that killed her.

They let her home to die with dignity, sent nurses to help ease her final days. But it was Frank who carried the burden of her death. She was too drugged to know what was going on. He had held her hand, wiped her face, talked to her even though he doubted she heard.

And now she was gone, it was he who tended her resting place, digging out the weeds, taking away dead flowers and replacing them with fresh. He had nothing else to do.

He felt a sudden, aching emptiness, as if Daphne had taken a part of him with her. He missed her terribly. There were times when he would do nothing but cry countless silent questions to God. Why had she left him? How long must he wait before joining her?

He made himself stop. He knew the answer to the first question; the second would be revealed when the time came. Frank closed his eyes, tried to relax. God help anybody who passed by and saw him. He would look like a corpse, sprawled out in the long grass, surrounded by monuments to death. The thought cheered him slightly.

The village of Bethesda was a good five minute walk away, and the graveyard, surrounded as it was by trees and hedgerows, seemed protected from noise. It was the most peaceful place Frank knew of, and he luxuriated in the silence.

When he opened his eyes, the first thing he noticed was that the strange mist still masked the sun; the second was the young girl who stood motionless, staring at him.

He must have drifted off to sleep at some stage because the path which circled the church was made of loose gravel and surely he would have otherwise heard her approach. Her sudden presence made his heart skip unpleasantly, but she looked more startled than he felt.

'Hello,' he said, sitting up. 'Lovely day.'

The girl said nothing.

'Are you lost?'

Bethesda, in the shadow of the Brecon Beacons, attracted many summer visitors. Perhaps the girl was staying in the camp-site down the road and had lost her way while taking a walk.

'If you're looking for the village, just follow the road,' Frank said, nodding at the gate.

Still the girl failed to answer. She was young, blonde and pretty, but now she looked frightened. Frank hoped he had not startled her.

The girl turned and ran for the gate, and as she went through it she vanished.

Frank blinked. The girl had not turned a corner, or passed behind a tree. She had simply *disappeared.* He shook his head. Had he lain in the heat for too long? Perhaps it was time to go home. The idea was unappealing. There was nothing to go home *for* these days.

No, he would stay a while, work on the grave some more. There were always things to be done.

He picked up the small gardening fork from where he had left it embedded in the sun-hardened earth. Then he crouched and began digging at weeds which seemed to reappear immediately he had cleared them.

As he worked, he glanced idly around the graveyard, secretly pleased that he at least was making an effort. The other plots were in need of repair; the headstone next to Daphne's was so covered in moss and dirt that the name it bore was illegible. Laziness, sheer laziness.

There. The weeds were gone, torn from the ground they had infested and dropped into a pile ready for burning.

Frank straightened, and was struck by a wave of dizziness. His vision darkened and cleared, and he felt an odd sense of dislocation, as if he had been momentarily frozen in time.

The earth covering his wife's remains pulsed and shifted as fresh shoots forced their way through; the pile of weeds he had cleared browned and rotted, the air instantly ripe with the cloying stench of decaying vegetation.

He knew something was terribly wrong. Frank's hand gripped the headstone; it was his anchor in a strange storm. He had a vision of blonde hair and freckles, and then she was there again.

'Who *are* you?' he demanded. The girl remained silent. She stood unmoving on the path and seemed to be looking through him. Was she somehow responsible for the strangeness in the air?

Frank suddenly knew beyond doubt that the child was dead. 'Please,' he cried. 'Leave me alone!'

She continued to watch him in that disconcertingly blank way. Frank felt a great and inexplicable upwelling of pity. If she was dead, then she was a ghost. Unhappy, perhaps lost, and certainly not a threat. It was doubtful she even saw him. The feeling of terror relaxed its grip, and the world returned to normal.

He held out his hands. 'Is there anything I can do?'

He felt stupid. If the poor child could not see him, what made him think she could hear his voice? He took a tentative step forward, and the girl shrank back.

She could see him.

'Don't be scared,' Frank said. 'I won't hurt you. I only - '

Once again the girl spun away from him, began running. This time Frank followed.

Reaching the gate, the girl paused to look back. Then she stepped through the gap in the old stone walls and flickered out of existence. Even though he had seen it once before, the sight still made Frank falter as he pursued.

He waited just inside the gateway, feeling foolish. What if he stepped through and the girl was there, afraid, her disappearance due to nothing stranger than old eyes playing tricks?

He had been so convinced she was dead; now the more he thought about it, the more ridiculous it seemed.

What had come over him? The poor child probably thought him a madman and could even now be running to report his bizarre behaviour to her parents or the police.

He had to find her and explain. *Please don't be afraid. It's my wife, you see... I haven't really been the same since she died...* He hoped the girl would understand.

Frank stepped through the gate, and into emptiness.

There was no country lane, no trees, no fields. There was nothing, an eternity of blackness where Bethesda should have been. The place was darker than the night sky, devoid even of stars. The only sound was a faint sighing, like a wind from far away.

Frank moaned softly and tried to step forward, but an invisible barrier stood in his way. His heart hammered in his chest, and his mouth was dry. He was beyond fear. He simply felt lost and alone.

He turned and walked back through the gate. Feeling the sun on his neck but casting no shadow, he made his way to Daphne's grave. It was overgrown again, choked with weeds and brambles. The plot next to it was equally neglected, its inscription illegible still.

Frank pressed his hand against the cool stone. He picked up his fork and began scraping away the moss and dirt which concealed the details underneath. As he worked he felt the world shrink around him. There were no sounds at all, nor a breath of wind on his exposed flesh. He felt nothing. He kept working at the headstone until it was clear, until the name it bore was revealed as his own.

Together at Twilight-Time

by

Joan M Wilder

20th March 1980

Started work at Twilight-Time Residential Home for the Elderly. It's not really my scene, I've no patience at all, especially at the moment, but I'm desperate. Flat broke. God, it's a huge gloomy place, a great Gothic mansion straight out of 'Night of the Living Dead'. Keep expecting to see Peter Cushing pop out from behind a pillar. Instead - Attilla The Hun - the resident matron. She lurks round every commode, behind every zimmer, like the personification of the misery of Old Age itself. And every night she blows a silly trumpet at teatime. Like the Piper at the gates of Death. Who will still be here tomorrow? Now you see them now you don't. If I was depressed before coming here, this place is like a blast of cold air from the grave. It reeks of Death. Decay and despair hang in the air along with the stench of urine and disinfectant. There should be a placard above the main door - Abandon Hope All Ye Who Enter Here. For this is Journey's End.

In the lounge, they sit propped up, in various stages of semi-consciousness, mouths open, heads slumped on laps, surrounded by false teeth, biscuit crumbs and torn-up tissues. In Sybil's case, it's chewed-up polos. She crunches them, and spits them all over the floor. Or over Mrs Brent who keeps asking if she can go home to see her Mother. No, Mrs Brent, you can't go home, not ever. And she looks up, bemused, with half a sticky polo on her forehead. Then she sits and whimpers, this eighty-nine year old ex-Sunday School teacher who married a Vicar.

27th March 1980

Today, at breakfast, Mrs Powdrill fell off her chair. Matron made a great fuss, false cow, because she'd just made her walk from her room to the Dining Room. Mrs Powdrill is ninety two, blind, and has a chest like a rattlesnake. But she forced her to walk, blasting her verbally the whole way, until Mrs Powdrill peed herself out by the desk. When she crumpled in a pathetic heap of porridge-streaked spectacles and pink beads, under the table, there was a stampede for a wheel-chair.

Wheel them out, wheel them in. Plonk them on commodes, wipe their bums. Feed it in one end, mop it up the other.

'Oh I want to die. Let me die, please God...' wails Mrs Biddulph every moment of every day.

'You can't die today Mrs B, we haven't got time. You'll have to wait, like the rest of us...' And she stands gazing longingly at a vase that could double as a urn, wishing she was in it.

'How's Harry?' Someone asks at dinner.

'Harry died two weeks ago Mabel.' And Mabel drops her meatball on the floor.

'I want my dinner...' she wails, and Harry's memory doesn't stand a chance.

Walter is fiddling again. Twiddling radiator knobs and swatting spiders on the ceiling. When he's on the rampage there's a trail of running taps throughout the building and toilets blocked with Together at Twilight-Time leaflets. He was a teacher once. Now he pees in the sink and in his slippers.

Hylda is throwing peas all over the dining-room.

'Bitch,' she mutters.

'You stink...' to Matron who breezes past oozing charm with a sledge-hammer.

'Pardon, my darling?'

'Arsehole,' she says and laughs maniacally. Quite a culture shock here for anyone with any breeding. Like Mrs Ferneyhough, who pauses in her braggings about her four sons who are doctors and lawyers etc to remove a pea from her tapioca. Her room is filled with sunny grinning photographs of sunny grinning offspring. Offspring getting on with their lives.

20th June 1980

I was right. Went to the Doctor yesterday and I'm pregnant. The worst has happened. I'm forty years old for God's sake, what a mess. Gerry doesn't want to know. Saw him last night and he wants me to get rid of it. If I don't he'll scarper, back to Helen. Bastard. They're all bastards. I don't know what to do.

It's catching you know, the indifference here. I, too, am beginning to find the old buggers insufferable. They're so selfish. Buzzers going every five minutes. Nurse! Nurse! Get me on the commode, get me off the commode. Toilet please. Teeth please. Scratch my back. I've dropped a grape. Give me a pill. Give me lots of pills... My back aches, they're so heavy. My leg aches.

25th June 1980

Today while I was up in the old wing I saw Mrs Nelson. Well, she was in that room anyway. She's so pathetic, creeping about with huge haunted eyes and a withered leg. And so thin... She gave me quite a start when she came out from behind a screen, reminded me of the mad woman in Jane Eyre. She said a peculiar thing. She said: 'Don't do it. *Please* don't do it. Go through with it, before it's too late...'

'Don't do what?' I said, and she said:

'You know. You're in a terrible dilemma aren't you?' She gave me the creeps, because she seemed to know.

28th June 1980

Bert's birthday today. He sits, eyes unseeing - little black beads like a goldfish, surrounded by one card. A huge card - *To a Very Dear Dad.* Oh very dear I must say. And a stupid verse about wishing him a wonderful year ahead of happiness and good health and all his dearest dreams coming true. What a ridiculous irony. Bert dribbles all over it and his nose runs onto his cake.

I keep seeing Mrs Nelson. At the end of corridors and in dark little alcoves. She jumps out on me and says eerie things like: 'This is your last chance dear... don't kill her. Don't kill Emma.' And then today: 'I nearly had a baby once. But I killed her. And look where I am now... I didn't want to give up my life. I was so selfish. And now I'm all alone... Don't do it.'

I went downstairs white and shaking, and then Julie scared me even more. She said Mrs Nelson had died two years ago. Come to think of it, I haven't seen her downstairs at all.

I've seen a ghost. Mrs Nelson is a ghost. And she's trying to tell me something.

30th June 1980

I've made up my mind. I'm going to do it. I mean, you give up your life, your job, your independence, your freedom - and Gerry. I'll lose him if I keep it. And for what? Look what happens to you. All these people here, dumped by their kids.

20th July 1980

There. It's done. All over. Two days in a cold clinical place on a conveyor belt of frightened women. All gone. Now nothingness, emptiness. Remorse, self-reproach. I didn't bargain on feeling like this.

25th August 1980

Left Twilight-Time today. I'm upwardly mobile now. Nothing to hold me back now, I'm moving on. Saw Mrs Nelson once more last week. She was sad, very sad. She kept saying:

'Buffy killed Emma. And now she's alone, all alone.' Poor old sod. Must have had a miscarriage years ago.

1st October 1980

Gerry's left me anyway. Gone back to his wife. Never mind, I've got a new job now. And a future. Once I've had the operation on my leg and got it fixed. I still think about... you know. There's an emptiness there. A numbness. I wonder if she would have had blonde hair, my little Emma? Now why did I think of that name?

28th June 2010
Saw Mrs Nelson again today. After thirty years, she's returned to Twilight-Time. Only she's not Mrs Nelson after all. She's Buffy. And I'm looking at her now. Looking at the straggly hair and Belsen-like arms. And she drags her left leg behind her.

She has no sunny grinning photographs in her room. She has no pictures of Emma who dumped her. Because Emma didn't dump her. She wouldn't have... if she'd been born.

She's just seen a ghost. A ghost of a forty year old Care Assistant with a mind in turmoil.

'Don't do it Buffy...' she breathes. 'Have your baby before it's too late.'

But *I'm* Buffy aren't I? And it *is* too late. For *I'm* the ghost, not her. The ghost from her future.

The mournful whine of a silly trumpet wails down the hall. Teatime. Together at Twilight-Time. I live here now you see.

I look into those cold haunted eyes in the mirror and I think: I nearly had a baby once. But I killed her... and look where I am now.

Changes

by

J Woosnam

Roger turned off the motorway and on to the familiar 'B' road. As he drove past the Primary School he had attended in his youth, he sighed heavily.

In ten minutes he would be at his Father's house, but in what condition would he find him? It was his recent concern for his Father that had prompted him to make the three hour journey.

His Mother had passed away fifteen years previously, and after the initial shock and grief that followed the bereavement, his Father had settled into life as a widower. He had slowly regained his zest and returned to his favourite hobby of bowls. He had an active mind, and kept his interest in current affairs.

Although insisting that he did not wish to intrude in Roger's family life, he always took an interest in their activities. He worshipped his grandchildren Laura and Peter and was usually persuaded to spend a fortnight each year at Roger's home.

Roger was proud of the way his Father had adapted to his new lifestyle, and pleased that even as the years passed he never used phrases like 'I'm ready to go any time now' or 'It's time they shot us old one's' as some of his friends parents did.

Lately however, things had changed, his letters had stopped, and Roger could not get a reply when telephoning. On the odd occasion his Father had answered the phone, he had seemed impatient and eager to finish the conversation.

He had told Roger that he had not written because he had nothing to say. 'Not even your latest bowls tournament Dad?' Roger had enquired, but his Father had muttered quickly, 'I haven't played bowls for a few weeks.'

Roger, hiding his anxiety, ended the call casually, but decided to make an unannounced visit at the weekend.

He turned into Bartholemew Road and brought the car to a stop outside number six. He got out and opened the garden gate.

He wished that his heartbeat hadn't quickened, as he wanted to appear as natural as possible. He knocked on the door and waited. There was no reply, he knocked again, still no reply. Worriedly he reached in his pocket for his key. He opened the door stepped into the hall and called out. There was no answer, his mouth became increasingly dry, his palms were perspiring as he imagined the sight that could befall his eyes.

The search proved fruitless, and he moved onto the garden. Still no sign of his Father.

Mr Sullivan, the next door neighbour was watering his roses and looked over the fence.

'Hello Roger, looking for Dad?'

'Yes I'm surprised he's not here, although he didn't know I was coming.'

'I saw him go out about twenty minutes ago,' said Mr Sullivan.

'Do you know where he was going?' Roger asked, straining to look unperturbed.

Mr Sullivan put down his watering can and walked purposely toward the fence. As he came closer a frown formed on his face.

Rogers heart quickened again.

'To tell the truth lad, I've been a bit worried about him this last month or so, sometimes he seems in a trance. He goes out most days but never says where, I know it's not to the green as he never takes his bowling bag.'

'I've been concerned myself Mr Sullivan,' Roger said no longer hiding his distress, 'that's why I came today. I think I'll go and look for him.'

'Yes but where?' asked Mr Sullivan.

'I don't know, but I can't hang around fretting,' said Roger.

'Well all the best lad.' Mr Sullivan turned back to his roses. Then abruptly looked up again. 'It might be a long shot Roger, but last weekend he mentioned what a lovely view there is, from the old railway bridge. You could try there.'

Roger nodded his agreement and went back into Bartholemew Road.

Out on the pavement he began to run. His dry throat and perspiring hands had returned, and were now accompanied by wobbling legs and a mind that swirled with unpleasant thoughts. Why hadn't he said he was unhappy? Perhaps he'd discovered he was seriously ill. What if he planned to do something silly? His head thumped. He hadn't realized he was almost at the bridge. Totally exhausted, he had to stop. He leaned against the wall and bent forward trying to regain his breath. He took several deep gulps of air and slowly raised his head.

He blinked, then blinked again, falling back against the wall he heaved a huge sigh of relief, he had found his Father, but he was not alone.

He was sitting next to a lady of about the same age. His arm draped around her shoulder. They both looked relaxed and happy. The lady was talking animatedly, his Father listening and smiling.

Roger took a couple of backward steps, he was smiling but didn't wish to be seen.

The reason for his Father's strange behaviour, was now wonderfully apparent.

He would let him divulge his secret in his own time.

The Love of Pinocchio

by

David Jones

Four women, clad in black, stood weeping at a row of white marble tombs in an Italian village cemetery. Although sharing a common grief their reasons for such grief were quite different...

The garish midday sun hung in a cloudless azure sky, scorching the deserted narrow streets of grubby, uniform whitewashed cottages each with their faded orange terra-cotta roofs. Shimmering in the heat haze the countless vineyards and olive groves which spread out like a patchwork quilt over the distant lowlands took on an almost mirage quality. It was siesta time in the tiny Southern Italian village of Taresia.

Luigi Lavarello, permanent smile on his face, peered through the hanging bead curtain into the gloom of a dingy bar known to locals as La Canteena. Dressed in a grey gabardine suit two sizes too big, the jacket of which framed an expansive flowery necktie, he sauntered into the almost deserted bar.

Passing the rows of empty tables he made his way towards a group of teenagers huddled around the jukebox.

'Hi, gang.'

Having already eyed his entrance with distain the group of youths engrossed in the pounding out of the latest American rock and roll beat, deemed it unnecessary to acknowledge his arrival. Finally though, one of the group glanced up and spat out a contemptuous greeting.

'Well if it isn't our very own village idiot, Pinocchio.'

'Hiya Toni. Guess what I've been doing this morning, helping Mama to make the wine.'

Toni Patruccho, self-elected leader of the gang of village youngsters revelled in his role as arch tormentor of the little man. While others chose simply to ignore the widow woman's simple son, Toni seized every opportunity to ridicule him.

'Big deal bird brain. Well listen, while you've been getting pips between your toes you've missed the arrival of the lovely Angelica.' He nodded towards a young girl measuring out a Millefiori behind the bar.

'Hey, Angelica, meet Luigi, otherwise known as Pinocchio because...' he paused and stubbed a finger towards the little man's face '... of this incredibly big nose of his.'

The girl looked up and smiled. As her flashing dark brown eyes met Luigi's gaze the little man's heart thumped.

'Give him a coke will you?' Toni continued. 'D'you know he spends half of his life in here, yet has never been known to buy a drink.'

Luigi still staring at the dark-haired beauty behind the bar, stepped back and attempted to hoist his small frame onto a nearby stool. Crash! The little man overbalanced and fell backwards sending the stool spinning across the sawdust covered floor. Immediately hoots of derision rang out. Of all the teenagers, Toni laughed longest and loudest. Amid the cacophonous jeering and laughter Angelica's plea on behalf of the little man went unheard.

'Good old Pinocchio! Go on do it again,' Toni urged.

Luigi still spreadeagled across the bar floor grinned and picking himself up proceeded to mimic his previous pitiful antics. Unable to contain her embarrassment Angelica's face flushed with anger.

'Stop it, stop it!' she screamed, 'why don't you leave the poor man alone. You ought to be ashamed of yourselves, especially you Toni.'

An uneasy silence descended on the bar.

'I'm sorry, Toni,' pleaded Luigi, 'did I do wrong?'

Fixing the little man with a stony glare Toni snarled, 'you're pathetic!' and stormed out.

Some days later Luigi seeing Toni in the piazza, called after him excitedly.

'Toni, Toni, where've you been?'

'Look Pinocchio, I'm in a hurry,' snapped Toni, 'what is it?'

'I've got a secret to tell you, but first you must promise not to tell anyone. Promise?'

'Yeh, yeh, promise, what is it?'

'I'm in love Toni. I love Angelica and I think she loves me. She always talks to me and yesterday she said I was cute. I want to marry her Toni, I want to marry her.'

A faint trace of a smile fell on the youth's face.

'That right? Well listen, I shouldn't be telling you this Pinocchio, but yesterday when I was in the bar, Angelica told me of all the men in the village she found you the most attractive.'

Luigi's face beamed.

'Really?'

'Really, in fact, don't tell her I told you this, but she said she'd like to take you to bed.'

To the despair of his elderly mother, Luigi began neglecting his chores and took to spending every available moment at La Canteena. Propped up against the bar for hours at a time he gazed longingly at the girl of his dreams. At first he was happy to be rewarded with a kind word and a smile that melted his heart. Eventually though with Toni's words still ringing in his ears, he became bolder. Overcome by desire he blurted out, 'Angelica, I love you, I know you love me, can't we go upstairs together?'

Repulsed by the little man's suggestion of a night of passion, Angelica burst into tears.

'You pig,' she sobbed, 'how could you think I was that sort of girl? Get out of here, I never want to see you again.'

'I'm sorry, I'm sorry,' the bewildered Luigi cried, 'I didn't mean to upset you, I would rather kill myself than hurt you.'

He continued to beg her forgiveness with such sincerity that the kind-hearted girl relented and forgave him. Firm friends again, he resumed his bar-side vigil, gazing yearningly and chatting incessantly. When he told how beautiful she was, she would smile and when he talked of marriage, she would just laugh it off. Eventually however, his persistence again became too much and one day she left the job at La Canteena, never to return.

When Angelica's disappearance became know around the village, Toni confronted the distressed Luigi.

'Decided to do away with her did you Pinocchio? And all because you couldn't have your wicked way.'

Not suspecting he was again the butt of one of Toni's cruel jokes, Luigi hysterically pleaded his innocence.

'No, no! I loved her, she was my fiancee, we were to be married.'

Already distraught by the girl's disappearance, Luigi now became guilt ridden by the cruel allegations of the accusing Toni. He moped around the village talking of the fiancee that had left him to anyone who would listen.

The following day, unable to contain his grief any longer he stormed into the village police station. The bewildered officers looked on as the little man screamed, 'I'm going to kill myself. I can't go on living without my beloved fiancee Angelica, I can't go on without her.'

'So, poor Pinocchio has been jilted eh?' mocked one of the police officers, 'perhaps she didn't want a half-wit for a husband. Now stop wasting our time and be on your way home to your mother.'

'But you don't understand,' cried Luigi, 'nobody understands, I've got feelings. I loved her don't you see?'

The officers looked on in horror as suddenly he tore open his jacket to reveal pockets stuffed with sticks of dynamite. Warning them not to try and stop him he ran out of the police station. Outside, pausing momentarily, he turned and glanced through tear-filled eyes towards La Canteena.

'I'll show them,' he muttered, 'and her too.'

Sobbing uncontrollably he continued to make his way down the main street leading out of the village.

Fearful that the little man might just be crazy enough to carry out his threat, two officers were sent to disarm him at the first opportunity. On the outskirts of the village, thinking the time was right, the two policemen pounced. In the ensuing struggle Luigi, hand pressed firmly inside his jacket, broke free. Stumbling to make his getaway he took but two faltering steps. The peace of the village was rocked by an explosion which shook it to its very foundations.

And so, at the tiny cemetery, four women wept. One was Luigi's mother who had loved her son throughout his tortured life. Two were the widows of the policemen killed in the blast and the fourth was Angelica, who wept for the simple man she could not love.

Untitled

by

Samantha Dow

Closing time. The large inn doors slammed shut behind him, kicking out the lingering few that had refused to take heed of the last order bell. He pulled the collar stiffly up around his neck and dug frozen fingers into the comfort of fur lined pockets, nodding his goodbyes to the stumbling couple laughing their way down the street.

The hushed breeze rushed through the waving leaves and raced up to the mount to kiss the dark, sombre sky. Its icy breath embraced his cheek and he shuddered further into his jacket. He had stayed too late, should have been home over an hour ago but time had slipped greasily by and besides, he had no reason to return to the cold, lonely house that held nothing more than a few distant memories and the lingering smell of cheap perfume. His life had been a wasted one and it always looked worse though the bottom of an empty pint glass.

He stumbled up the kerb, his head reeling with brief disorientation. Somewhere in the distance an alley cat mewed pitifully on the back-yard walls accompanied with a curt yell of protest. It scampered away with a cymbal overture of dustbin lids.

Silence, and with it came despair.

The temperature suddenly dropped a couple of degrees and the wind picked up a howl. The head of the statue was just visible through the curdling mist and with some knotting dread he realised he would now have to pass it, have to brush past the toeless feet and look up once more to a crumbling face that had aged into a menacing leer.

The mist congealed low over this area of town, inexplicably so but had done for centuries and was not questioned anymore. Children, out late at night played chicken down this lane, daring adrenalin high action men to run blindly to touch the statue then pound back to the safety of warm cosy fires and patiently waiting parents.

His house had no open fire to run back to and no one to worry should he be late. He had to walk down this lane now, alone. Had to pass that dominating, toeless, fingerless, hollow-faced statue that had been beaten with the cruel winds of time and should he look up, see the over-enlarged pits where the eyes once saw and the slithering crack across the originally welcoming smile transform into a sinister grimace.

He hesitated. The wind was biting into his face, mocking his welling fear and suddenly sharpening his dulled senses. It was ten minutes to home, he could even count the steps. Eyes were drawn magnetically upwards and the slow recognition that it was watching him sent an icy bolt up his spine.

He wished he had never accepted that last pint, wished he had never set foot in the pub and he wished hard that he hadn't so foolishly embarked upon this route. Still, it was only a lane, a lane with a myth and weren't myths a product of an over-active imagination?

With a cannon ball in his stomach and the blood rushing in his ears he began to count towards the old turnpike, a welcoming landmark.

It grinned.

Slow reluctant steps echoed against the dewy wall. His feet kicked up the groping fog and he softened his breath so as not to hinder his sense of hearing. The cold had invaded the warmth of his coat and his fingers felt raw in the arctic depths of his pocket. From somewhere behind he sensed the glare burn into his back.

Eyes directly down, skimming the cobbles as his feet stretched over them, an awareness of another presence invaded the loneliness and his pace quickened. Step twelve, step fourteen, not far to the end, step fifteen. His feet stumbled, tumbled, falling through space, his head reeled and with a sobering thump he hit the ground, watery spray covered his face.

He cursed himself at his idiocy. Had to take it steady, no rush. Slowly clambering to his feet he cautiously checked behind him. Nothing, just the shadowy outline of the wall and the knowledge of the tall monstrosity now blanketed by the thickening gloom. His superstitious imagination saw it leap to life, his nervous stare saw nothing.

Footsteps counted briskly, the tip of the turnpike was just visible and he could feel the tension relax in his stomach, not far now, not long until he was into the light. The streetlamps had banished the despair, the fear and the night crawlers would soon shine gloriously above him.

The hair on his neck bristled. Something moved, scuttered in the corner of his eye. Something was behind him, something was shuffling, following him. Numb fingers clenched and his breath was shakily drawn inwards.

Step twenty two, no step twenty eight, he'd lost count, his pace was too fast. Ears as sharp as a hounds he took in every decibel of noise trembling irrationally when he heard the distinct sound of feet upon cobbles. The footfalls shuffled faster as he increased his speed, background to his hackney gait. His stomach knotted, his breath became laboured, he could feel eyes bore into his back, sightless eyes that would twinkle as the crack smiled and he knew that those long fingerless arms would reach stonily out to touch him if he should...

Light.

Never had a yellow bulb seem so welcoming, its glow melted the mist as it reached out with ethereal rays. He felt relief as it hit him and he turned down into the terraced row that was blacked out for the night. Civilisation, modern amenities, legends didn't exist in a world of megabytes and catalytic converters. He could calm down now, the effect of the alcohol had given him a rough ride and he would laugh about it in the morning when the sun would rise to extinguish all shadowy creatures.

But it was dark. Still had to make the last leg home. He wasn't safe yet, he knew it wasn't afraid.

Slow, soft, muffled shuffling invaded the quiet.

His stomach lurched. It was following him, wanting him. He yearned to run but numbing limbs failed to respond, desolate to spirit to the house and outpace this thing, he needed so badly to get away from it.

Street-lamps mocked him with their false sense of security, their brightness only blurred his vision. Twice he stumbled carelessly over a raised flagstone and twice he heard it laugh. Couldn't walk any faster, he was running out of breath, the drink in his stomach had turned to acid and his head thumped violently.

It was gaining ground, louder, closer, nearer.

Fear took a long rein in his head and it reared out of control. Unable to cry out he beat his hands wildly above him trying to distract it, to drown out the monotonous, steady slide of each threatening step.

The acrid smell tweaked his nostrils. It was right behind him, he could feel the coldness, the dampness of the earth on its breath and the musty odour that surrounded its decaying form. He could feel each putrid sigh raise the tiny hairs on his neck. His shoulder quivered and he knew that heavy fingerless stump of a hand was beckoning him around.

Feet stopped dead.

Slowly, with growing foreboding and curiosity he was compelled to turn, to face what monstrosity awaited him, to understand the true meaning of fear pounding in his heart.

He spun around. He stopped. His mind numbed and from the wide open jaw came the hiss of a miscarried scream. It was selfishly whipped away by the billowing wind and drawn forever in amongst the gloating, churning fog.

The Visitor

by

Enid Phillips

The house is still standing.

People live in it, and as far as I am aware, nothing spooky or untoward happens there. But it did.

It happened to me...

I remember the wind.

A high shrieky wind that whipped indifferent grizzly rain to a blind fury against my bedroom window panes.

I remember too, my small son. Fretful, croaky voiced.

'I'm hot Mummy. My throat hurts. My chest feels tight.'

'I know it does darling.'

Propping him up, I wipe the perspiration off his flushed face. I measure linctus on to a spoon.

'Here drink this sweetie. It will chase that horrid cough away.'

He gulped the medicine down. Grimacing as he swallowed. Fever had increased his thirst.

'Can I have another drink please Mum?'

He drank deeply from the glass that I held for him.

'Thanks Mum.'

I tucked him in and made him comfortable.

Keeping my voice cheerful, reassuring, to mask anxiety and bone weary fatigue, I said, 'Goodnight son, you will sleep soundly now until morning.'

I returned to my room and to my warm bed.

The night settled in to a pattern of restless tossing and turning, coupled with frequent trips to minister to my sick child.

I recall that first light was seeping through the windows. I lay wide awake stubbornly resolving not to respond yet again to a renewed bout of coughing from my son. This time I was staying put, determined to get some rest, some sleep, before beginning a new day.

The wind howled on.

Gradually I became aware of a drop in my room's temperature. A bone chilling numbness spread through my limbs.

Why was I cold? Was it because I was tired? Had the heating failed?

My limbs began to twitch. I clenched my teeth to stop them chattering. The room became colder and colder. Suddenly I saw her framed in my doorway. Who was she? What was she?

As she entered my room she brought with her such intense cold and terror that I was rendered incapable of movement, or coherent thought.

The lady had a pale luminous complexion. Her face was oval shaped with high cheek bones. The lips were set, unsmiling. Her eyes were dark pools of shadow. Snow white hair was arranged high on her head. Her hands were pale, clasped waist high in front of her. She wore a long dark gown with lace set over a high necked collar. The gown was fastened at the neck by a large brooch, possibly a cameo. I could not see her feet.

Her gaze was fixed, purposeful, looking straight ahead not at me.

Only my eyes moved, monitoring her slow seemingly eternal progress across my room. The woman glided past the bed, deigning not a glance at the frozen mortal that was me.

On reaching the wall she disappeared through the closed doors of my airing cupboard, only to reappear almost immediately, arms outstretched before her. They bore a ghostly burden, for she held in thick neat folds, a blanket. A blanket made from deep gray shadows. Soundlessly, she glided once more past my bed.

Crossing the room she went out of the door and turned towards my son's room. On her departure warmth returned, coherent thought became possible. Fear for my son overrode every other emotion.

Swinging numb limbs out of bed, slipperless, gownless, I hastened to his room. There was no trace of my visitor, or her ghostly blanket. Only the curtains flapping in and out, through wide open windows. My son lay fast asleep, still coughing. His bare chest exposed to the icy blast, his pyjama jacket, together with the bed clothes, lay in an untidy heap on the floor.

Visitor forgotten, I set quickly to work restoring warmth and order to my son and the room. As I worked it began to dawn on me that had the lady not jolted me out of bed, the consequences to my feverish son might have been disastrous. Was she his guardian angel? Or mine?

I shall never know, for I have never seen her since.

Incidentally, my son had opened the windows and shed his clothes, to cool off. I may also add he suffered no ill effects and recovered fully...

Tunnel of Love

by

Gordon Haines

Manfred stopped digging as footsteps sounded above his head. He lay perfectly still as he had no way of knowing whether the Border Guards would use the listening equipment they sometimes brought with them. After what seemed like a lifetime, he could hear them moving on, their muffled steps receding into the distance. Manfred breathed a sigh of relief and resumed his task. Two hours later, exhausted and hungry, he rested a while before dragging himself tortuously back to the tunnel entrance in West Berlin. Emerging from the allotment shed that provided cover for his covert operation, he dusted himself down and wearily made his way home.

As he walked along, he wondered how much longer all this would take? Should he allow others to share the task? Although the tunnel would be dug more quickly, could he risk the possibility of someone informing for a substantial reward? He was still mulling these thoughts around in his mind when he reached home, had a meal, and fell asleep. Upon waking, he still dwelt on these factors and decided to analyse the situation and reach a conclusion.

Firstly, speed was of the essence. He dearly wanted to be reunited with his beloved Hannelore, his girlfriend, and he was determined that the child she was expecting was not to be born in the East. That gave him four months to complete the task, and with forty metres still to go, there was no way he could complete the project unaided. There was nothing for it, he had to involve others. He suddenly remembered. A couple of his student friends had idly talked about tunnels to freedom. Would they be still interested? Would they inform? Since theirs would be an ideological motive, he could discount the latter. The idea grew in his head and all manner of things flashed before him. Perhaps a shift system of digging! In which case a ventilation arrangement would have to be devised to cope with the extra demand for air. His existing air holes, sufficient for one, would hardly be adequate for sustained excavation. Then there was the problem of a higher volume of soil. His present method consisted of filling sacks and hauling them behind him at the end of his stint. Shoring of the tunnel? Provision of lighting? These and other details continued to dominate his thoughts until that evening when he was able to resolve them at a meeting with his friends.

In a quiet corner of the Cafe Kranzler, now relocated in West Berlin, the three young men talked in subdued tones. By the smile on Manfred's face it was obvious that things were going well. His engineering student friend Helmut was enthusing about installing trunking, worked by bellows, to act as a ventilation system and since the tunnel needed support, he envisaged a rail arrangement whereby soil could be removed as it was dug. In return for this expertise, Helmut and Gunther wanted to bring their relatives out through the tunnel. Manfred readily agreed, but baulked at the idea that to pay for the materials and equipment required to complete the project, they allow 'fee-paying' passengers.

'Security, what about security?' Manfred interrupted, 'You know the Stasi are everywhere.'

One of his friends said quietly, 'If we vet them religiously, the secret police won't know about it.'

Manfred was unimpressed. He'd heard tales of members of families being set against each other, friends and workmates mistrusting one another and so it went on. In short, no-one could be trusted. He even began, in his mind, to question the loyalty of those he was seated with. Had they changed their political outlook? Had the 'Cold War' got to them? Were they stooges for the Stasi? He had to think! He rose quickly, telling them that it was his tunnel and he had to think about it. He announced that he would let them know the following evening.

In bed that night, Manfred tossed and turned agonising over his decision. He so wanted the tunnel to be completed, yet he couldn't risk treachery. The possibility of imprisonment or even being shot was the penalty for trying to escape the GDR. Had he the right to subject his beloved Hannelore to these consequences were the escape attempt to be discovered? He racked his brains to think of another method of freeing his loved one, but discounted them one by one, for was not the museum at 'Checkpoint Charlie' full of successful, and more ominous, unsuccessful ideas. No, it was the tunnel or nothing. He resolved to tell his friends that with adequate safeguards he would agree to 'passengers' in order to finance the venture.

Over coffee in the cafe, Manfred was stipulating what was to qualify people to join in the escape. 'They must have no family left in the East so no pressure can be brought to bear upon them in the event of discovery of our plans. Also, every effort must be made to enquire into their background. Anything that might make them or us vulnerable must be unearthed.' Finally, satisfied that he had taken every step to ensure the safety and success of the operation, Manfred left his friends to contact with the utmost discretion the families wishing to flee and to arrange for the requisites to speed their burrowing.

Now that the tunnel was to be completed 'professionally', Manfred decided to switch his attention to the escape planning itself. Having already routed the tunnel to emerge in a shop cellar without the knowledge of the occupants, he had to check that no change of ownership had, or was about to occur. This entailed having to take extraordinary steps to elicit the information so as not to arouse suspicion. The activity of the 'Grepos' - the Border Guards, was intense, and were a building to become unoccupied, a thorough search was undertaken.

Over a period, Hannelore, in a series of coded letters, was able to convey to Manfred information concerning the cobbler's shop in a street adjoining the border. It appeared that the owner, a bachelor, was elderly and had no apparent family. When Hannelore told him that Herr Schmidt also had a flat for rent, he was exultant.

'Move in within a few days and I will come and visit you to make some final arrangements,' Manfred enthused in his secret code. As a citizen of West Berlin he was permitted to make periodic day-time twelve-hour visits. He could say so much more during the time they were able to spend together than in many censored letters.

Once having moved to the flat, Hannelore started to do chores for the old man and therefore had the run of the house. It seemed that her landlord never used his basement so she was able to store her spare furniture there as a cover for their later nefarious activities.

The tunnel was progressing well. By now equipment had been acquired and, by Manfred's reckoning, only a month away from completion. His friends had been fortunate in obtaining 'sponsors', and it was simply a matter of time. Manfred, able to leave the tunnelling to others, devoted his time solely to the detailed planning necessary for 'F' for Freedom Day.

Eleven persons were to attempt the escape and Manfred's plan was for them to meet at Hannelore's over a period of several hours to avoid arousing suspicion. To obviate last-moment problems, Manfred decided to interview all involved, vetting them personally, and to explain in detail what was required of them. Some of the mothers didn't like the idea of their younger children having to be sedated. He also had to test each of them for claustrophobia. Luckily, no-one failed. It had to be impressed upon them, positively no luggage, only what could be carried upon the person. Manfred gave a wry smile at this last demand, for he knew that human nature being what it is, some would want to bring the kitchen sink. Dark clothing of dungaree type was specified, and after a host of minor details had been examined, Manfred was satisfied.

With only a few days to go, the problem of Herr Schmidt was the only one remaining. So far, he had no inkling of the situation. What to do? Involve him in the escape bid and seek his co-operation, or drug him? Manfred was in a quandary. Upon due deliberation, he sought the views of Hannelore.

'I couldn't possibly see Werner drugged, I've got to know him so well. What if we were to get the dose wrong? Let's find out, in a roundabout way of course, what his politics are.'

Manfred's face was impassive. 'We've got to be so very careful, any hint about what's going on before we're sure of him and we would jeopardise the whole thing.'

After much consideration, they reached the conclusion that they had no alternative. Gently, they gradually probed until it became obvious that he was decidedly anti-Communist.

Having been taken into their confidence, he convulsed with laughter when told about the knock-out drops.

'That would have destroyed my faith in human nature, if that's possible in this miserable existence of ours,' their friend Werner exclaimed.

The last hurdle surmounted, Manfred went home singing for tomorrow was 'F' Day.

The breakthrough happened on schedule, and as Werner Schmidt was no longer a threat, the escapees were positioned in various rooms. Although having been warned about excess baggage, many had parcels and bundles of possessions. Manfred thought it prudent not to deprive them of these until the last moment, so as not to upset the elderly of them.

As 'Captain of the Tunnel', Manfred was the last to leave. Taking one last look around the now empty cellar, he shook hands with and thanked the cobbler profusely. Cocking his pistol, he disappeared into the entrance. Some way into the darkness Manfred found his passage inexplicably blocked. Frantically, he clawed at the earth in all directions, but to no avail. Some tremendous weight had caused the tunnel to collapse, but Manfred would never know the reason. Minutes later he would be dead. That day, for the first time as protection against trigger-happy escapers, the Grenze Polizei had introduced armoured vehicles into 'No Man's Land'. A wheel had compacted the tunnel at its only weak spot. Manfred backed out laboriously to be confronted by a knot of 'Grepos', their guns levelled. Foolishly drawing his own pistol, Manfred was cut down in a hail of bullets. Werner had the gruesome task of identifying his lifeless body. The next day, the Ninth of November, 1989, the Berlin Wall came down.

The Dawnless Morning

by

Graham Binning

The alarm clock bounced about on the bedside cabinet as usual this morning. I struggled to remove my legs from under the duvet, it was not as easy as it should have been. Sitting on the edge of the bed trying to rub the sleep from my eyes with the heel of my hands I was swaying about as if drunk yet I'm tee-total.

Suddenly I was wide awake. Something was wrong here, something was very wrong indeed.

I grabbed the clock and stared at the hands. Seven o'clock but it was still dark. As it was well into the second half of May it should have been bright especially in my bedroom which was to the east.

Reaching for the curtains was difficult. What's happened to my co-ordination, I thought. Peering out of the window all I could see was darkness, not a light anywhere. 'It's an eclipse of the sun,' I told myself. 'I've heard it affects people in different ways.'

Diving back across the bed I switched on the bedside light, nothing happened. Sod it! I thought, the bulb's gone. I tried the radio, not a sound.

The sudden realisation that it was cold, more like November than May, struck me. I could, by now, feel the panic starting to build up. My pulse rate was quickening, beads of sweat appeared on my brow and started a chain reaction down my face and neck. I was cold but I was sweating. If it had been an eclipse it would have been over by now. My brain raced. What was happening? Good *God!* I thought, I've been asleep for six months, it's now nearly winter instead of late spring.

'Get a grip of yourself,' I almost shouted. 'Sit down and analyse the situation. There must be a rational explanation for what's happening here.' By now I was talking to myself, out loud. A sure sign of instability.

If I'd been asleep for six months, by now I'd have more than just the faint stubble that currently graced my chin and I'd be pretty hungry, and rather thin. It's time to freshen up, I thought, then I'll be able to think better.

As I staggered through to the bathroom I must have bounced off all the walls, pieces of furniture and doorways in the house. It felt like walking the decks of a rolling ship on the high seas.

By now I had become accustomed to the darkness and could see quite well by the light from the stars and the moon. That was another thing, the moon was in the wrong place.

Having freshened up I was now in a position to really get to grips with the frightening situation that I was in.

The staggering and lack of co-ordination could have been due to some sort of food poisoning, 'Botulism' the thought struck me. Am I starting to see double? It was difficult to tell in the meagre light around me. Has the onset of paralysis begun? I began to run my fingers over my face, I could feel the tips of them quivering. The panic was returning. What was I thinking about? I'm always careful with what I eat and anyway I never eat canned foods. I ruled out botulism.

Suddenly like a hammer blow to the skull it struck me.

I dived back into the bathroom and filled the wash-basin. Into the kitchen, I grabbed the matches, back to the bathroom and as I pulled the plug to release the water I dropped a match on to the surface and by the light of another I watched the little piece of wood in the whirlpool travelling in an anti-clockwise direction, faster and faster till it disappeared down the centre of the vortex. It should have gone clockwise.

Somehow the northern and southern hemispheres have changed places overnight. The Earth's axis must have tilted through one hundred and eighty degrees.

If this is the beginning of the end how come there's been no warning?

The only other possibility I could think of was that I'd been kidnapped by some alien space ship. I dismissed the thought as quickly as it was hatched. By now I could see that the house was as if it had been ransacked. That would tie up with the tilting theory.

My co-ordination was slowly coming back and as I made my way into the bedroom I managed to do so without bouncing off any of the furniture. However, I must have caught my foot on the dishevelled rug as I stumbled and struck my head on the bedside cabinet knocking myself out.

When I came round I was lying in a pool of sweat, by the side of my bed. There was a trickle of blood on my brow, that must have been when I struck my head as I fell.

I lay there for a while gathering my thoughts. Gradually I could feel the smile growing across my face. What a relief! It's all been a nightmare. It's the middle of the night. I've fallen out of bed.

I instinctively reached for the alarm clock.

Two minutes to seven!

'It's still dark, it shouldn't be. It wasn't a dream. It's true!' I was shouting.

I leapt to the curtains and flung them wide.

My panic was now extreme. Pitch dark!

As I stood there rooted to the spot the realisation dawned.

I'd been telling my next door neighbour for months now to have his shed roof made more secure. It was that which had been blown off in the night and was now completely covering my window.

I fell back in a helpless heap on to my bed, the sense of relief was overpowering as I laughed out loud in near hysteria.

I wonder what I'll dream tonight? I thought.

Cry of the Cormorant

by

Shirley Vaughan

I watched the cormorant as it struggled desperately for life. Its once glossy plumage a cloying mass; its eyes wide, terrified; the slender beak open as it tried frantically to get some air into its already oil-filled lungs. For a moment it stood still, gasping, and then tried again to move further up the beach. I held my breath. It was of course, useless. It had no strength; no air could penetrate the gaping mouth; no one was near to hear its feeble croaking as it stood there, waiting for death.

Suddenly the camera panned up and away from the cormorant, sweeping across the surface of the water. The huge oil slick moved slowly and menacingly through the once tranquil waters of the Gulf, like a monstrous, black slug, devouring everything in its path - plants, fish, flotsam, sand, nothing escaped its voracious appetite.

Three thousand miles away, I stared horrified at the screen. Was this the place I knew so well, where I'd swum and skied and laughed - was this the place? This stinking edifice - dramatic proof of man's madness.

The plight of the cormorant - so familiar in the Gulf - had stirred memories.

I remember the day - it must have been about six years ago - when Saddam Hussein's army was fighting another war on another front - when the Gulf States were hardly known, and the oil-rich sheikhdoms basked in the hot sun, enjoying the fruits of their new wealth. It was a Friday - the Moslem weekend - and we had planned to spend the day with some friends on their boat. As it was high summer, and the temperature threatened to hit 112 Fahrenheit, we were up early to enjoy the best of the day before the sun got too high and the heat intolerable.

We piled everything into the car - towels, skis, sun-creams, water, a cold-bag of salads and fresh fruit, and a large thermos of ice-cold Pimms. The streets were deserted as we drove off towards the beach - most people were still enjoying the luxury of a lie-in. On the way, we stopped at the little bakery by the side of the road. I got out and bought some Arab bread - gazing fascinated as always at the traditional brick oven and the dexterity of the baker as he tossed the freshly baked bread onto his tiny work surface. It smelt delicious.

Our friends were already on the beach loading up the boat. It never ceased to amaze me how much stuff we took for just one day on the water, and I remember there was much laughter and bantering about the vast quantities of food and drink we had between us. With everything stowed away, and while the morning sun was still comparatively low in the cloudless sky, we left the humidity of the beach, and headed out to sea, the boat gliding effortlessly across the satin-smooth water. It was an idyllic morning. A heat haze rose from the sea, shimmering in the glare of the sun, distorting familiar images and enveloping the horizon in a moist and eerie light.

The water-skiing was good - it always was in the Gulf - the sea glassy calm with never a ripple to break the momentum as we hurtled across the water. With the sun rising ever higher, and the heat and humidity soaring, we decided to eat an early lunch, further out still, where we knew the water was deeper - and cooler. This was the place.

We were chatting quietly, enjoying a glass or two of Pimms, when we became aware of a gentle nudging sound along the side of the boat. At first we ignored it thinking it was a piece of driftwood, but as the nudging became more determined, we looked over the side - there just beneath the surface, circling the boat, brushing the sides, were four dolphins. We'd all seen them before - it was common knowledge that they liked human company, and often swam alongside the dhows as they chugged along the fishing lanes right out in the middle of the Gulf. These though were comparatively close to shore. Had they too come in search of cooler water? Or were we trespassing on their territory? Whatever it was, they certainly seemed very friendly, even playful, as they rolled over and over, and darted underneath the boat, jumping out of the water on the other side, their silver-grey bodies glistening as the sun caught a fin, a tail, a head.

We watched fascinated, as these beautiful and intelligent creatures swam around us - every movement graceful.

I do not know whose idea it was, but we all decided to get in the water. I thought the sudden disturbance of four adults diving into the sea so close to them, would have frightened the dolphins - but it didn't. As we swam slowly away from the boat, the dolphins joined us - diving in and out of the water; gliding effortlessly beneath us; swimming round us, and joy of joys alongside us. To have a dolphin swim by your side, is a very moving and humbling experience - for me, a moment captured forever in my memory. The dolphin seemed quite unafraid as it swam ever closer to me, watching me as I swam, following me when I dived under water, and always gently nudging me, curious perhaps at this rare contact as man and beast swam together. We were all laughing, calling out to each other, excited and exhilarated, when, as suddenly as they had appeared, they were gone. The brief, wonderful, magical moment, was over.

I stared unseeingly at the flickering images on the screen. I didn't hear the whine of aircraft engines or the roar of gunfire. I didn't see the soldiers hungry for action, or the dead and wounded. The rhetoric was ignored, the anguish of war unheeded. I saw only the violation of Nature, and that hideous black mass creeping like death across the tranquil waters of the Gulf. I heard the feeble cry of the dying cormorant. Was this the place, I wondered, where I had swum with dolphins?

A Green Hour Among Strangers

by

A Davies

The likeness was remarkable. She stared fixedly at the picture for a moment then glanced up at the mirror. Thin lips puckering into a worried pout, half-closed eyes without a spark of hope, face an unhealthy ivory - they could have been twins.

The barmaid waited in stolid silence for an order. Good customer, this. Regular as clockwork. Never spent more than an hour in that uncomfortable wrought-iron chair backing onto the window. The hanging light with its green tasselled shade would give her face an unearthly glow. Claire shivered. Maybe she had been watching too many late-night horror movies.

'Same again?'

She felt it necessary to break the uncomfortable silence. Admittedly business was slack, as always at this time of day but she was anxious to get back to the colour magazine on the counter. After all, reading matter was not intended for the clients along with the mignons morceaux.

Madeleine nodded briefly. Speech, movement - all too much of an effort. She longed to reach for the bottle and take it back to the table with her, to feel its coolness against her forehead just as she could feel the reassuring chill of the marble bar-top under her outspread hands. Too much effort. This precious hour was needed for escape.

'You wanted four fucking kids. Get out and earn some money, then. I don't propose to keep them.'

She shuddered and closed her eyes. Some memories remained, however effectively the Pernod had obliterated others. The best had gone first...when the children were small and Vincent hadn't minded so much, provided they were kept out of his way. All gone. The present held nothing but grief and regret, and the need to find a way out.

This hour among strangers was no longer enough. At the end of it, she had to go back. She gulped feverishly and made an ineffectual effort to focus on the old-fashioned watch around her neck. It gleamed against the black blouse but refused to stop swinging. She was unaware that her hunched shoulders were shaking.

'Another five minutes, if you're thinking of going at the usual time.'

Madeleine did not look up immediately, but raised her empty glass with a free hand. She did not feel able to walk to the bar this time. Oblivion seemed within reach and the welcome apathy weighed down her shoulders until they were stilled. Once she would have stayed at home, hiding in the understairs cupboard in order to snatch a drink - or three - after the children had gone to bed. If Vincent had noticed her absence, he was not sufficiently interested to query it.

Now the children were older and she could no longer risk discovery. She told nobody where she was going and nobody was interested enough to ask. Money had been found from somewhere.

Claire sidled round the counter in an effort to avoid attracting attention. She was embarrassingly aware that her long black skirt and high-necked white blouse made her appear as if she had expected to be serving behind the bar at the Folies-Bergere. It was no use. One other table was still occupied.

'What's wrong with us, darlin'? We don't get no personal attention. 'ave to collect our own.'

'Prefer the ladies, do you, Claire? There's a name for little girls like you!'

Claire shrugged and, ignoring the comments, poured a refill. Madeleine's expression did not change. The longed-for time was approaching. Tonight she would not return home.

The room was smoke-filled now. An inappropriate mobile over her head stirred and tinkled as the red entrance door opened on the evening's arrivals. Madeleine did not move. She could sense her dream world taking over.

The familiar greenish light, giving an underwater appearance to the surrounding walls, crept into her consciousness even as she became aware that the dry atmosphere had insulated her from pain with its styptic calm.

Time had retreated, and in her mind she was back in the Green Room.

Disregarding the little boys, sprawled across the vast bed, black-capped, like a tumble of kittens, she felt totally convinced that she needed to restore order to her own world first. She glanced at her daughter, sitting in neat placidity, one leg tucked beneath her and stilled hands linked in her lap. Long hair was swept back from the large pale forehead and secured by a blue Alice-band. The even bluer eyes gazed back at her steadily. Madeleine was content.

In a far corner of the room, only half-concealed by a screen, was a pile of household refuse. Was her family responsible, she wondered, or had it been left by former occupants? There was no smell. For the moment it could be disregarded. Outside the window she noticed with unconcerned detachment a small yard filled with weeds and rusting debris. Pushing up the lower frame, she climbed over the sill, needing to satisfy her curiosity about the flaccid blankness that lay beyond.

As she moved forward, she became aware of criss-crossed lines of washing; row upon row of white shirts, flapping barriers of sheeting and beyond, far beyond, a high fence of wire netting. The neighbouring yards were identical. The stereotyping moved her to a feeling of indignation.

Returning to the Green Room, she noticed a slight change. The remaining space on the bed was piled high with personal and household possessions, over which her husband stood guard with his usual steady mad gaze. She skirted past him and kissed each child in turn, ignoring the appeal in their eyes. An open door leading onto a brightly painted corridor showed her a way of escape.

To her right, the walls remained green and flakey but to her left they glowed red and yellow. She glanced briefly behind her and noticed without curiosity that the family remained in a frozen tableau.

'This way for the Punch and Judy show!'

Passers-by jostled her into a lobby but she felt no need to watch the performance. The small, the weak, the defenceless and the just would all be under sentence of death. Punch would set the world to rights. That's the way to do it!

With a growing sense of adventure, she turned back, fighting against persuasive bodies until she found an empty corridor. 'Why follow the crowd?' she reasoned with herself. Having gained freedom, she was determined to use it wisely.

Pausing at an intersection, she could hear a rustling of fabric and childish laughter. It seemed to be all around her. Making a random choice, she pushed open a pair of swing doors. Just ahead of her was an oriental screen, glistening with those same reds and yellows she had noted on the wall of her chosen route.

Now the sounds seemed even closer. Although the performance area was concealed by the screen, Madeleine made her way along a rear wall shielded by gold silken curtains until, through a small gap, she had a view of the child audience.

· There was a small coloured girl in the front row that attracted her attention immediately. Bright pink frilly dress and matching hair ribbon. Little fingers crammed excitedly in a laughing mouth as she gazed with enchanted eyes at the unseen performers. Madeleine thought of her own daughter, so pale and calm, trapped in a dumb show of a very different kind.

She wanted to stay, cocooned in her own silky niche, and share this experience with the children in front of her. No personal consciousness would remain to torment her. She could dream unthinkingly, float unknowingly and, if necessary, give herself up to the friendly hands that were now gripping her shoulders.

'Time you were going home, love.'

That one voice sounded familiar, but not the others that were pushing the gentleness of the dream-show further and further into the recesses of Madeleine's consciousness.

'Take yer 'ands off of her, Claire. You don't know where she's been.'

'Way beyond, I should reckon. 'Ow many Pernods does she put away in a night?'

'Give 'er a chance - she only ever stays an hour. Inn't that right, Claire?'

'That stuff gets 'em like that - rots the mind, gives you bad dreams.'

Madeleine shrugged off the helping hands and deliberately turned to the mirror behind the bar. Beyond the reflection of a pale-face, black-clad stranger, she could see her tormentors, all with identical faces. They didn't worry her. There were too many around like them to waste the energy of caring.

She knew herself for what she was, at last. If she could keep that other familiar face before her, she was safe. With a slight enquiring raise of the brow towards Claire, she picked up the magazine in delicate, black-gloved fingers and moved with a slow, firm step toward the swing doors. The garishly patterned red and yellow walls of the vestibule did not make her flinch. Instead she welcomed the sight of them with the first smile of the evening and walked confidently out into the night.

Too Young, I Suppose

by

Joseph Mann

My mother said she was leaving but she had always said that, ever since I could remember. They had seemed to get on, my mother and father, in between the shouting there was kissing and affection, after the kissing came the shouting. Yet they had stayed together this long so why couldn't it be like that forever. My father would always rant about 'him' but I could never understand who he was referring to. I would ask my mother who 'him' was but she would more often than not tell me to mind my own business; due to being too young, I suppose.

I'd try and keep out of their way once the shouting started but it wasn't easy, my mother would move around the house trying to get away but my father would stalk after her as if a bird after its prey. He would shout and scream, mainly about 'him', I would listen to try and find out what he meant but to no avail. Due to being too young, I suppose.

I can still remember vividly the time when Mrs Young came in crying her eyes out and my father turned to my mother and shouted 'look what you've done now.' Mrs Young stayed for a couple of hours, through most of that time she cried, my father comforting her for my mother had gone out, slamming the door behind her. It was very late when she arrived home again, but my father was waiting up for her and they started shouting again. My mother said she was leaving but she never talked to me about it, never. Due to being too young, I suppose.

Since that day, me and my father have been alone, never seeing my mother, not once. Mrs Young pops in now and again, they seem to be close, she's alright, but not like my mother. I ask my father where she is, he always says he doesn't know. I often ask him why she left, but he always evades the question, never tells me. Due to being too young, I suppose.

Apocalypse in the Fog

by

Bernard Coghlan

It was a cold and foggy late December day. But not too cold for a brisk walk along the magnificent stretch of broad, sandy, North Devon beach. The tide was out and, because of the fog, I was unable to see the tide-line but I could hear the muted roar of the breaking surf somewhere out in the grey mists. I set off across the firm sand towards the distant sound.

As I walked on the fog seemed to thicken. People in couples and small groups appeared out of the mist, crossed my path, then disappeared again. A pair of dogs ran out of the murk, circled me and sniffed my legs. I greeted them and they allowed me to pat their heads before running back into the fog. They reappeared a few seconds later with an attractive girl wearing a brightly coloured anorak and tight jeans tucked into calf-length boots. She gave me a sweet smile and a cheerful 'Good afternoon'. I responded to her warm friendliness in a like manner. Her dulcet vision faded into the obscuring greyness.

Sounds were muffled and distorted by the fog. Even the piercing calls of the ubiquitous herring gulls lost their echoing quality. The noise of the surf was louder now and seemed to be all around me but I could see nothing beyond the never changing grey circle of damp sand on which I walked. It was an eerie feeling. Almost as if my very existence was restricted to a tiny island that moved with me as I moved.

I must have walked a good half-mile before I reached the tide-line. The first sighting was of a thin, foam-flecked ripple, hissing across the sand towards me. Next, the creaming breakers chasing each other landwards. Until finally, at the very limit of visibility, the curling, crashing, Atlantic rollers, breaking into roaring avalanches of foam. I turned and walked along the beach parallel to the waves.

I passed the waterproofed and sweater bulked form of a gum-booted fisherman, standing behind his sand-spiked beachcaster watching the fine, almost invisible line that vanished into the mist above the surf-line, for the first signs of a biting fish.

I had walked for perhaps another half mile, or perhaps more. There was no way of judging distances in my isolated, fifty-yard world. I saw a lone oyster-catcher paddling amongst the wavelets on his scarlet legs. Probing the sand for cockles with his long, red, clown's nose bill.

It was then that I sensed a new sound. Faint and far away, unseen and without direction. I felt, rather than heard, the low, rhythmic, rapid drumbeat approaching through the fog. It was getting louder with each passing second. Rising above the continuous thunder of the surf. I stopped and listened. What on God's Earth could it be? Whatever it was, was rapidly closing in on me. But from which direction? I peered intently into the fog all around me, straining my eyes to see through the grey curtains of mist, hoping to get a glimpse of whatever it was that was coming towards me through the murk. Suddenly I was startled by a shrill 'pee-eep, pee-eep'. I swung around to seaward and saw the black and white barred wings of the oyster-catcher flashing low over the wave tops, away from the invisible threat. It was very close now. The sounds were rising to a thundering crescendo and now there were new sounds, even more menacing than the ones first heard. Short, sharp, snorting sounds. Like the heavy, laboured breathing of some fast moving creature but multiplied several times. Most frightening of all were the wild, animal calls that somehow sounded strangely human.

'Yah, yah, cumon, go, go, yip.'

It was as though the unknown menace had several voices, all shouting at once.

Icy fingers of fear closed around my heart. Then, panic stricken, I began to run. Away from the sea. Back towards the sea front, the car parks and hotels. Where there would be people. Where I would be safe. Fearfully I glanced back over my shoulder as I ran and saw the curtain of fog torn apart by the forms of galloping horses.

There were four of them. Their riders crouched low over the horses' withers, were shouting to urge their mounts on. Wet sand and sea spray flew all around them from their iron shod hooves. The snorting breaths from their flared nostrils were like jets of steam in the cold, damp air. They passed close behind me. I felt the sands tremble beneath my feet from the thundering hooves.

The last horse was a grey, its white helmeted rider wore a white jacket and breeches. He turned his head to look at me as he passed. Were they dark riding goggles he was wearing? Or were they black, empty, skeletal eye sockets that were turned towards me?

Then they were gone. The sound of their hoof-beats receding into the fog. A long forgotten verse from the Book of Revelations came into my mind.

'And I looked, and behold a pale horse: and his name that sat on him was Death...'

I shuddered, and kept running.

The attack came suddenly. All at once there was a tightness in my chest and I found it hard to breathe. The pain started in my left arm and spread rapidly down to my wrist and upwards to my neck. I stopped and clutched my arm, gripping it tightly to my body in an attempt to ease the sudden agony. Then, like a spear-thrust, it seared through my chest. The sheer magnitude of the pain forced me to my knees and I gasped for breath. The walls of fog seemed to be closing in all around me. The very thickness of it making breathing impossible. It even seemed to be getting inside my brain, blurring my vision and deadening all sounds. The only thing I was conscious of was the all pervading agony that was growing in my chest as though someone was relentlessly tightening a steel band around my body. As a large shaggy dog bounded at me out of the mists, a dark hole opened in the sand in front of me.

'Cerberus,' I gasped, 'the Guardian of Hades.'

I pitched forward and fell into the bottomless abyss of the Pit.

I floated upwards from the darkness into a strange light. The mists were still there all around me, but now the greyness had turned to red. The fog, the sand, the faces and bodies that bent over mine were all tinted red. Blood red. To one side of me were crimson fires, burning brightly and pouring blood coloured smoke into the fog. On the other side a crowd of people stood, silently watching. Were they the souls of others who had been cast down into the Pit? I remembered then, the rest of the Apocalyptic quotation.

'...and Hell followed with him.'

The pain in my chest and arm was still there but dulled now. There was something over my nose and mouth but I was able to breathe more easily. As though from far away I heard a voice.

'He's coming round. I think you got to him just in time.' A face swam into focus above me. The face smiled. I recognised the smile and tried to smile back. 'Hello again.' I croaked. My voice strangely weak and muffled, even to my own ears.

I became aware of another sound. A heavy mechanical roar and a beating of giant wings. The smoke and fog whirled and wreathed all around. Everyone was looking upwards. The souls were backing away from me, as though in fear. What new menace was descending upon me? There was a mighty rush of wind and particles of sand flew all around, stinging eyes and exposed skin. More half remembered verses from Revelations formed themselves in my mind as the clouds and mists disintegrated.

'And I saw a mighty angel come down from Heaven... and when he cried, seven thunders uttered their voices.'

Cold, unreasoning fear grew in my stomach again as the gigantic yellow dragonfly settled on the sand beyond the red flares. I was picked up, carried to the roaring monster and lifted into its belly. Straps were tightened around me and then, with a mighty roar, the dragon leapt into the air. Carrying me heaven-wards towards the light. A crewman leaned over me, adjusting the oxygen mask on my face. He touched the side of my throat with his fingers to check my pulse. I saw that he had a squadron badge on his flying suit. It was of a small, red, horned devil with a barbed tail. Below it was embroidered the legend - '666 sqn'.

'... Let him that hath understanding count the number of the beast: for it is the number of a man: and his number is Six hundred three-score and six.' I began to scream.

Waiting in Line

by

Terry R Provis

Well, he looked such a nice chap didn't he. Not that you can tell what a bloke's like just by looking at him. I mean, look at politicians, you wouldn't think butter would melt in their mouths at election time. The rest of the time they couldn't give tuppence. And they were such a lovely couple, they seemed to have everything going for them.

For a start, they had a lovely house. Detached, you know. In that really nice area by the park. You didn't have to drive through a maze of parked cars to reach their drive, I can tell you.

I remember when they invited Doug and me round for drinks one day. We knew it would be a bit dressy, so we took the trouble to tidy ourselves up a bit. Well, it was like going into one of those showhomes they have on those new housing estates. Everything exactly in its place, all looking new and clean. It seemed a shame to spoil it by sitting down on the chairs. I remember going upstairs to use the bathroom halfway through the evening. I was surrounded by tiles, floor to ceiling. Every surface was so clean I was afraid to use the toilet. But she made us feel so welcome, obviously went to a lot of trouble preparing all that lovely food, it turned into a really nice evening. He seemed a bit quiet, even then, but I thought it was because he'd had a bit of a difficult day at the office. You know, like they say. He had a good job, though, arranged life insurance, or something like that. He kidded Doug that he ought to have some, saying they were both well covered, but you know Doug. Anyway, he earned a lot of money, and he made sure she had the best of everything. Never one to stint. That's what makes it all so difficult to understand. Seeing they had so much going for them.

By the way, are you saving those coupons? You know you've got to come in here every week and spend a hell of a lot of money to take full advantage of them, but I think a holiday in Hawaii is worth putting yourself out for, don't you? Doug says he's always wanted to go there and if that means he's got to eat double portions of Corn Flakes every morning for the next two months, then it's a price he's willing to pay. Mind you, with our luck, they'll finish the promotion when we've got about fifty pounds left to go. Have you ever noticed how they do that? I think it's quite deliberate. It makes them look good without actually costing them anything. I mean, I've never met anyone who's actually won one of those prizes, have you?

Anyway, where was I? Oh yes, between them, with her working as well, they must have been coining it in. She had a good job too, you know, must have been earning almost as much as him, and that's saying something. I suppose when life seems to be that easy, people get bored. I suppose her getting pregnant must have changed their routine quite a bit. I think it came as a bit of a shock. Well, he didn't seem exactly overjoyed at the prospect, although she was definitely looking forward to it. She was positively radiant for a while. I met her in here one day, she was pushing the trolley round with a permanent smile on her face. Of course, when she gave up work, they would have missed the extra income, even though she was going to get her job back after the birth. But I think it was the change in lifestyle that upset him. No more free and easy stuff. Less money and the prospect of waking up at three in the morning to change nappies didn't seem to be his cup of tea. He definitely wasn't pleased about it, even though he did his best to put on a brave face.

Oh, I see you're trying those new tea granules. I think the adverts they put on the television for them are really good. Course, my favourite is the one for the Electric Company, you know, where they have those Pandas sitting around saying how much better their home is thanks to Central Heating. So clever, whoever thinks them up. Doug says it must take them ages to train Pandas to do that. He's joking of course, - at least, I think he's joking. Not that adverts would ever persuade me to buy anything, I believe in making up my own mind on things. I can recommend that new Washing Powder, by the way, it does make the clothes smell nice, just like they say it does.

Anyway, when we heard she'd lost the baby you couldn't help but see she was really broken hearted. Absolutely shattered. Him? It didn't seem to affect him at all. Quite relieved if you ask me. It gave him the chance to go back to his old lifestyle, when money provided the cushion for everything. But she was never the same girl after that. She seemed to lose that sparkle, that little extra she used to have. That must have been when he took up with that secretary of his. How many times have I read of cases like that? And after all that poor girl had been through. You'd think she would have noticed, with all the time he was spending at that office of his. You can only use the excuse of pressure of work for so long, can't you. And it's just like they say, the woman at home is always the last to find out. God, I yearned to tell her some days, but it wasn't my business, I wasn't going to interfere, they had enough problems without my adding to them. I think that was when the rows started to happen.

Do you think that little boy is going to eat all that chocolate he's carrying? I think you can spoil kids if you give in too much to all their whims. Mind you, that could go for all of us. I think it would be nice if Doug gave in to one of my whims now and then. We all need a little pampering every so often, something to make us feel important. The trouble is, the ones we're living with are too busy waiting for us to make them feel important, and so we go on waiting for each other to make the first move. Silly isn't it?

I remember one of the worst rows they had. It seems as though half the street heard it, talk about voices being raised, they must have been hoarse for a week after that one. We all thought it was one of those things, a lover's tiff, we couldn't believe a couple so attached to each other could fall out so badly. But then the invitations stopped. Nobody was invited to their house after that. I was disappointed for one. It wasn't that I was scrounging, I always took my welcome, I just enjoyed the company, and I suppose I liked to see a young couple, you know, getting on in the world. It's too late for Doug and me. After that, we didn't seem to see all that much of them. He would go to work early and it would be quite late by the time he got back. Probably worn out by his secretary. Anyway, She just seemed to cut herself off. Hardly ever went out as far as I knew.

You know, these big supermarkets are all very well, but I can't help feeling we miss the corner shop. Well, it's all so impersonal isn't it? You never get to speak to any of these assistants, unless they've moved something and you want to know where they've hidden it. It just adds to the loneliness of life. Your entertainment is the TV, your car is run off an assembly line, the chances are you work for a large company 'cause all the small ones have gone broke, and you do your shopping with all the masses in a place like this. There's no room for the personal touch anymore is there? We're just herded around like sheep. Sorry, Doug would say I'm on my soap box again.

I'll never forget that day I saw her in the Post Office. She looked as if she'd just done ten rounds with Frank Bruno. Her eye was the colour of that Blackcurrant cheesecake. She looked as if she'd been crying all night, which she probably had. I asked her if there was anything I could do to help but she cut me dead. Didn't want anything to do with me. That hurt, I can tell you, so I just left her alone. I regret that now, of course, but at the time I just kept thinking of all those nice times we'd spent together and I was so upset she didn't seem to want to know me. She'd changed, everybody said that, but you can hardly blame her, she must have been going through hell. Funny thing was, I saw him a couple of days later, and he ignored me as well. It was as though I never existed for either of them.

Have you ever noticed how the other queue always moves quicker? The light's flashing over our check-out, that's always bad news. We'll be here for at least another ten minutes. That lady in the blue coat has forgotten her cheque card. Honestly, you'd think they'd get her to stand to one side so the rest of us can get through, I mean, fancy coming in here and stacking your trolley with all that without even checking you've got the means to pay for it. That's what I can't stand about these places, all these people, I just want to do my shopping in peace and quiet and go home. Is that too much to ask?

So I suppose they went from being the talk of the street to - well, being the talk of the street, if you know what I mean. My neighbour heard the sound of furniture being crashed around one night, she was on the point of calling the police but her husband told her to mind her own business. It was just after that one or two of us began to get the feeling that something was seriously wrong.

Well, for a start the house went so quiet, nobody heard a thing, and that seemed unnatural after all the noise of the previous few days. We didn't even see a light on at night. And then there was the absence of any coming and going. I mean, I'm not one to pry, but I felt I should check if anyone was using the house or whether they'd gone away, you know, a second honeymoon or something, to patch things up. The silence was positively eerie.

Well, when the police told us what had happened, I couldn't believe it. I shall miss her, I mean, she was always so full of life wasn't she? It seems hard to think we won't see her again. I wonder if they'll ask about that patch in their garden. Doug said it's none of our business but you can't help thinking about it, can you. I don't suppose we'll see a couple like that again.

The Umbilical Cord

by

Lorna Balchin

A son is a son, till he takes a wife, a daughter is a daughter all of her life. Who said that?

My daughter is like a boomerang. I throw her away, she comes bouncing back.

My husband and I heaved a big sigh, when my daughter walked down the isle a radiant bride. Free at last of the umbilical cord.

No more daughter leaving ironing board out, cluttering up the kitchen, various items of discarded garments thrown on the floor, after I had washed them. 'Can't wear those, mum, they make me look fat,' she'd cry. 'Oh to look fat like that,' I'd murmur, looking at her size ten figure.

No more hunting under the bed for bits and pieces lost out of my make-up bag, where madam had dropped them and was 'much too busy' to retrieve them; high-heeled shoes kicked off in the hallway lying in wait for husband to fall over them; bathroom door locked for hours while daughter has bubble bath.

Yes, we heaved big sighs.

'What to do now,' says husband.

'Don't know,' says I. 'Get a part time job I suppose.' I feel that I've been made redundant from motherhood.

I take a look at the house, quiet, tidy - *empty!* No, I musn't say that. I have husband's undivided attention. We are free of responsibility. The world's our oyster.

After a couple of months, I start to enjoy this sense of freedom, this tranquillity. Daughter is still there in the background, talking on the phone, sending little notes, flowers, invites to coffee mornings. Then I felt daughter's unrest. Couldn't put my finger on it. I just felt she was unhappy.

I fretted to husband. 'Leave well alone, she has to stand on her own two feet,' he says.

Time passes, and I still worry. Umbilical cord seems to be dangling from me somehow.

Then out of the blue comes a phone call, 'Mum, may, I come back home? I'm leaving him.' 'Him' being her husband. 'I'm bored. Bored. Bored. He's making me old before my time.' No amount of persuasion could make her 'stand by her man'. So back she came and took over our lives again. I was secretly pleased because I had missed her so. My husband was a darling and I loved him very much but something had been missing. My daughter. Married life hadn't changed her way of living, chaos surrounds us once again. Divorce. Goodbye Son-in-law. Pity, I'd quite liked him. Boring, but nice.

We settled down into the old routine. She dropping, me picking up.

Then along comes *'The real thing'* and off she trots, wedding number two.

Husband breathes bigger sigh of relief. He's getting older - can't handle it.

Time goes by and the *'Real thing'* starts dishing out black eyes, and I yank very hard on the umbilical cord and bring daughter back into the fold, only this time accompanied by her first born. More chaos, but oh how I adore my little grandson. Divorce, Goodbye Son-in-law and good riddance.

We're back to playing happy families again.

Then the icy fingers of death reach out to me and hit me hard. My beloved husband is killed in a car crash. My world comes to an end.

I'm dragged back into the land of the living by my daughter. My salvation. Four days, four months, four years, I lose all track of time. I don't know how long its been but I start to feel again. I have to. The umbilical cord is still attached, and I have someone who needs me. I start to live, life goes on.

Then the inevitable happens. *'Dreamboat'* comes sailing into her life and nine years and three more children later, daughter is drowning in a sea of depression, and I throw her my life line, the umbilical cord.

So now I have daughter and four beautiful grandchildren running amok in my life. No time for moping and crying. I'm too busy being mum again.

I'm getting old now, can't bend like I used to. I sink into a chair and sigh, 'who will look after me?' Daughter smiles, 'Why me of course, Mum.'

The Squirrel

by

Ivor Jones

It had been one of those long hot summers, just like the ones Joe remembered as a boy. Joe paced the room like a caged tiger and sighed deeply. Why was he feeling so restless?

He stopped at the kitchen window and stared sightlessly at the distant hills and from somewhere deep within, a dim and distant memory stirred. In his mind's eye Joe saw the gangling youth of many summers past, take careful aim and slowly-ever so slowly, squeeze the trigger of the gun which nestled expertly against the youth's shoulder.

A solitary feather spun heavenwards in a crazy arc and waltzed gracefully earthwards again as the young cock-pheasant quivered once and tumbled out the clear blue sky. Joe never missed.

The melancholy wail of a distant train drew Joe back to reality. A pulse flickered rapidly beneath the freckled skin of Joe's temple as his perceptibly trembling hand reached up for the dust covered Crossmann rifle. Enough was enough, the gauntlet had been thrown down and Joe was determined to take it up.

The cause of Joe's agitation was his fifteen year old nephew. Every night for the past two weeks he had brought Joe a fat little rabbit. Each one unspoilt and unmarked except for the small neat hole in the milky opaqueness of the once so bright and watchful eye.

The spoils would be ritually laid out on the kitchen table in a strategic ploy designed to undermine Joe's manhood and prowess of old. 'Bet you never did that Joe.' The nephew was barely able to conceal a sly smirk of satisfaction as he noticed the pulse on Joe's temple move into overdrive. Joe swallowed hard.

It was more than a body could stand and so on that warm August evening Joe found himself settled sniper like on a small rocky outcrop above Grey's wood. The air grew still, the silence interrupted only by the monotonous drone of a lazy bluebottle which buzzed irritatingly around Joe's camouflaged anorak. Wood pigeons feeling once again secure flew with squeaking wings, low in the sky.

Joe shifted uncomfortably, trying to forget about the viciously persistent cramp that nagged toothache like in the small of his back. Time drifted quietly by and the blood red sun settled comfortably into the hollow of the hill where Joe lay. His mind drifted unconsciously to boyhood scenes where he was once again 'Cochise' noble Apache warrior, blood brother to Burt Lancaster, did he ever feel like this?

Joe was jerked back to reality by the small sound of rattling gravel. He turned and struggled to focus his fifty-four year old eyes but they were out of practice. Joe blinked once-then blinked again and saw in the distant haze a movement slowly resolve itself into the shape of a small grey squirrel.

The creature purposefully made its way along the path towards Joe, oblivious of his presence and of the glistening barrel of the Crossmann rifle pointed directly at its small grey head.

The adrenalin flowed freely as Joe's finger imperceptibly tightened on the trigger. 'Breathe out slowly and squeeze... that's it Joe' he said to himself. Joe laughed silently as he anticipated the expression on his nephew's face.

The squirrel stopped, sat up, its great bush of a tail flicking nervously from side to side. Joe hesitated, and in the same moment a small black face with glittering yellowed eyes appeared out of the rocks above. The squirrel turned to the silent sound and was gone an eternity before the cat landed on the empty path.

The chase was fast and furious, yet the issue was never in doubt as the squirrel moved with the practiced agility of a Welsh inside half, easily frustrating the cat's best efforts.

A convenient sapling provided a refuge from where the squirrel mercilessly taunted its cold eyed adversary. From tip to tail the cat's body quivered with suppressed rage until finally aware of its own impotence it padded into the deepening shadows with an unconvincing air of nonchalance.

The gun felt heavy in Joe's arms as he stared admiringly at the little grey creature, for it was indeed a thing of spirit and beauty. Joe slowly lowered the gun to the ground and smiled within himself. A small stone clattered noisily down the path. Joe turned to the empty sky and saw that he was alone.

Back in the familiar surroundings of his comfortable kitchen, Joe felt warm and at peace with the world once again. His demon had been exorcised.

The click of the lifting latch caused Joe to turn and see the kitchen door slowly open. 'Bet you never did that Joe.' The nephew tauntingly swung the lifeless form of a small grey animal by its great bushy tail so that its bloodied coat brushed against Joe's skin. The pulse in Joe's temple throbbed with painful intensity and exploded into life. Joe smiled a strange sort of smile as he reached slowly-ever so slowly for the glistening Crossmann rifle.